Assignment
in
Oran

Assignment
in
Oran

SUSAN C. TURNER

Assignment in Oran
by Susan C. Turner

2024 Harry Douglas Press Paperback Edition
Copyright © 2024 by Susan C. Turner
All rights reserved

Published in the United States of America

Harry Douglas Press
704 West Swann Avenue
Tampa, FL 33606
USA
www.harrydouglaspress.com

ISBNs:
978-0-9847232-9-4 (softcover)
979-8-9904900-0-0 (eBook)

Printed in the United States of America

Cover and Interior design: 1106 Design

For Nancy Little
my dear friend

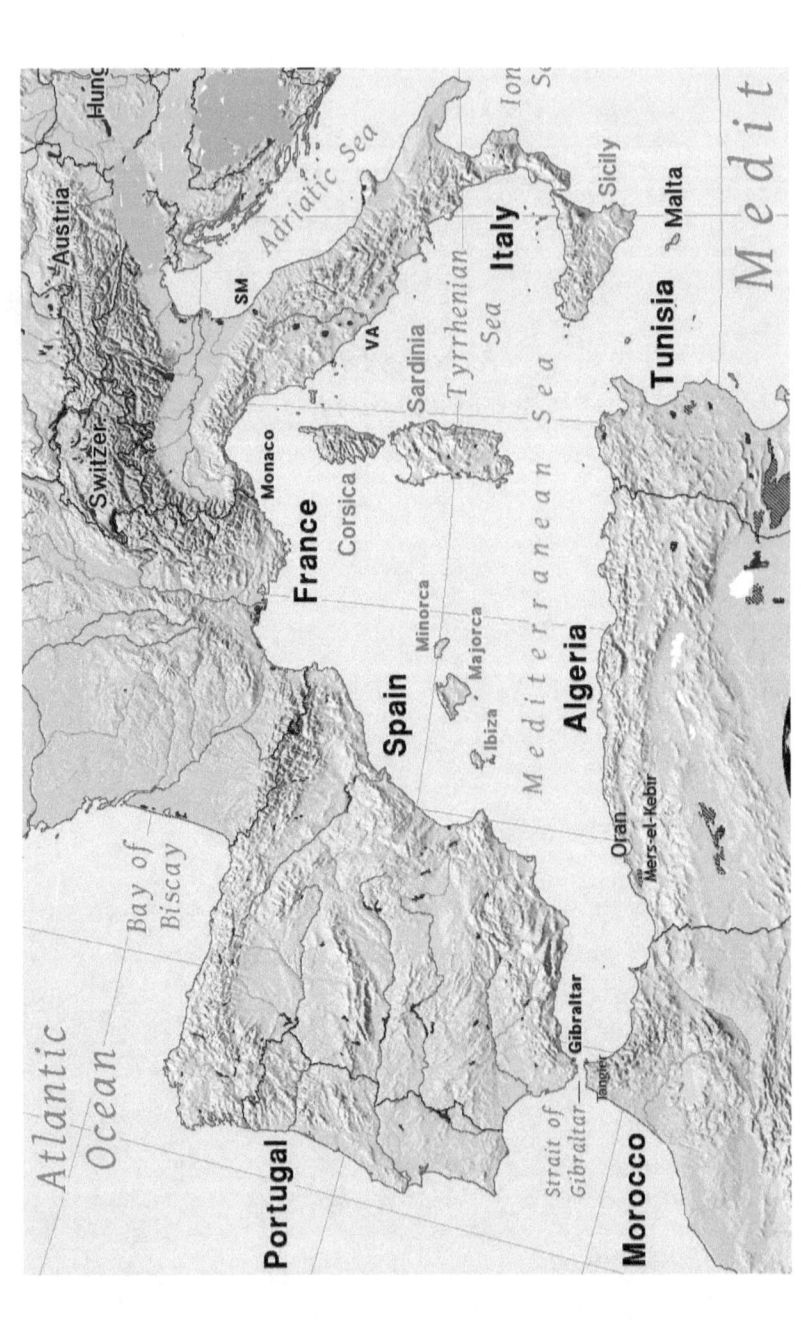

A warm wind out of the south smells quietly of the sea.
Against a flawless sky, blue-tailed swallows dip and glide
like dancers on glass.
It is a day like no other.
The kind of day that makes one wish to hold time still,
a day that makes one believe the world is pure and fine.

Chapter One

7 **June 1939, San Siro Racecourse, Milan.** Harry Douglas straightens the knot on his tie and raises his eyes to the line of spectator boxes where Italy's racing elite are known to pass luxurious afternoons between the sixteenth pole and the finish line. His gaze travels to box number two where a figure dressed in the palest yellow—with matching elbow gloves and a feathered hat—shines bright against the dark interior. She leans out across the railing, head to one side, one gloved hand shielding her eyes, the other resting on the rail. Over her shoulder, she says something to the man standing behind her. He points to the lead pony that guides, without hesitation or hurry, a dozen sleek thoroughbreds to the track.

Though the hat's brim casts a shadow, Harry easily identifies the elegant silhouette as Gabriella Terzo. Her brother Lorenzo, in a splendidly tailored summer suit, lounges against the column that separates the adjacent box from their own. He holds a pair of Zeiss binoculars and scans the line of horses passing below him, observing, Harry assumes, the small man astride Apelle, Lorenzo's entry in the biggest purse race of the season.

The rider in Terzo lemon-and-black looks fit and in complete command of the long-legged chestnut gelding. Yesterday, Apelle was listed as the likely winner, but a well-timed rumor of the jockey's illness caused the horse's odds to plummet overnight, anointing Ursone as the favorite. Harry does not envy the diminutive rider atop Apelle. Weeks ago when Gabriella introduced Harry, her brother gave no indication that he was, in any way, a merciful man. Nor, days later, at their second encounter, that he had the slightest remembrance of their first meeting.

Not that Harry minded. In his line of work, a mark's poor memory serves a distinct advantage.

When Gabriella looks down in his direction, a rush of emotion catches him by surprise. He waves and then adjusts the brim of his hat to a rakish tilt. *Jimmy Cagney.* Gabriella laughs, returns the wave, and stares down at him for a long moment—expectantly, he thinks—before she indicates the stairs that lead to the box's entry.

Two days ago, over a sumptuous lunch in the gardens of Ristorante Don Lisander, she invited him to join her family and friends to watch today's featured race. He climbs the stone steps to the richly carved door that separates wealthy owners from less fortunate enthusiasts. Money and position determine the owners' distance from the wire, and Harry is again reminded of the Terzo family's influence. When he reaches the landing, he stops and listens to the low hum of voices inside. Before he turns the knob, he checks the lie of his tie.

A host of people mill about. Visibly prosperous. Harry recognizes no one. He reaches into his pocket for his pipe—an automatic habit—and turns it over in his hand. He scans the pastel dresses and suits of cream and tan until he catches sight of her and begins to move toward the elevated railing she sits upon. He nods to Giovanni Agnelli, heir to the Fiat empire, and avoids a line of uniformed servants carrying silver platters laden with fruits and roasted vegetables, lobster tails, and meats covered in bubbling sauces. A tenor in a white apron sings as he dispenses drinks. A few steps farther on, there is a sitting area with leather chairs and lush carpets and colorful umbrellas that provide shade. Waiters are quick to light cigarettes and distribute champagne in yellow and black crystal goblets, no doubt anticipating a victorious Apelle.

Lorenzo stands apart, studying the slow progress of the twelve thoroughbreds toward the green slotted gate. When he lowers the field glasses, Harry pauses in front of him and nods, expecting the courtesy of acknowledgment—a cool formality, perhaps—but he gets only a grunt and a frown. Lorenzo averts his eyes and stalks around the box, a tiger in a cage. It seems apparent, to even the most casual observer, that Lorenzo Terzo consumes himself with his own importance.

Harry watches Gabriella laugh at a comment someone has made. She turns, meets his eyes and waves him to her.

"I don't want to interrupt," he says.

"No matter." She takes his arm and leads him to a shaded sitting area. "Let me introduce you to my mother Vivianna," says Gabriella.

He takes the gloved hand. "A pleasure, Signora Terzo."

"I understand you're a racing fan, Mr. Douglas. Please sit down." Harry lowers himself into an empty chair. Vivianna Terzo, a patrician beauty in middle age, lives a rarefied life. Strands of silver mark her perfectly coiffed dark hair. She wears a smart linen suit, a striped pattern of muted yellow and black. She and Gabriella bear a striking resemblance.

"By happenstance, Signora. I know more about auto engines than racehorses, nothing of note compared to your husband's and your son's expertise, of course. They appear to be successful at both forms of sport."

"So they say." She raises her eyebrows and shrugs one shoulder elaborately. Her mouth belies a small smirk. "Surely you have a preference in this race."

"I placed a small wager on Vezzano."

"How peculiar. That horse, I am told, is a long shot. Sizable odds against. May I inquire as to your reasoning for such risk?"

"Of course. Odds aside, Vezzano comes from a long line of champions. In '01, his grandfather, Ajax, was named best horse in Europe. Bendetti's stable is due for a big win. The jockey Pietrino handles a horse better than any rider of his class. The track is dry and hard today. Vezzano runs well on a fast track."

Vivianna Terzo gives him a long look. "For someone who prefers automobiles, you possess a great deal of knowledge about horses. You have quite a talent for research. I must urge Gabriella to tell me more about Harry Douglas. Thus far, she's only shared your interest in acquiring some sort of engine."

Harry smiles. A warm breeze stirs around him. The horses and their riders wander casually toward the starting gate. There is a steady murmur of conversation. Gabriella has disappeared. Harry wishes to remain near her, to talk to her privately, but he knows what he wishes is impossible. He spots her arm-in-arm with a woman clad in a fashionably fitted lavender sheath. His eyes follow them as they walk to the front row and settle into their seats. Every now and then, Gabriella pauses to look back at him, a glint of humor in her eyes. Sunlight illuminates her face, and he is struck by the force of his attraction. He starts toward her and feels a hand on his arm.

Mick MacLeod raises the whiskey glass in his hand, a silent question. Harry shakes his head, eyes intent on Gabriella. Mick drops his voice a level. "Now's hardly the time, laddie, for one of your romances."

"When is the right time?"

"You know what I'm saying. There's work to be done."

"This looks like work to me." Harry grins and says, "Glad you made it on time."

"Is our favorite dictator in the box?"

"He was perched in box number one, a few feet from the spot where Lorenzo is standing, but I don't see him now. Can't imagine he'd miss this race." Harry scans the track just past the finish line. "Likely, he's making his way to the circle for the winner's presentation. All those bangles on his chest slow him down."

Mick swallows the last of his drink and looks around for a tray. "I'm more interested to see which of his new German and Austrian pals are around. Now that Il Duce and the Axis are official, we'll see a sharp increase in brass."

"Count on it. Just so they're here playing the ponies, and not making plans to march on the French border," says Harry.

A woman wearing a dramatically plumed wide-brimmed hat stands at a respectable distance, a few feet away. When Harry catches her glance, she gives him a weak smile. Stylish, well-heeled, matching gloves. Very much alone. A wealthy widow squandering her fortune at the track or seeking, perhaps, a temporary companion. Pencil in hand, she ponders a page in her racing form. A dubious activity, given this will be the final race of the day.

Harry and Mick fall silent as Rosso Terzo approaches and stands between them. Terzo is a small, stocky man with a heavy face and sagging jowls—the result of an overabundance of two-, possibly three-martini lunches. There is a practiced ease in his stance. He looks up at them. "Delighted you gentlemen could join us this afternoon. I trust we will be able to do business, Signor Douglas. It's not often we are asked to work for an American."

"Canadian."

Rosso Terzo shrugs. "North American." Gabriella's father speaks with a confident deliberation that Harry expects in a man with his reputation. The Terzo engineering firm and manufacturing companies are among the richest in northern Italy. "Gabriella mentioned you are in search of auto parts."

Harry laughs. "Something like that. I am in Milan for a serious look at the Alfa and Fiat engines. Then, to Alsace to see the Bugatti."

"Of course. Bugatti posted wins at both Monaco and Le Mans. Not easy to do. Who would not want to inquire about that success?"

"Bugatti also did well at Chimay two weeks ago."

"Ettore Bugatti was born here in Milan, you know. A pity his Alsace factories are officially French. How was Chimay?"

"Two wins in a row for Bugatti and Trintignant, their driver."

"What about the Silver Arrows?"

"They ensured a blistering pace. On Trinignant's heels the entire race."

"The Germans want to dominate, don't they?"

"Indeed," agrees Harry. *In many ways.*

"You own a fleet, then?" asks Rosso.

"Hardly a fleet. A few is a far better description." Harry acknowledges Mick. "Rosso Terzo, meet Mick MacLeod. Mick is a colleague of Humphrey Cook."

"Ah, the ERA crowd in Surrey. Fine engines. Fierce competition in the past few years. Any wins?"

"None to speak of," says Mick. "We're in early stages. We need to learn a thing or two from you Italian chaps."

Terzo smiles. "Do not expect us to share our secrets. Nevertheless, with the right agreement, we will design and build something extraordinary for you." He turns toward the oval track. "Today is a beautiful day for horses. Lorenzo's horse, Apelle, is running. We think he will do quite well."

A tall servant with a fringe of gray hair and highly polished black shoes comes to stand next to Terzo. The wealthy engineer reaches inside his jacket and extracts a glimmering gold pocket watch. When he uncovers it and speaks softly, the servant clears his throat and announces in a high thin voice. "Two minutes to post."

Terzo replaces the watch and bows slightly. "Time to take our seats, gentlemen. The race is about to be run."

While they wait for other guests to find favorable viewing spots, Harry and Mick survey the occupants who fill the front row.

Lorenzo bends close to his mother who sits straight in her chair, nodding absently, not looking at him. From the look on his face, he appears to be making an emphatic point. She gives a little shake of her head. He straightens and looks around at the other guests, as if to assure himself they have not witnessed the exchange. He meets Harry's eye, scowls, and goes to sit at the end of the row, apart from the family. His look is one of anger, Harry assesses. An emotion he finds more than curious for a man whose prized thoroughbred is expected to capture the premier purse race of the season.

"Who's sitting with the family?" asks Mick.

"Nico Lukas. Some sort of cousin. Next to an attractive woman. Long black hair. Dark glasses. Broad purple hat. Lavender dress. Lots of leg. Very cozy. She seems the more interested party."

Mick studies the woman in question. "She's Polish."

"Ours?"

A long pause. Another look in her direction. "She must be visiting from Warsaw. Her husband serves in the diplomatic corps."

Harry waits for more, but Mick checks his racing form and turns his attention to the starting gate. "Who've you got?"

"Number three, Vezzano."

"The long shot. I should have known. Safe money's on Ursone. Post six, plenty of room up the middle."

"So now you're a loathsome odds-on man? A hedger. No money there."

"You're all about the risk, laddie. The big score," says Mick.

"Keeps the wolf from the door. On occasion."

Harry recognizes—the result of any number of unsuccessful wagers to date—the three slot as far from the track's best starting position. He figures Vezzano is up to it. At least the big brown bay won't be trapped on the inside.

Harry's glance falls on the dark-haired woman in purple. She leans forward to tap the ash from her cigarette, looks up, removes her sunglasses, and stares at Mick. Then, she ducks her head and turns over the racing form in her lap. She does not look again in their direction.

On the rail, the crowd presses forward as the crew directs the horses into the starting gates. Vezzano initially balks, uncharacteristically reluctant. He rears up, the jockey Pietrino, barely hanging on. It takes four big men, linking hands, to make a cradle behind him, swaying and pushing his rear end, to move Vezzano into post three.

Mick gives Harry a nudge and whispers, "From the looks of that horse, you're dining on pigeon this week."

An instant later, Vezzano's gate slams shut, the bell rings, the speaker blares, "Partiré!" A roar rises from the grandstand, and the twelve rivals burst from their gates.

Apelle takes the lead. Vezzano breaks slower than the rest, running eighth of twelve. They all move left toward the rail and round the first turn. At the quarter pole, Vezzano drops to ninth and settles on the outside, off the pace, but staying in contention, conserving power—Harry trusts—for the marathon three thousand meters. The field spreads out, and Harry loses sight of the last few horses. A commentator is calling the race but Harry cannot hear over the shouting crowd.

Midway down the back straight, the big brown bay comes into view. Legs driving, Vezzano cruises past horse after horse, an unexpected display of speed. While the lesser animals begin to tire, Vezzano gains steadily on Apelle and the other leaders, Ursone among them. On the third turn, to save ground, Pietrino nudges Vezzano along the rail. The five and the eight box him in, leaving no clear path of escape. When Pietrino drops a perfectly timed whip on the bay's left flank, Vezzano digs hard and bursts off the inside, accelerating to a hole before it slams shut.

On the arc of the rail, Vezzano and Apelle run neck and neck, nose to nose, the bay bearing down on the inside. Great shouts and bellows rise up from the grandstand, the entirety of the Terzo box on its feet. Coming off the final turn, Apelle edges into the lead, but with one pull to his right, Pietrino straightens his horse away for a furious run to the finish. Inside the sixteenth pole, Vezzano flawlessly takes control, two lengths ahead of his spent challenger. In record-book time, the big brown bay crosses the finish line, the undeniable and unlikely winner of the fiftieth running of the Gran Premio di Milano.

The jockey in the lemon-yellow cap finishes a distant third, six lengths behind the winner, and four lengths behind second-place Ursone. The celebratory crystal swiftly disappears.

Rosso Terzo remains seated. One by one, departing friends stop and murmur the ritual words of gratitude for Terzo's generosity. Then, there is silence as guests press toward the main door, anxious, it seems, to escape the displeasure of Apelle's angry owner. When Harry reaches the doorway, he hesitates in order to button his jacket, and becomes aware of eyes upon him. Behind, he hears a sharp loud laugh and feels a heavy hand on his shoulder. Mick is a few steps ahead, so Harry turns, startled when Lorenzo Terzo intrudes into the small space that separates them.

"We have not met," he says. Too loudly, he adds, "Who are you?"

"Indeed we have met," says Harry. "On two occasions, both in the company of Gabriella. The name's Douglas, Harry Douglas." He takes a step back and sticks out his hand.

Lorenzo removes a cigarette from the pocket of his jacket, inspects it thoroughly. "Gabriella," he repeats. He places the cigarette between his lips and extracts a gold lighter. Harry notices a dramatic monogram of raised gold. Lorenzo cups his hand around the flame and takes a few deep pulls. In no hurry, it seems. "What kind of name is Douglas?"

"Canadian." Harry does not explain. For a moment, they stare steadily at each other.

Lorenzo sniffs. "You laid money on Vezzano. Why is that?"

Harry wonders why it matters. "Pure luck," he says with a slow smile. "Like many things in this life."

The crowd moves toward the exit gates. Harry cranes his neck to glance back at the Terzo box. The guests have disappeared. Servants efficiently fold and stack chairs and hurry off with the silver platters. The Terzos, accompanied by Nico Lukas, engage in animated conversation with Il Duce himself, who has returned from the award dais and now is seated in a ceremonial chair adorned especially for the occasion.

"Gabriella is a bonnie lass," Mick says. "Is she part of the assignment?"

Harry avoids his partner's meaning. "She's beautiful and smart. Irresistible, by the way. I've known the woman little more than a month. She thinks I'm a worthless playboy, a big-spender auto enthusiast bent on buying custom auto engines for my racing fleet. Doesn't mean I'm not paying attention." He glances again at the group gathered in box number one. "When have I missed a dispatch?"

"Your memory's gone to lunch, Douglas."

Harry pretends not to hear. As his partner loves to remind him, Harry Douglas possesses—among his many talents—any number of failings. Within the space of a minute, he can rightly recount a bounty of injudicious decisions, particularly when it comes to women.

Harrison Jacob Douglas and Michael Fergus MacLeod started their careers in the summer of 1933, raw recruits in the King's service. In appearance and temperament, the two men are starkly different. Mick, a red-cheeked Scots highlander with an infectious grin and wry wit, knows how to ask the right questions, where to search, what to watch for. His burly look and ginger hair hide a thoroughly analytical brain. Harry, on the other hand, is a handsome dark-haired Canadian, slender and fit, known by reputation for his limited restraint. Slightly off the rails. Incidents of alcohol and womanizing, both of which have ended badly. Still, there exists—without reserve—a tough trust between the two men, a built-in loyalty, an easy teamwork, a shared language of glances and nods. On more than one assignment—Mai Ceu, Tirana, Budapest—Harry and Mick have fought side by side, each silently counting on the other's intelligence and courage. The Scotsman is a rough Edinburgh street fighter, a fearless man with his fists. Harry, on the face of it the more urbane, is every bit as steely and dangerous. When things get rough, there is no fleeing the foxhole. No excuses. Each has risked his life for the other. And undoubtedly will again.

Their light banter masks the underlying seriousness of their work, their meeting today far from accidental. From postings around Milan and Rome, Douglas, MacLeod, and a small group of British agents monitor the activities of Mussolini's government. In the past few months, those activities have proved most interesting. OVRA—Mussolini's secret police—has stepped up its murderous tactics, and Italy's youth organizations have increased recruitment, re-emphasizing their hardline messages.

Less than three weeks ago, in an elaborate ceremony in Berlin, Italy officially aligned itself with Hitler's machine, putting to rest all speculation of alliance with Britain and France. Hitler's intricate game of political chess plays on. Anti-fascists in Italy, anticipating far worse, have packed up their children and fled to France.

"It's clear you're interested in a bit more than auto parts," says Mick. "Maybe she is, too. That's all I'm saying."

"No reason to lose sleep over it. She's way out of my reach, surrounded by lean-muscled Italian chaps who keep Battaglia and Canali in business."

"Rough, competing with the Romeos, is it?"

"The good life agrees with them. They spend their days practicing their backhands. Errol Flynns with St. Tropez tans."

"Wee bit pretty for my blood."

Harry bends down to tie his shoe and waits for the last of the crowd to pass before he speaks. "In any case, the Terzos are worth a look."

"Start with brother Lorenzo. You met him before today?"

"Twice. I first met Gabriella at the Agnelli plant where I had shown up for a tour. On the same day, Lorenzo was attending a meeting at the plant. She introduced us. Two days later in a restaurant where Gabriella had arranged to meet for dinner, she introduced us again. On both occasions, Lorenzo appeared preoccupied, abrupt to the point of rudeness. Arrogance is the last trait he lacks. I got the impression he wasn't too pleased to run into us and doesn't care much for foreigners."

"English-speaking foreigners?"

"Wouldn't surprise me."

"Married?"

"Apparently not."

"Friends?"

"Lorenzo and his pals own half the factories in northern Italy. Mussolini supporters. Pro-German to boot," says Harry.

"Pro-German or pro-Nazi?"

"Lorenzo lines his pockets however he can. As long as his bank account grows, I suspect he has no interest in political ideology. Besides, almost all of Europe now claims to be pro-Nazi. They've swallowed the propaganda. When the Führer's car glides past, they wave the flag, raise the arm in salute. No harm in that, they say. No harm in survival."

"Go on," says Mick.

"Lorenzo is Gabriella's only and older brother. Father's only son. In line to inherit the family engineering firms as well as half the manufacturing plants. You met Rosso. He's the designer and the brains. He leads and manages the engineers."

"What does young Lorenzo do while he awaits this inheritance?"

"So-called president of Terzo/Farber, jointly owned with a German chap named Georg Farber. Strictly in-house, hushed production policy. Two years ago, Lorenzo emerged as president when Farber stepped down, no longer interested. Farber's in his seventies, lives in a penthouse in Monaco most of the year. Rumor has it, with a progression of extremely attractive young women."

"How did Farber get so lucky?" asks Mick.

"Made big money during the Great War. Munitions. Ball bearings, that sort of output. Grabs for, holds on tight to every reichsmark. A rigid anti-communist. Hates the idea of any alliance with the Russians."

"So our boy Lorenzo presides over a company that, not so long ago, manufactured wartime munitions. Small world, isn't it? Any idea if he's in the game now?" asks Mick.

"Can't imagine Farber would have objections, given past history. I'm betting they have a few defense contracts. For reasons she's not disclosed, Gabriella refuses to work for either Farber or Lorenzo. Hence, her employment with the Agnellis, old family friends, at the Fiat factory near Turin."

"We have, it seems, an abundance of friendly coalitions," says Mick.

"Looks that way. Many of Fiat's engine parts are designed by Terzo Engineering and produced at Terzo/Farber Manufacturing." Harry is reminded of the aircraft engines Fiat produced for the Spanish Nationalists. "A tight bunch, these fascists."

They step inside a small café. Each orders a cappuccino. They find a table in the corner, away from the door, out of earshot. Mick lowers his voice. "Can we locate the factories? Has to be more than one."

"I'm aware of at least two. One west of Milan, a few kilometers from Novara. Another in Genoa, along the docks. When I inquired about production time and shipping requirements for my imaginary engines, Gabriella offered to make some introductions. I held back, best not to appear too eager, said I wanted to do a bit more research and include a colleague."

"Set it up for next week. Tell her your colleague has business in the north until Monday. The Genoa plant is promising. Outlet to the sea, transport hub. Access to both plants would be better. I'm betting there are more than two. Let's pin down locations and get a quick notion of production schedules."

"Fair enough. You can stay out of sight for a day or two. A weekend in Monaco?"

Mick finishes the last of his cappuccino. "Fat chance. What about the cousin?"

"I'm getting to that," says Harry.

"Can't fathom why Broadway wants us to keep an eye on a slick little wop who reeks of brilliantine."

"Nico Lukas. Gabriella mentioned him in passing, so I checked his background. Our aromatic little guinea is an Alpini officer with special arrangements. He comes and goes as he pleases. Today, he was more interested in crowd watching than the race."

"What do you suppose that's about?" Mick raises his eyebrows.

"Got me. Murky loyalties? Opportunities?"

"Clear soon enough."

Chapter Two

Six months later. Harry's next confrontation with Lorenzo Terzo is not without warning. Harry and Gabriella dine in Turin, then spend a romantic night at the Sitea, an elegant midtown hotel—marble floors, golden sconces, tall windows, historic paintings, grand pianos, quiet alcoves—known for hosting artists and celebrities. The Sitea has a reputation for discretion, waiters who possess unfortunate memories when it comes to names, faces, and lovers.

Over an after-dinner drink in the classy deco-style bar, Gabriella introduces Harry to Beno Masone, Agnelli's vice president for operations. Masone exudes the aura of the medieval prince—lustrous dark curls and a languid posture, smooth bronzed skin that matches his manner. Harry dislikes him on sight. Over carefully iced Negronis and pricey Toscano cigars, Masone probes Harry's knowledge of European racetracks and Kentucky tobacco. After a drawn-out conversation that all but excludes Gabriella, Masone invites Harry to a private card game the following evening. With little hesitation, Harry accepts, mainly to rid them of Masone's presence. Equally compelling, the invitation presents an ideal opportunity to garner details of Agnelli production schedules.

Later that night, in the dark luxury of their room, after he slips his hand under her shimmering black satin dress and they slowly undress, Harry's tuxedo and Gabriella's stockings lie on the floor. In an oversized bath, slick with fragrant bubbles, the two lovers are blissfully exhausted, exquisite forms of torture fresh on their minds. He runs a finger down the length of her spine.

"Let's fly to Majorca. To Palma. Or Portugal," she says. "Oh yes, Portugal. In Sagres, there is a beautiful little house on the edge of the world with stone steps down to the sea. No one will know us. It will be our hideaway." She kisses him suddenly, her voice abruptly changed. "I wish you'd said no. About tomorrow night. I don't like it."

"It's a card game," he says, thankful he need not respond to her dreamlike proposal.

"A game is oftentimes about more than cards."

"All right, it's high-stakes poker. A game all the same."

"Not to my brother."

"What does Lorenzo have to say about it?"

"He's a regular player. You've been invited to a regular game."

"I don't see the harm."

"You will."

The following night at precisely nine o'clock, a white-jacketed bellman accompanies him to the closely guarded hotel penthouse. A second bellman ushers him into the private suite, requests his drink order and directs him down a softly lighted entryway to a broad balcony where a stunning view of city lights and four men in hand-tailored business suits await. In a loose circle, the men swirl their cocktails and review the day's events, cigarettes between their fingers. Their conversation turns to women.

"I suppose I could have jumped her, had it for nothing," Harry hears one man say, "but it was hardly worth the effort."

"Don't tell me you didn't get into that great ass," says another. "I would have taken it."

Both men are laughing when Masone interrupts, makes the introductions and steers the conversation to horse racing.

"Do you suppose the Reich will close Longchamp?"

"A pity if they do."

"Why would they? They enjoy their hobbies."

"They'll require entertainment. Not that Paris wants for it."

"They'll want to show the locals who's making the decisions."

"Ah, here's Lorenzo now."

They proceed inside and gather at a table on the edge of the living space, the city still visible below them. Inlaid on the table surface are outlines for chips and cards, drinks and ashtrays. Six black leather chairs surround the table. In swift order, the men remove their suit jackets—whisked away by observant attendants—and secure their usual places. Out of courtesy, Harry waits for the last man to be seated—shame on the new chap who sits in another's spot—then assumes the empty chair, which, by bad luck or design, is situated on Lorenzo's left.

As is his custom, Harry studies the room. The men are young industrialists—ball bearings, chemicals, concrete—not yet seasoned in their positions. Vice presidents of this or that. Masone, the smoothest and most relaxed of the group, wears a crisp—even at this hour—white shirt rolled tidily at the sleeves, necktie loosely but artfully arranged at the collar, arms at rest on the tabletop. On Masone's left, Antonio Alessi fits Harry's notion of an ancient Norse huntsman. Closely cropped white-blond hair, muscled, ramrod straight posture, strong jaw, and sun-weathered skin, all of which give the distinct impression of a man who thrives in the cold. A man who knows how to survive. His is not a relaxed countenance, but one of watchful alertness. His eyes an icy shade of blue.

Next to Alessi and across from Harry, Pascal Romano—Romo—removes his tie and flings it onto a vacant chair, frees one end of a shirttail from his ample waistline, downs the remainder of his gin and tonic and promptly orders another. He has a lazy eye and a rugby player's shoulders, a man who takes up more than his share of space. The sweat on his forehead and the volume of his voice—too loud for the waiter's proximity—cause Harry to contemplate the number of drinks Romano consumed before he arrived. Leo Moretti places a hand on Romano's shoulder and squeezes. An attempt, Harry guesses, at quieting his friend. "Damn, Romo. Skin over bones. Put some meat on, brother. Feel this, Lorenzo. He's wasting away."

Romano directs an obscene gesture at Moretti. "Fuck you, Leo. You couldn't save a mouse from drowning. And you'll never get in that gnocca's ass."

Moretti is a small man with a hooknose and thick eyebrows that obscure the bridge of his nose. He keeps up a steady chatter of conversation—football scores, train delays—as the others stub out their cigarettes and separate their chips. His thumbs thump the table in a rhythm Harry recognizes from schoolyard days. Leo Moretti is the joker and nervous peacemaker in the group. Lustful, but unsuccessful with women. He reminds Harry of a minor con man.

Lorenzo leans back in his chair, slowly removes a cigarette and taps it on the outside of its gold case, waits for the

attendant to appear and provide the flame. He has not spoken
since he sat down. He does not remove his suit jacket, waving
the attendant away.

"Not staying, Lorenzo?" Masone inquires.

Lorenzo gives Masone a cold glance, takes a drag on the
cigarette, and blows a ring of smoke toward a smiling Madonna
on the ceiling. "Of course I'm staying."

"We have a guest player tonight."

"I noticed."

"Let me make the introduction."

"We've met." Lorenzo does not look at Harry.

The other men fall silent. Alessi shifts in his chair. Head down,
Moretti plays with his chips. Masone stiffens just a fraction,
realizing he has committed an error. "Well then, we shall begin."

Harry signals the waiter to replenish his glass. Lorenzo's
rudeness will not hinder his work. These men are the reason he
is here. They will let slip, given the right opening, information
of value. It is obvious that Lorenzo's mood matters to them, and
his displeasure at Harry's presence unsettles them. The president
of Terzo/Farber Manufacturing means a great deal of business
for each man, inside bids for their companies, a constant stream
of revenue for their products.

As the game unfolds, Harry learns just what sort of men they
are and how far they will go to curry Lorenzo's favor.

Possessed of a keen memory for cards, an observant eye,
and a competitive character, Harry comes to realize, after three
hours of lopsided play, that such qualities hold no advantage in
this game. Lorenzo's mood has improved in direct correlation
to his chip count.

Moretti's coil of cigarette smoke floats in the air. He has dropped out early in the betting and stands away from the table observing the play, feigning interest. A sweet-smelling Turkish Murad dangles from the corner of his mouth, the earlier nervous energy gone. While the others consider their cards, Harry decides to find out exactly how Lorenzo's winnings have so quickly accumulated.

In the hole, Harry holds a jack and a four, both hearts. His next four cards are dealt—two black kings, another red jack, and a nine of hearts. He is looking at two pair, kings high. A solid hand, possibilities for another king or jack. With any luck, a full house. As things stand, he will need three of a kind.

Lorenzo's hole cards are a mystery, of course, but a tidy string of hearts lies exposed, five, six, seven, eight. Possible straight flush. The nine of hearts or the four will win it. Purely impossible. Harry holds both cards. Lorenzo's luck, or whatever it is, has finally run out.

By the next round, the room is heavy with the fog of cigarette smoke and the peat of strong Scottish whiskey. Yellow rings of light cast shadows on the ceiling overhead. A faraway train whistles. A fortune in lire lies in the pot. Only Lorenzo and Harry remain in the game. The dealer, Romano, slaps the last cards down, an amused expression on his face. Lorenzo first, then Harry. Before Harry picks up the card, he takes a long look at the other men. Moretti, erect now in profile, one eye turned toward them, a forgotten cigarette dangling from his fingers; Masone still and alert, hand wrapped around a freshly made Negroni; Alessi leaning on the doorframe, one foot cocked up against the door behind him, one hand in his pocket, an unreadable expression on his weathered face.

Harry cannot say exactly what it is, but something—a purely animal sense he recognized long ago, an instinct he has learned never to dismiss—is wrong. A nameless tension in the room. A dark secret awaiting revelation. The tiny click of poker chips comes from across the table. Harry lifts his card. King of diamonds. Full house, kings over jacks. Only a few hands will beat it, including the unattainable straight flush.

It is Lorenzo's bet. "All in," he says too quickly.

He does not look at Harry or the other men, but directs his eyes away from the pot toward a far corner of the room and settles back into the comfort of his leather chair, an air of confidence in the tilt of his chin. He reaches for his cigarette and sucks a long, contented draw.

Harry has to admit, there is no telltale remorse in the movement of Lorenzo's body. No involuntary tic. No message to reveal the foolishness of his announcement. The man has a superb bluff. Harry will give him that. For the fraction of a second, Harry contemplates folding. No one the wiser. After all, winning is not the reason he is here. *You're holding a full house, for Christ's sake. How often does that come along?* He waits for the struggle within him to fade.

The other men, with no pretense at indifference, watch Harry.

"Call," says Harry and matches Lorenzo's chip count.

Unhurried, Lorenzo places the cigarette into the ashtray, makes a show of slowly flicking the ash a time or two. With the same deliberate hand, he turns up the last card and grins at Pascal Romano. A glowing four of hearts completes his straight flush.

Harry recalls Gabriella's words. *You will.* His eyes stray to the open balcony door, the lights of the city against the black of night. *You need to get the hell out of here.* An escape to Sagres now seems a fine idea. He wonders what time it is, where she is. He could check his watch, fold his cards, collect his jacket, and go in search of her. Yet, here it is, the unavoidable. If he allows Lorenzo to get away with this, Harry will lose something of himself. One man does not allow another to openly cheat him.

The other men do not alter their positions or their expressions. They wait silently. Harry fixes his gaze on Romano. There is clear warning in the dealer's eyes.

Harry looks to Masone, his tone pleasant, positive. "You could have warned me what kind of game we're playing." Masone turns his head aside, a look of evasion. Feigned bewilderment, perhaps. Eyes averted, he gulps the Negroni.

Lorenzo voices the unspoken question. A menacing sneer, "What the hell does that mean?"

Harry smiles, turns up the first and last cards he was dealt, the jack of hearts and the king of diamonds. "It means you're the luckiest son of a bitch at this table." Lorenzo grunts, his smug expression spreading, two meticulously manicured hands anxious to gather the pot. Harry chooses that moment to turn up his remaining card and place it precisely—vertical side to vertical side—next to Lorenzo's. "It appears a very odd deck you chaps are dealing."

A sudden bellow shocks the air. A snared animal realizes his fate and curses his captor. A crystal ashtray shatters against the opposite wall, crumpled cigarettes and their ashes suspended in diagonal shafts of light. Lorenzo leaps to his feet, fists pounding the air, chair slamming backward onto the floor. "You call me a cheat?"

Harry nods. "A most definite yes."

That ill-advised response is how it begins and how it ends.

Afterward, Harry does not recall specific details of the beating that leaves him sprawled face down in the stairwell two floors below the penthouse door. Consciousness emerges, the stench of floor sealant and his own bile under his nose, a scattering of wooden poker chips around his head. Flashes of Romano gripping his elbows. Moretti rushing to close the window curtains. The snap of a door lock. Lorenzo cocking his fist, right arm swinging in an arc, delivering frenzied blows. Masone hollering something indistinguishable, grabbing Lorenzo's arm. Alessi stone-faced, watching impassively from the doorway, at some point crushing a cigarette underfoot, and moving toward the group.

Harry's jaw stings and his ribs ache, the result of a vicious kick, he recalls. "Get him out. Get him out of here." Masone was hollering. "Get him out of here." Harry will never know if Masone was referring to Lorenzo or Harry. He sits up, removes a handkerchief from his pocket, and daubs the blood on his lower lip.

Herein lies a lesson. Never sit for a game with a gang of thugs, particularly if they're disguised in bespoke suits and pointy Italian shoes.

Chapter Three

May 1940. The German army corners the French army and the British Expeditionary Force at Dunkirk. Agents Douglas and MacLeod are dispatched to Paris to explore the French government's rumored exodus to Bordeaux. They find a regime in disarray, the mood in Paris divisive, and the French army, Europe's largest and finest, on the verge of collapse. By 28 May, the British War Cabinet, apprised of the same news from multiple reliable sources, reaches the dismal conclusion that their major ally lay dying. Section Six—known to employees and critics alike as Broadway, the official location of its London headquarters—focuses its attention on the military buildup along the French-Italian border. The two agents are sent quickly back to Milan, their mission clear: Secure information for the commencement of RAF precision bombing raids on automotive and aero-engine factories in northern Italy.

On the stroke of noon, church bells toll on the Piazza di Roma in the twelfth-century village of Castell'Arquato. Hundreds of brilliant yellow daffodils and orange lilies perfume the air of Santa Maria Assunta Church. Slices of sunlight dapple the ancient frescoed walls. The bride is undeniably beautiful, but to Harry's mind, Gabriella Terzo is the most dazzling woman on display. Easily the best-looking woman in the crowd, she has enormous chestnut eyes, flawless olive-gold skin, and thick auburn hair swept high on her head, an errant tendril escaping casually down the back of her exquisite silken gown. Of late, Harry and Gabriella are frequently seen together at Milan's elite social events. What began as simple desire has grown into something more complex. Harry is not sure exactly how or when it happened, but here it is.

In another life, they might marry, have children, and grow old in a cozy house in a small village in the Dolomite foothills. Not this lifetime. At best, Harry's is an uncertain existence. He lives a life of secrecy and perpetual disguise, one that, by design, inhabits the lives of others. Abrupt departures, hurriedly packed bags, and trains in the dead of night require no obstacles. No vulnerabilities to exploit. By necessity, he tells himself, his heart must go untouched. He dares not acknowledge his purer inclinations and is more than reluctant—in this immediate circumstance—to accompany Gabriella to the wedding of her dearest childhood friend. An isolated village at the foot of the Piacenza Hills means expectations of open and endless conversations with Gabriella's friends and family. Not to mention prolonged encounters with the likes of Lorenzo Terzo and Nico Lukas. Every sentence will be weighed, each gesture considered.

As Harry expects, a sumptuous outdoor banquet and operatic feast, interminably long hours of celebration, follow the ceremony. Enormous tables clothed in white linen hold lobsters, clams, osso buco, risotto alla Milanese, and buckets of expensive

French champagnes. Under ancient tulip trees, a joyful bride and groom seem to float in graceful dance to the orchestra's Cole Porter tunes. Tenor Giovanni Martelli himself—the greatest Italian Otello—thrills the bride and her guests with arias from Mozart, Verdi, and Donizetti.

Hours later, when the sun's last edge slips below the horizon and the blue of the sky begins to darken, a sleek black Mercedes appears, an extravagant orange bow sprawled across its highly polished bonnet, and sweeps off the bride and groom to an undisclosed estate in a remote region of the Po Valley, leaving their guests to feast and dance long into the warm, violet night.

Away from the crowd, Harry and Gabriella stroll across the arched stone bridge that joins the banks of the Arda River. Midway, the water passes beneath them. On their right, a sea of soft wheat disappears into clouds of purple and gold. On their left rises the soaring tower of the town fortress. Smells of earthen wheat and a slow gurgle of fresh flowing water fill the twilight.

"Gabby, we agreed you'd go to Lugano."

"Of course," she assures him. "It's arranged. I will take a leave and move to Nico's apartment in Ticino. It's a lovely place near the Via Nassa."

"Your cousin Nico?"

"Yes, Nico, whom you've managed to avoid all afternoon." She stares down into the water. "Actually, he's sort of a half cousin," she adds absently.

Half, whole. The finer points of Gabriella's familial relationship with Nico Lukas make little difference to him. Harry's official responsibilities, however, involve investigating the man. He has managed to keep Nico in sight the greater part of the day. Throughout the reception, a parade of guests—men,

women, even a child or two—have vied for Nico's attention.
He treats each one with exacting attention, piercing blue eyes
focused on the person to whom he is speaking, seemingly
nothing withheld. A wide grin, bursts of laughter at the right
moments, dutiful waltzes with plump matrons and graceless
teenagers. Nico Lukas is, on the surface, charming, magnetic. In
the darker corners of Harry's mind, Lukas appears as a smooth
rock gleaming with flecks of gold that attracts admirers and
collectors. Lift the rock and an ugly tangle of worms squirms
into the light. The thought of Gabriella living in his apartment
annoys Harry no end.

Her eyes wander and rest upon a burbling heap of stones in
the middle of the black water. "He doesn't go there anymore,"
she says hurriedly. "Since the alliance, he's lived in Rome. I can
stay as long as I like."

Moving higher on the ladder, is he? Harry takes her hand, kisses
her fingers. "You promised me you'd be in Switzerland by now."

"And I promised Mr. Agnelli I'd finish a project for the firm.
I cannot leave him with no one. One word of honor competes
with another, does it not? You must understand, these people are
good to me. They are like my family. Besides, Lorenzo has no
idea of this move. I must handle my brother carefully."

Compared to Gabriella's safety, Lorenzo's opinion means
nothing. A flash of worry awakens within him. "This project,
how long will it take? An hour? A day?"

"A few days only."

"A few days."

"What difference will it make?" she asks. "What are you
saying?" She continues across the bridge, pulling him with her,
laughing at her effort.

"I'm saying it's important you're in Switzerland. It's no secret France is about to fall. You can't be anywhere near the French-Italian border."

Gently, she twists his sleeve so they are facing each other. She places her hands under the lapels of his jacket and moves closer. She smiles. "I think this is our first quarrel." The warmth of her body arouses him. Her wide eyes stare into his, insistent, firm in their resolve. She speaks slowly, softly. "A geography lesson. The French border is eighty kilometers, fifty miles at least, from Turin. Unlikely we'll have Frenchmen storming a Fiat factory." Another teasing smile. "You know how they love their Peugots." She laughs, the dimple on her cheek deepening.

Harry knows the depleted French Army, defeated in the north, will not be arriving anywhere anytime soon. He has no confidence in France's dwindling military resources. He is more worried about the three hundred thousand Italian troops poised on the French border and the British bombers that await instructions.

"Tell me the days you'll be in Turin." He knows his tone is harsh, but the situation is urgent, and he must assure that she will be out of danger.

She pauses, looks over his shoulder into the field beyond. "Today is Tuesday, is it not? We leave here tomorrow. So, I will work Thursday and Friday only. By Saturday, I am in Lugano. Safe and snug and longing to hear from you."

"Saturday the eighth. Is that right? And you won't leave again."

"I just said it, didn't I? What is wrong with you?"

"I need to know you're safe." He is exasperated at her delay. He cannot make her understand.

Her expression changes, the impish grin gone. "Has it not occurred to you I'm equally anxious for you? That I have no idea where you are? That this frightens me?"

"I don't know where I am one day to the next."

She laces her fingers through his, her body still pressed against him. He can feel her studying him. She holds his eyes. "You are a man of secrets. I ask no questions, but I have few illusions about what you do. You don't say it, but I know Harry Douglas isn't entirely safe in my country."

He wraps her in his arms, savoring her warmth. He carries her with him wherever he goes. The raw perfume of her body. The sound of her voice. The gold of her skin. A nonsensical feeling something like love. "Your country isn't safe for anyone at the moment." They stand together without moving, as if the slightest twitch will cause a fragile moment to shatter.

Finally, she pushes from his arms and opens her mouth as though to say something, but shakes her head. "This conflict, this danger—whatever you wish to call it—it won't last forever."

If not forever, a long, long time. He foresees the inevitable war that stretches ahead, and knows they will—in one form or another—share in it. He fears that Gabriella has not yet acknowledged the plague that spreads across Europe, the sickness that surrounds them.

She will see it soon enough. This time, the wolf is coming.

Chapter Four

10 **June 1940.** On Monday, at two in the afternoon, from the balcony of Rome's Palazzo Venezia, across from the National Monument of Victor Emmanuel II, Italian dictator Benito Mussolini—resplendent in black hat and uniform, ribbons and medals of gold crowding his chest, supremely confident in his absolute power—surveys the mob below him. A quarter million Romans, his fierce rabid supporters, raise their fists in the air. Black bands encircle the bicep of every sleeve. They carry red posters with Nazi symbols and hoist Italian flags. With riotous intensity, they chant slogans of war and lift their faces to the man on the balcony. In 1936, from this very spot, he promised an Italian empire like that of ancient Rome, one that stretches from the Strait of Gibraltar in the west to the Strait of Hormuz in the east. Four years later, allied with the most powerful man in Europe, he is one step closer to achieving the empire's glorious resurrection. Fascist banners hang everywhere. Streets are clogged, shops shuttered, schools closed. Italian and German radio stations and all frequencies in German-occupied Poland,

Luxemburg, Belgium, Bohemia, and Moravia are set to broadcast Mussolini's declaration of war on Britain and France.

Less than twelve hours after Mussolini's announcement, thirty-six RAF Whitleys, on a midnight bombing run, unload seventy tons of explosives on industrial targets in Turin and more than fifty tons on manufacturing warehouses on Genoa's docklands. The raid claims fifteen civilians. On Wednesday morning, 12 June, the lead news item in Milan's *Corriere della Sera* lists the dead.

> *. . . Among the casualties are prominent aero-engineer Signor Rosso Terzo and his daughter, Signorina Gabriella Terzo. The pair left Milan just after eleven o'clock Monday evening following a celebratory dinner with the Terzo and Agnelli families. Signorina Terzo, Public Relations Director for Agnelli Fiat, had resigned her position in preparation for a move to Lugano, Switzerland. Her father is said to have driven her to the Agnelli factory to retrieve a box of personal items. Investigators speculate a bomb fragment severed the car's braking mechanism, sending it into the railing at a high rate of speed. According to Lorenzo Terzo, son of Rosso and brother of Gabriella, the two died instantly.*

Harry paces the narrow street behind Milan Cathedral, a hollow feeling deep in his gut. Abandoning every caution, he spent the better part of the night inside the massive Duomo. Under dark haloed angels and their trumpets, amid flickering votive candles that cast ominous shadows, he stood vigil at her casket. He prepares himself for the coming hours, intensely aware of the hostility he will face.

His connection with the Terzo family is finished, severed four days ago on a dark stretch of highway. In the wee hours, it crossed his mind to slip away, to trade a lover's devotion for the responsibilities of war. But Gabriella is here. For a few hours longer, he will not desert her, no matter the cost.

Hours before the Requiem Mass convenes, Harry stands hat in hand in a palatial sitting room of the Terzo estate, summoned there by Gabriella's mother, Vivianna. Grief has taken its toll, her face a ghostly pale. She kisses his cheek. One thin hand holds the sleeve of his coat; the other clutches a flat white box.

She holds out the box. "She went back for this."

He places his hat on a side table and accepts the offering. *What could possibly have been so important? At midnight? Why has her mother summoned me to explain it?* Gently, he squeezes Signora Terzo's hand, and she releases the box to him. He feels her watching his face as he lifts the lid and finds, to his utter surprise, a silk necktie. Thoroughbreds racing across a background of the purest blue. "I don't understand. Why would she?" He pauses, reflective. "For this?" He seeks the right word, "Something so insignificant?"

Vivianna Terzo walks to the window that looks out over the garden, a long pink line of roses in bloom under a gray sky. He knows her as a strikingly forceful woman—worthy of her noble name—and is stunned by her image, fragile and stooped, diminished with the burden of grief, sorrow written in her demeanor, her spirit shriveled. She does not seek to disguise it.

At the wedding reception a mere ten days ago, they sat an arm's distance apart, close enough for him to admire the line of her cheek and breathe in the subtle scent of expensive Chanel. After dinner they danced—Gabriella with her father, Harry with Signora Terzo—to a Glenn Miller medley. The four of them had laughed—simply, happily—at the orchestra's interpretation of *Little Brown Jug.* On that day, Vivianna Terzo stood tall, round, and filled with life's joys.

Now, she stands thin and quiet, gazing out at a distant place. She moves to a brocaded couch in the middle of the room and sits, her back against the pillows. She motions for Harry to join her and looks down at the shaky hands folded in her lap. Her voice chokes with emotion.

"Gabriella and I liked to go out walking. Since she was a little girl, it was our time together. Just the two of us. No one else. She was my sweet lively child. Always the brightest light in my life." Her hands flutter, and she presses them tightly together.

An Italian mother who confesses to preferring daughter over son. There are few who admit to such a choice.

"We would admire the shop windows. Stop at the Grand Hotel for cups of chocolate. Find a table on the loggia, watch the crowds, and create funny stories about those who passed by. A week ago, a few days after the wedding celebration, she told me she was leaving for a while. Until these government disagreements—as she called them—were resolved. Though she did not give it voice, I knew you had something to do with this decision. It was so unlike her to choose to leave me. To leave her family. On that day, I hated you for taking her away. I begged her to stay. God has thoroughly punished me for that plea. Placing my need over hers. My dear Gabriella, the obedient daughter. If only she had paid her mother no mind."

Signora Terzo struggles to continue her story, a distant look in her eyes. "Not knowing when we would again have our little ritual, we walked for a few hours more. On the Via Manzoni in a small shop, there were ties arranged in the window."

She stops and shakes her head. Clearing it of some errant thought. "They were smart ties. Unusual colors and scenes. Gabriella studied each one. She spied this one, and she laughed. I close my eyes and hear her now. Quite suddenly, that beautiful gasp of joy. 'This one is meant for Harry,' she said. 'No one else shall have it. Horses running under a perfect blue sky reminds me of San Siro. The Gran Premio,' she said. It was a stunning day, if you recall. Before the race began, before you arrived, she looked down and there you were looking up at her. You removed your hat and waved. She said she knew then that she would love you. So . . ." Vivianna Terzo sits very still. It is an interminable moment, a deep sadness between them. "It was her exquisite memory of you. How could she leave it behind?"

How little I know of love. Lives change. Worlds end. For want of a simple tie.

She opens his hand and places a string of rosary beads into his palm. Her voice, when she finally speaks, is almost unrecognizable. "Partire è un pó morire. To part is to die a little. There is an agony that comes with living without them." She looks down at her now empty hand. "Will I never see you again, Harry Douglas?"

He senses she does not expect an answer, not one that will satisfy either of them. Wise enough to keep silent, he gets up and lifts her to her feet, feels the lightness of her bones, and wonders how one loses such strength in so short a time. They stand for a long moment, looking at each other. In her eyes is a look of suffering so intense it makes him draw back. She has told him what she wishes him to know. Now she is no longer present, but somewhere else entirely.

In that instant, he feels Gabriella surrounding him, pressing in, reminding him of the hard reality of her death, his own masquerade in the face of her professed love, his inability to save her, his foolishness in believing he could. Without a word, he retrieves his hat and tucks the beads and the tie into the pocket of his jacket.

The impenetrable Lorenzo appears just inside the doorway, a cold anger in his eyes, rage thinly disguised. In his mother's presence, Lorenzo does not speak nor meet Harry's eyes. Harry speculates that this will not be their final encounter. Here is a man easily driven to violence. Experience tells Harry that Gabriella's brother relishes an approving and supportive audience. Until the requisite spectators appear, Lorenzo Terzo will simmer in his hatred.

Harry closes the door to the sitting room and finds the hallway to the front entrance.

An hour later, he squares his shoulders and emerges into an open piazza to wait among the mourners. He steps into the vast interior of the cathedral. Heavy scents of wax, incense and tragedy fill the air. The caskets of his lover and her father stand on biers in the center of the sanctuary—surrounded by burning candles and crosses draped in black—moved from the small sepulchral chapel where Harry found them the night before. He pauses in the shadows until a grim-faced Lorenzo and his mother are seated. The translucent black veil covering Vivianna's head and shoulders renders her invisible.

Not wishing to walk the endless aisle past Terzo family members and their bejeweled friends—those with whom he danced and sang days before—he finds a seat in a back pew and sits down to await the organ's entrance processional. The world passes in slow motion. He feels an immeasurable sadness, a peculiar numbness, his nerve endings undone.

In a large plot in a corner of the Terzo estate, they bury them side by side. Harry looks toward the Terzo home and recognizes the garden window where Vivianna stood. In the days ahead, no doubt she will spend interminable hours rooted there, gazing at those she loves.

There is an incessant drizzle in the gray sky, and he finds a place under the canopy that protects the open graves. The family's priest, Father Frisetti, stands nearby, waiting for the others to gather. Harry approaches him.

"Lorenzo is grief-stricken," Frisetti says. "Bursting with anger at the English bombs. It is the way he deals with his pain. Much as I try to dissuade him, he is bent on vengeance."

"I'm here, Father," says Harry, "to honor Gabriella's life and mourn her death. Her brother does not concern me."

"He is a powerful man," says the priest. "Power is his opiate." He adds quietly, "I am aware there is bad blood between you."

Bad blood doesn't tell the half of it.

After Father Frisetti pronounces the Rites of Committal, after the faithful intone their prayers of farewell, after the last bits of dirt are shoveled onto the coffins of Gabriella and her father, Lorenzo and Harry stand face-to-face. The dampness has flattened their hair, and thin streams of water accentuate their faces. Lorenzo's fists close with fierce intensity.

"What the hell are you doing here?" he snaps.

In the weary lines of Lorenzo's face, Harry sees not grief, but hatred. He does not fault Lorenzo for wanting to squeeze the life from him. Harry understands the need all too well.

There is no doubt in his mind. *The guilt is entirely mine. My naïve promise of protection. Believing I could wrap her safely in Switzerland while war descended upon us. My arrogance, my idiocy, caused her death.* No matter that he thought she was safely away. No matter that Gabriella decided to drive that particular highway on that particular night. If she were here, she would insist the responsibility was hers alone, that she chose her own fate. But Harry's gut tells him something different. It is he who supplied the coordinates for the drop. He who targeted the Agnelli and Terzo factories. He who is to blame as surely as if his hand released the latch on the weapons bay and sent bombs plummeting from the sky. He who cannot change the road she drove that night. He who cannot grab her and pull her back from those irrevocable choices each of them made. He who cannot save her from the terror of the final moments of her life.

In Lorenzo's place, Harry would ache to kill that man. Without hesitation, he would already have completed the deed.

Harry holds Lorenzo's stare, refuses to look away. "I am here to pay my respects. A mourner filled with grief. Like you."

Lorenzo's jaw hardens. "You're nothing like me," he snarls. "My sister, my father are dead."

Many of the mourners have gone. Still, a silent field of tight black umbrellas hunch against the rain that splatters the earth. Attracted by the scent of violence, they gather. Harry waits wordlessly. The small crowd will bolster Lorenzo's fury. He spits at Harry's feet, starts forward, puts himself in Harry's face. "Your bombs found their target. A revered man and his daughter. How dare you stand here? How dare you watch us grieve? You will pay for what you've done."

Lorenzo backs up and widens the distance between them. Harry feels the heat and rage recede. Lorenzo calls out, in a voice calculatedly loud enough for the others to hear, "Get the hell out of my country, you British bastard."

"Canadian. I'm a Canadian bastard," Harry responds. "It matters what we're called."

Chapter Five

16 **June 1940.** A statement regarding France's imminent collapse and the urgent need to prevent French equipment falling into German or Italian hands is delivered across Europe and Northern Africa. The British Foreign Office orders its agents to proceed immediately to discover the locations of all vessels of the French fleet. Desperate for word of the number and type of French ships in each port and their exact positions, British intelligence dispatches agents to southern France, French territories in North Africa, and Alexandria.

Near midnight, flying east from an airfield north of Marseilles, six RAF Wellingtons find their targets on Genoa's docklands and, farther north, west of Milan on the outskirts of Novara. Six manufacturing plants are leveled to the ground.

No one will sell Harry a ticket to Toulon. Hordes of travelers—shoulder to shoulder, bags on their backs, boxes at their feet, unable to go, unwilling to stay—jam the station. It is a chaotic scene. The situation is critical. Trains from Porta Garibaldi are packed with French citizens, frantic to reach home before the Italians permanently close the border to them. After spending years in and around Italy, Harry still cannot fathom the Italian code. The Italians—unlike the Germans—do not move swiftly regarding such things. Nor does consistency reign. Thus far, Italian officials at French border stations have simply tightened travel between the two countries. It is the way Italians operate: Make things unpleasant, frustrate people—their own citizens included—with delays. Hours and hours of delays. There are no detentions or arrests. Harry notices a slow exodus—automobiles, bicycles, on foot—along the roads west of Milan. Those who can afford a ticket board the trains and trust they will make it beyond the border.

After an endless line, Harry buys a ticket for Chambery and finds an empty place in a second-class car among a family of five, a young mother and four children, all under the age of eight, he is soon to learn. Their belongings spill across two benches and clutter the center aisle. In a dark suit carrying one bag and standing alone, Harry is a figure out of the ordinary.

"Pardón, monsieur." The woman senses his presence, pats the bottom of her youngest child, and begins to move aside the blanket that covers the child's legs.

"No need, madam. This seat will do." He nudges past her and sits down next to a sleepy small boy with a broad face, bangs cut straight across his forehead. A homemade haircut, if ever he saw one. "I don't wish to disturb you or your children."

"You are alone?" she asks, her voice husky. Her long dark hair and wide eyes, her voice, send a jolt through him. Gabriella smiling, that quick flash in her eyes. Joyously alive. His fingers in her hair.

The image leaves him speechless for an instant. "Yes," he manages.

In a half whisper, she asks, "Will they detain us at the border, do you think?"

"Likely not. What will the carabinieri do with dozens of small French children?" He tries to make light of her question, reassure her with a smile. *They'll dump the lot of us on the Italian side and run straight back to Milan.* Given the present circumstances, he doubts a French train will be waiting across the border.

"Where are you traveling to?" he asks, hoping the family will not have far to walk on the narrow mountain roads. How can she possibly carry her children and their heap of belongings for any distance?

"My family lives near Modane, a few kilometers from the border," she says. "If we can cross, they will meet us."

He feels a strange feeling of relief, as if, for a moment, the family has been his responsibility. The boy takes that moment to nuzzle against Harry and rest his head, eyes closed, in Harry's lap. "You will be fine, then, madam."

If the train drops its passengers at the border, Harry has little expectation of getting to Toulon, no chance of meeting Mick on time. Only a handful of Alpine passes are safe for motor vehicles. The other route is the coast road. He suspects it is already officially closed. That leaves the mule trails, difficult but doable. He thinks about the woman's comment. From the border, he can walk to Modane. With a little luck, he can catch a train south to Marseilles, then east to Toulon. It will take longer, but at least he will get there.

"Your husband is there?" He assumes she has a husband.

She bites her lip, blinks rapidly before she meets his eyes. "He works in Milan." She looks ready to say more, but closes her mouth quickly. A tic of alarm.

A blue-uniformed official smelling of foul cigarettes stands above him, hand extended, the address and tone formal. "Per favore, il passaporto, signor."

Harry rearranges the sleeping boy, stands, reaches into his jacket.

The official flips through several pages, focuses on the dates of entry and exit stamps. "Norte Americano. What is your destination?"

"Chamonix," Harry lies.

"Skiing in June?" Pursed lips.

"Afraid not," says Harry. "Much as I'd wish it. I've come from a business meeting in Milan."

The man looks harshly at mother and children. He slaps shut the passport—a busy man—hands it to Harry. "You will get your wish. A snowstorm has settled in the last few days. What is this business you are in?"

"Sawdust. I'm in the sawdust business."

The official's mustache—trimmed to perfection—twitches. He moves his eyes up and down Harry's suit, unsure perhaps, whether he looks the part of a sawdust salesman. "In Milan? Sawdust?"

Harry smiles, unfailingly polite. "It was a follow-up visit. Trouble-shooting, we call it. Our client was not satisfied with his delivery."

"And the name of your client?"

"Terzo. The Terzo Sawdust Plant. Perhaps you've heard of it. Not very imaginative title. But understandable, given what they produce."

The official narrows his eyes. He looks sideways at the mother and children, their messy heap of possessions. "There are seats in the first-class cars, signor. You may wish to relocate there," he says with a smirk.

Harry wants to knock the smirk from the man's face. Instead, he sits down, gathers the sleeping boy into his lap, "Grazie, signor. I am quite content."

He leans back against the seat, the accumulated strain of sleepless hours and Gabriella's death hitting him full on. Too exhausted to move, he begins to doze, a growing strip of darkness overtaking him until he ceases to be conscious of the anxious conversations of his fellow passengers or the rhythmic rumbling of the train's wheels.

He holds her image in his mind as he fades into sleep.

When he awakens, the temperature in the car has dropped significantly, ice crystals in starlike patterns on the glass. The family huddles together for warmth, the boy curled under Harry's arm. They hear the shriek of metal on metal, and the train begins to slow. As Harry foresaw, the train stops a hundred yards short of the border—refusing to enter French territory. Into a ferocious cold and great cloud of fog, the engineer unloads his passengers. Hand-in-hand with the child, Harry disembarks. The snow is knee-deep, the chill seeping into bone. Harry scoops up the boy, lifts him onto his shoulders, and shepherds the child's shivering family into France.

The track behind them is empty before they cross the border.

Chapter Six

"Dio cane!" Lorenzo's face is red with fury. He paces the length of his office and back. "The Genoa plant is rubble. The entire production wing in Novara is destroyed."

"You could use some sleep." Nico lifts two small cigars from a silver box on Lorenzo's desk. He places one in the pocket of his jacket, lights the other and hands it to Lorenzo.

"You have to do it." Lorenzo grabs Nico's arm.

"What?"

"I'm not talking about pissing on the bastard. I want him dead."

Nico disengages Lorenzo's grip and makes his way to a leather sofa that stretches along one wall.

The lion resumes his pace; the cigar twists in his hand. "He boarded a train at Porta Garibaldi this morning. The train stopped, as expected, this side of the border. He walked into Modane and asked about trains to Toulon or Marseilles," says Lorenzo.

Nico lounges on the couch, removes the second cigar from his pocket, runs it under his nose, lights it, and smokes for a moment.

He moves the ashtray closer. "You've given him a shadow? Or this information fell from the sky?"

"The French are easily terrorized these days. A bit of prompting, information comes available."

Nico raises his eyebrows. "Remind me never to get in your way, cousin." He smokes again. "So, he's on his way south."

"Not by train. Between the exodus and the blizzard, they're all jammed."

"The roads are impassable as well. How else can he travel?"

"Mule, bicycle. One of Hannibal's elephants. How the hell would I know?"

"You're not giving me much."

"You have to do some on your own," Lorenzo snaps. "The Alpini have crossed the border. Ask your friends. You must have contacts. It's not so long ago."

Nico shakes his head, says nothing for a few moments. "They've got their problems fighting the snowstorms. Major delays to Grenoble. Heavy artillery cannot navigate the pass. Tanks and trucks are stuck on the roads. They make more progress near Sospel, but Douglas cannot be that far south. I suspect he's cooling his balls in Modane."

"Go to Modane, then. Goddamn it. Find him. Destroy the English bastard. Pezzo di merda!"

Nico tries to redirect Lorenzo's tirade. "What about the factories?"

"I reached Farber by phone. He will have to be convinced to rebuild. Monaco has changed the old man. I thought he was in my pocket, but his dick's gone soft, says he is unsure of his allegiance. Who gives a damn about fucking allegiance? Allegiance to what? Hitler is on the move. He's going to devour France and

Britain and secure the whole of western fucking Europe. Terzo/
Farber has to survive. We must be capable of responding to the
Reich's needs. Farber does not understand. We must own those
contracts for German aircraft engines."

Lorenzo walks to the desk, unrolls the aero engine drawings
he has confiscated from his father's—now his—engineers. They
had been reluctant to part with them, said they were incomplete.
He took them anyway. He stares at the drawings, fingers tracing
the new engine's outline.

"Just shoot the bastard."

Chapter Seven

2 1 **and 22 June 1940.** Benito Mussolini sends his army into France. Three hundred thousand Italian troops cross the border. One column marches along the Mediterranean coast toward Nice, another through the Alps south of Chamonix at the Little Saint Bernard Pass. A third proceeds along the southern portion of the Little Maginot Line. The Alpini Corps advance on a twenty-five-mile front, assigned the task of capturing Chapieu, Setz, and Tignes and continuing the offensive into Albertville. This region is heavily fortified with armored formations at Solage, the Traversette forts at the border and the Bourg St. Maurice in the Isere River valley. French garrisons consist of a mere 3,000 men with 350 machine guns and less than adequate ammunition. For three days, there is rain and snow and dense fog. The Alpini Corps take up positions stretching southward from the Seign Pass.

Harry's years in service taught him to exclude the unnecessary. The morning he left Milan, he emptied the contents of his apartment into a small duffel bag, slipped the key into the owner's box, and walked out the front gate, knowing he would never open it again. On his person, he carries a combat knife fitted for the sheaf that now weighs against his spine and a loaded .38 service revolver for his shoulder holster. He slipped extra cartridges and an Alpine map into a jacket pocket and a small pair of binoculars into an inside pocket. A small holster strapped to his ankle holds a lightweight Baby Browning pocket pistol, acquired in Ethiopia from a Frenchman—after considerable whining—who lost the last poker hand and had no cash to pay his wager. The Frenchman owed him more than the gun was worth, but Harry settled the bet all the same. The well-crafted pistol has become Harry's favorite, weighing half a pound, flawless at close range, able to dump six rounds in less than two seconds.

Finding no hope of boarding a train in Modane and less chance of hiring a car or even a mule, he has no choice but to take the only route left open. His destination is Briancon—as the crow flies, thirty-five kilometers to the southwest, farther inland from the Italian border—where he is almost certain to find a train— passenger or freight—that will carry him to Toulon. Luckily, the summer trails from Modane to Briancon are well marked and, in normal weather, well used by scores of sun-thirsty hikers. His map indicates rest huts at three intervals along the way. A briskly paced walker, the map directs, can travel the distance in eleven hours, though the route's challenges include rugged glaciers of three-thousand meters and jagged chasms nearly as deep.

He has been on the move for days. If his body is to last through the next hours, he will need to conserve energy. Harry has never hiked the French Alps, and in many months, he has not challenged certain muscles, but snows and icy winds are more than familiar to him.

Harry's was a grim, austere childhood marked by the absence of familial love and shared with a hotchpotch of seasonal strangers. His scowling father, a successful dairy farmer with five hundred acres in northern Ontario, lives near a village named St. Charles. In winter, subzero wind gusts rearrange the largest of snowdrifts. From the age of twelve, Harry rose at the cock's crow, labored in all seasons without payment, and shared the same backbreaking work that every hired farmhand bore. In a world of hard men, Harry learned their unwritten laws for survival. Stand up for yourself. But don't be an arrogant bastard. Curse when it feels right. But don't be a crude troublemaker. Drink your share of cheap liquor when the bottle is passed. But don't be a loathsome drunk. Take your beating at the card table when your turn comes. But don't be a shark's fool. Above all, when asked about your lot in life, smile a wide grin and state the firm belief that life is no harder than you will it to be. A man gets what he gets. A man earns what he earns. A man knows what it means to be a man.

Years later, when Harry made his escape to McGill University, he shed the coarse language and pungent aroma that came with such an upbringing. But he held fast to the working man's prized laws for survival and the mettle they inspired.

After four years, he graduated in the middle—lower middle, truth be told—of his class. Out of the classroom, there was no questioning his achievements. Through discipline and grit, he became the Redmen's fastest and most acclaimed downhiller. The best of the best. An ace with a wind-burned face and moves as smooth as if he had been born with skis on his feet. Harry's study time was spent memorizing every bump and perfecting every turn on Mont Tremblant's most challenging runs. Released from Earth's gravity, he launched off steep embankments, somersaulted ravines, soared over snow-laden treetops. At night, he grew wise in other ways. Frequent visits to countless—too many to recall—après-ski bars earned him a fluent, slangy French, and a five o'clock habit for potent homemade brews.

When the snows melted, his pursuits turned to European politics and to the violence and grace of the boxing ring. Though twice as resolute in this indoor world, he gathered no titles. No accolades accrued. His rewards consisted of a pair of finely carved shoulders and a reputation for ferocity. Every sparring partner wore his father's face.

When talent-spotters for the British Secret Service—sculpted goatees and exclusive preparatory school manners evident in spades—scoured the Commonwealth for those who had not roamed the same circles as they, those who did not trouble themselves with gentlemanly codes of right and wrong, those whose talents they did not possess, they discovered one of the most complete men they'd ever got hold of. Harry Douglas traded the fogs and chills of the Canadian plains for the fogs and chills of the British Isles. In so doing, Harry discovered a place where he belonged and the better parts of himself.

In Jacque's Sentier de Randonnée, a small sporting shop in Modane, Harry stops long enough to purchase equipment required for the journey. The merchant—an unshaven septuagenarian with deep-socketed eyes, a mass of greasy gray curls, a cigarette clenched in his teeth—warns him against heading into the mountains until the storm has well passed. Tobacco smoke drifts from his oversized nostrils. The entire region, the shop owner says, has endured three days of blizzard. Gale-force winds in the higher elevations have surely altered or closed portions of the trail. No hikers dare it now.

"I'm not going far," says Harry, "just to Briancon."

Harry collects from the shelves a fur-lined jacket and wool pants, heavy gloves, goggles, cold-weather hiking boots, a thick neck scarf, a ski hat with earflaps, a two-sided rucksack, a compass, a flashlight and batteries, and a canteen with a wide shoulder strap. At the street market, he fills half the sack with dried fruit, meat, cheese and bread, a tin of matches, a tin of skin salve, and small bits of cloth and dried wood. He changes into the cold-weather gear, packs the other half of the rucksack with his street clothes, and stands at the entrance to what he believes to be the hiking route—a narrow ribbon of trail that curves up to the right—that will take him south. In his haste, he is certain of only two things: He has little more than twenty-four hours to reach Toulon. And there is no way to contact Mick or others in his service. He is entirely on his own.

Fingers of a drowsy fog crawl over the mountains. It is late June, nightfall hours away, plenty of time to find his way to the first hut, some six kilometers distant. There, he will sleep for a few hours, and then set off again with the fresh light.

Harry walks at least a mile up a rutted trail, each footstep crunching in the crisp dry snow. The steady beat of his boots pushes him forward. He eases around large boulders in his path. Icicles cling to overhanging rocks, so that he has to knock them loose before he steps under them, careful to avoid the newly jagged edges. He reaches the top of a ridge, just below the clouds, and leans against a rock to ease the weight of his pack. In his left shoulder, an old ache stirs—reliving a catastrophic fall, a fractured scapula—on an icy slope in the Laurentian

Mountains. He breathes through his teeth and adjusts the pack. Already his clothes cling in a thin cold sweat. He tilts back his head and searches the white slope, touched by its strange solitude. This world is deceptively quiet, no signs of living presence. He finds no words to describe the wild sight of mountain, wind, and sky.

The weather is ever-changing, a thick white cloud, a shrieking raw wind, a spot of blue sky and fading sunlight, a gauzy glow and moments of calm, then ominous pockets of stinging snow, and wisps of cloud again. He angles his walk away from the wind, but it wraps around him nonetheless. The trail is steep and snowy—he has underestimated its sharpness and the depth of snow—with nothing but piles of rock between him and a vertical drop of several hundred feet. He imagines himself falling, swallowed by the abyss.

An hour later, the trail dissolves into a cold gray mist, the path now empty, the markers buried beneath mounds of snow. The sky darkens, and he glimpses the beginning of a faint roundness of moon behind a haze of cloud. He has expended great effort and made snaillike progress. Climbing at a sharp angle, a wet wind now howling against him, he watches a fresh gathering of clouds race toward him, a clear promise. The dim light is fading, and he plants each step carefully, feeling a new urgency to reach the hut before this latest storm lands. The image of avalanche crosses his mind. He looks up at a sudden break in the clouds and scans an unbroken landscape of white.

The rucksack, heavier with a layer of wet snow, shifts on his shoulders, his hat and neck scarf coated with ice. His leg muscles begin to spasm and stiffen. Turning back is out of the question. He comes upon a narrower auxiliary trail that goes some distance down and to the left, where he spots an opening in the rocks, possibly an ice cave. At the least, he might rest out of the wind, inhale a few breaths of warm air and use the binoculars to search for the hut before darkness falls completely. But that brief respite is time wasted and there is danger of falling, likely an inability to retrace his steps, particularly if the incoming storm dumps snow on the narrow path. He cannot afford to wander aimlessly, even for a moment. His breath comes in shallow gasps, the air grown thin. The steeply graded main trail looms above him, subject to the bitter wind—his lungs already two blocks of ice. Without sufficient oxygen, the climb will test his limits. The merchant assured him the trail leads to the rest hut. It sounded like the truth. He thinks briefly of the consequences if the merchant was mistaken.

He ties the earflaps tight around his goggles, tucks his chin into the fur of the jacket, and rewinds the scarf—layering it around nose and mouth so that each inhalation of breath will gather a small degree of warmth. The storm is coming in fast. He has to keep moving so that his legs do not become immobile. He focuses on gaining a tiny bit of earth, one step after another, up the mountain. These rest huts are built on level ground, he remembers. In due course, then, the trail must level off. Cold common sense, it is. *Clever, Douglas. No time for word play.* He occupies his brain by conjuring up bits of popular songs and begins to hum the tune for "My Prayer"—not the slower Ink Spots version, but Norma Bruni's adapted upbeat Italian tango.

The light mist becomes a fog so dense he cannot see the trail at his feet. He recognizes he now stands in the middle of the storm cloud. The air hardens. Wind wails in his ears and whips aside the scarf. A cold snow pelts his goggles. His face burns.

He can no longer see which way to go and his first instinct is to stop, but—fully aware this is the worst move he can make—he slows his pace and keeps his head down, turns his back to the wind and finds the compass inside his glove, straining to hold it steady. Exhausted and hypothermic, he struggles for a point of reference. South, fix on south, the way is south, he says aloud. Do not wander aimlessly. The wind grabs his words and bears them away above the endless mountains. The slope sharpens anew, and he inches upward, his side to the wind, the snow stinging his face, the back of his legs beginning to burn. The wind shrieks, pushing him forward one moment, pulling him back the next.

What transpires next is never entirely clear in Harry's memory. He cannot sort out what happened on that trail and what he imagined. From a great distance, he has vague recollections. Muddled fragments of time seek and fail to arrange in precise—or believable—ways. He remembers the sharp cold, his hands and feet near frozen, his legs numb, his face raw, his throat icy hot, the growing blackness. He falls in the snow, unable to rise, the wind pressing down his efforts. The snow so cold—colder than anywhere he has ever been—that it feels hard upon his face. He gives himself no choice but to keep moving. He crawls forward, upward, desperate, refusing to stop, the cold bone deep, snow gathering around him. He is shivering violently, his mind unable to mark time or place. Two minutes or twenty? How far has he crawled? Shall he stop and give up his place in this world?

He senses a swirling wind and snow, and feels a narrow fissure—wide enough to pull himself up, and stand between the ice-laden rocks—then a larger crack wide enough to step through. Inside the darkened space, his muscles lock and harden, and he begins to shake. He has a sensation of sinking. He gasps for breath, and descends into a black hole that holds him fast. There is a still silence. His mind fades to nothing. He is no longer fully conscious.

A ghostly image against the rock comes forward to meet him, her hand outstretched, her hair that rich auburn hue, her face olive-gold, the air around her a sparkling cloud that blinds him. He extends his hand to touch her. "You mustn't give up," he hears her say.

Then, as if a stage curtain has risen to reveal the next scene, the storm—the blinding fog, biting wind and stinging snow—is gone. A dazzling moon bathes the pearly mountains against a velvet night; snow crystals shimmer in its light. Not twenty yards distant, a remote structure floats under the thousand stars that surround it. Shaking with relief, he manages to drag his leaden feet through the deep snow and push open the hut's weathered door. Four bunks line one wall. A metal counter stretches beneath the window. A pair of empty water buckets are stashed below. A shelf contains candles of assorted lengths, holders attached along three walls. The hut is dark and bitter, but the firepit—a round stone formation at the hut's center—is charred and smells of recent use. Just inside the door, a small closet protects a woodpile and well-worn ax. A half cord of wood—blessings from above—is stacked in one corner, and a box of sturdy wooden matches sits on a ledge.

Exhausted and barely conscious, he shrugs out of his pack, blows cold air into his hands and clumsily—muscles twitching—strikes a match to light a thick candle. He holds it close, inhaling the light, warming his nostrils, easing the paralysis in his throat. With time, his hands relax enough so that he can build a small fire. He kindles the flame, and when the hut grows warm, he strips off clothes and boots and crouches naked in the firelight, throwing log upon log into the orange flame until the heat envelops him, and he tastes acrid burning in the air. He moves closer to the fire until he can feel the bones in his hands begin to thaw. His face and lips throb from the intense heat. *What I'd pay for a stiff shot of whiskey.*

He organizes layers of clothing and boots, wet with sleet and snow, along the pit's rim. From the rucksack, he tears half a loaf of frozen bread and, with a poker, toasts it quickly on the open fire, the meat too hard to chew and he too tired to wait for it to thaw over the flames. He settles instead for softening several bits of icy cheese and a piece of dried fruit, chilled but edible. From the bunks, he drags two thin canvas mattresses to the edge of the pit, piles one atop the other and sits amid the soft crackling, savoring the warmth, until his breath and heartbeat return to a rhythm that feels like normal. The ache in his shoulders and knees begins to fade. A weathered wooden closet offers up two sets of boots and snow skis and six woolen blankets. He inspects the condition of the skis and wonders whether they had been carelessly forgotten, or if they served as spare equipment for an alpine ski squad. Snug beneath the warmed blankets, he is overtaken by an overwhelming sense of gratitude. For the first time in days, he sleeps.

In that icy black hour before sunrise, he awakens cold and shivering, the fire long since dead. According to his watch, it is four o'clock, twelve hours since he left Modane and started up this mule trail. He rekindles the fire, warming body and clothing and another chunk of hard bread before dressing for the next leg of the journey. He dreamed of that unlikely image in the cave. In the face of certain death, he had been spared by

Gabriella's golden spirit. It is a spiritual leap. An act of faith he has never possessed.

The soft pastels of an early alpine dawn brighten the window. The hiking map indicates Briancon is fifteen miles to the south, southwest. If the weather holds steady, and he skis the downhill segments, he can lop off a good portion of time, and reach the train station before noon. Against a dark sky, rosy streaks of light and a cluster of morning stars shine overhead, the moon a huge sphere close enough to touch. The air is clear and cold as he descends four wide wooden steps—he does not remember climbing them—and tucks in the newly warmed scarf around his chin. There is no wind, the only sound the crunch of his boots on the top layer of icy snow. An old supply sled, useful with a horse or mule, is propped against one wall. Regrettably, no such animal is available, and the sled has seen younger days.

He props his pack and the newfound skis against the door and picks his way along the length of the ridgeline on which the hut is perched. The rays of a weak sun emerge. He listens and hears—save the sound of his own breathing—a clear and profound silence. He takes in the depth of the valley and the stunning vista of mountains, peaks as far as he can see in all directions. White, barren, infinite, a land of white crags, without detail to give them scale, a disorienting environment that washes away depth. He gathers air into his lungs, bellows into the still white morning, and listens to the echo fade away.

At the bottom of a long deeply creviced gully is a thin ribbon of water, faint and far away. From this height, it is nigh impossible to gauge distance. According to the map, the Durance River flows six miles to the south, a distance he can cover at cruising speed in less than half an hour. On race days, when he barreled full-steam downhill on Tremblant's steepest trails, he had been clocked at close to seventy miles per hour. Wild rides on perfectly packed snow. On a mountain he knew better than the back of his own hand.

He retrieves the rucksack, ties on the skis, and begins his solitary journey down the mountain, savoring the familiar swish of skis on snow. His moves are instinctive, born from hours of practice and the power of repetition. In joyful rhythm, he dances effortlessly down the curve of the mountain, conscious only of the fluid movement of his body. A bird in flight. As close to heaven as earthbound bodies come. Momentum drives his speed, and in little more than ten minutes, he is halfway down the mountain. Atop a slim ledge, he catches his breath. As a light snow falls, he rests under an overhanging rock. An unusual patch of warmth—a high underground spring—allows him to warm his hands and produces a steady drip of water. He patiently tops off the canteen.

Minutes later, he steps out from the overhang and looks straight down. At the bottom of the slope lies the river. From afar, the slope had looked manageable all the way down, but up close, the terrain is more challenging than any he has skied. It is an unpredictable snowfield that demands more than skill. The ledge breaks off into a near vertical precipice, an unforgiving combination of ice and pitch. One wrong shift, one overcompensation, he will find himself in freefall, sliding with alarming speed, unable to right himself, his body crumpled and trapped in a hostile crevasse that hides its dead. Mercy neither given nor received.

Leaning in, the rock face holding him upright, he shuffles to his left to test the strength of a thick ice shelf that juts from a second ledge below his left ski. The shelf holds and he stands on one leg, using the mountain for support. Two more well-spaced ledges allow him to push from one to the other. When he manages only to inch along a third such perch, the time comes to turn his skis down the mountain.

The next sixty seconds will require the exactness of the watchmaker, the artistry of the ballet. He must keep to the north side of the gully, hit the tops of the rocks at precisely the right angle, and shift his weight at the split second of contact. He prays the storm dumped enough snow to provide the tiniest bit of traction. Otherwise, the skis will slip, and his body will tumble uncontrollably down the incline. He pushes toward the drop-off, inhales one long breath and exhales a burst of icy air.

Clacks of wood on ice. Gusts of swirling snow. Dizzying flashes of white. The skis plunge down, brushing the tip of each boulder, executing one meticulous turn after another. Less than ninety seconds later, the skis sink unceremoniously into a flat area of deep snow. A rush of water runs some distance below. The pounding of his heart tells him that he remains among the living.

The last mile leads straight to the riverbank. From there, he will discard the skis and cross the bridge over the Durance. Its southerly course intersects with the Guisane, the river that leads to the high plateau on which Briancon is built.

He hears the rumbling of distant thunder and first thinks it is a warning of an impending storm. But the sound continues as a regular chant, reverberating among the mountains.

Of course. The Italian army is coming through the Col de Montgenèvre pass, the border a mere two kilometers east. I can only hope a dozen French machine-gun nests await their arrival.

It is the lowest of the crossings between France and Italy. The pass is kept open in winter, but the blizzard's heavy snows must have blocked the road. The Italian equipment can't get through.

Mountain warfare in play, then, using all the elements at hand. The Alpini are notorious for it. Maneuver. Find the most difficult route, particularly in these seemingly impassable mountain regions. Search for routes that will outflank the French. Harry recalls Hannibal's storied trail through the Alps. The Carthaginian general and his war-elephant corps surprised his enemies.

He senses movement down below. The binoculars reveal a lone climber scaling the eastern slope. Unquestionably an expert mountaineer. Dressed in white. Equipped for snow. A disciplined quickness in the gestures. Alpini.

He did not count on company. Harry tosses the binoculars into the pack, stows it and the skis behind a clump of boulders and moves to the high ground, climbing farther up the mountain, looking for footholds among the steep icy terrain. Within minutes, he has disappeared into a thick cloud. His size-10 footprints—bait for the hunter—remain. The long upward slope is sheltered by a small rise with a high snowbank, and he stands behind it, listening. If the cloud lifts, he is an easy target for anyone firing from above.

From the small of his back, he withdraws the knife and waits, coiled and ready, inhaling soundless breaths. His hand wraps around the hilt of the knife. Concealed within the cloud, he sees nothing. The wind whips cold against his face.

A bullet snaps overhead.

The predator has found him. Out of the fog, distinct and startling, the heavy butt of a rifle delivers a brutal blow and a sharp slice of pain to Harry's cheek. Blood oozes into one eye. He steps sideways, enough time to bring up the knife and drive it into the attacker's shoulder, tearing sideways through muscle and tendon. His knife wears a ribbon of red. The attacker drops the rifle and grabs for Harry, one hand finds the soft bones of Harry's windpipe. Harry brings up his knee, hard, into the attacker's groin. The hand abruptly relaxes, but as Harry backs away, he loses his footing on the icy slope and cannot right himself. The knife slips from his grasp. As he slides backward down the steep incline, he feels for the Browning at his ankle, and yanks it free. He pulls the trigger, shooting blindly at the figure rushing toward him. Heat rises in his hand. There are sharp flashes of light when the pistol fires again. He hears three, four shots, then a dreadful cry followed by a long guttural gurgling. The attacker lurches forward, arms outstretched, head to one side, mouth gaping, a dark hole in his neck, a look of startled amusement. He trembles the slight shiver of death, his icy-blue eyes focused on one small spot of red on Harry's boot.

It is the last thing Antonio Alessi sees in this life.

Chapter Seven

June 1940. The Italian Regia Aeronautica bombs the city center of Marseilles, killing 143 and wounding almost as many. On 21 June, in both day and night raids, they bomb the Marseilles port. On 22 June, France reluctantly signs the Second Armistice at Compiègne, resulting in a division of France. Germany will occupy the north and west regions, closest to the English Channel. Italy will occupy and control the southeast, as far west as Nice.

The café is called Denise. It sits two blocks off the waterfront in the middle of a narrow street between a patisserie and a shop that develops photographs for Toulon's seaside tourists. Caravans of automobiles, trucks, bicycles, and overloaded carts flood the southern coast road, filled with people fleeing from the east, putting distance between themselves and the invading Italian army. They carry children, bundles of belongings, and the smell of despair.

In the twilight, two men—one in the costume of a dockworker who has just finished his shift, the other dressed in a seriously wrinkled gray traveling suit—sit at a table five steps from the curb, glasses of red wine and a bowl of empty mussel shells between them. For the third time in as many minutes, Harry checks his watch. "Who're we waiting for?"

"Dispatch said to sit tight until contact shows." Mick regards his friend and partner silently, pretends to scan the sidewalk before he speaks. "If it were me, I'd be holed up somewhere crying my heart out."

Harry counts the passing vehicles. In truth, her death has wounded him in a way he did not foresee. He shakes his head and gives a small shrug, the closest he comes to openly expressing his grief. "The last thing I need is an empty flat with time on my hands. I'm here. I'm working."

"Then what?"

"Then I'll work some more. Skip it. Worry about yourself."

Mick picks up a mussel shell and lobs it, careful to miss the heads of passing cyclists. "Mind explaining what happened to that aristocratic face?"

"I ran into a glacier."

"You should be more careful."

Harry finishes his wine. "Down to business."

Mick glances left and right, lowers his voice. "Yesterday, I walked the beach to the tourist area and hired a boat. Small craft. Rented out by the hour. I cruised the quays, noted names, vessel types, locations, crew positions. A genuine naval squadron, it looks to be. Close to forty ships in port. One carrier, four heavy cruisers, eleven subs, twelve large destroyers, eight supply ships, the rest chasers, patrol boats, one or two of each. Nothing came in or out yesterday, but two vessels look to be in prep: destroyer *Le-Corsaire* and the big one, aircraft carrier *Commandant Teste*.

Crews busy. Don't know where they're off to, but definitely on the move. Could be one escorting the other."

"All French navy? No swastikas or Il Duce banners?" asks Harry.

"Not at the moment. Doesn't mean they're not over the horizon. This fleet is well guarded by shore artillery, by the way. In any case, after filing the numbers, I popped in at a couple of cafés along the waterfront. Figured to find a few froggies with loose tongues."

"Who did you think would talk to you? You smell like rotten fish."

"That was jolly unkind."

The auto traffic has subsided. A line of bicycles piled high with possessions pedals past. Harry observes a couple—arm-in-arm, well dressed, thirtyish, seemingly blasé in the midst of their country's turmoil—who stop on the sidewalk opposite their table. They examine the menu, and then move on.

"Decent intel?"

"Nothing at first. But the night wore on. As the cups increased, there were more than enough grumbles from our French sailor friends. Real sense of defeat, they have. Shock more than anything and fear. Under no circumstances do they want to be delivered to Hitler's service. To a man, they say they won't crew their ships for the Reich. Nothing short of revolution. Big talk. Could be true."

"Let's hope. We may be looking at a massive scuttle."

When it grows darker, Harry and Mick move inside the smoky café, order a drink and wait, listening to the babble of conversation around them. Worries about family and friends, about when the Italians will arrive, about which faraway place will provide safety. After another half hour and nothing to show for it, Harry and Mick have heard enough and get up to leave. The bartender sends half a bottle of table wine and gestures them to stay. Mick turns the wine bottle in his hand and reads the handwritten label. The well-dressed couple who passed by earlier enter the front door and occupy two stools at the bar.

A few moments later, a slender-framed woman steps from the shadows of a back hallway. Large dark glasses conceal her eyes.

Mick takes a moment to recognize her. Under his breath, loud enough only for Harry to hear. "Bloody hell. What's she doing here?"

Without hurry, she unties the knot under her chin and removes her scarf, a grand flourish. "Sorry to be late, boys. The roads are blocked with traffic. Hordes of people going God knows where. Let's have a drink." A deep and striking voice. She nods to a vacant table in the corner away from the eavesdroppers, then approaches the bar and orders a round of martinis. She and the bartender are acquainted. One or two men look up as she passes. Dressed in a form-fitting suit of brown linen with a thigh-high slit to her skirt and diaphanous sleeves, she is a darkly attractive woman.

"Churchill's favorite spy." Mick turns his head aside so she will not hear.

"Doesn't exactly blend in." Harry lowers his voice.

"She gets what she wants," Mick says. "Tough to her fingertips. Could sell sand to a Bedouin. Probably has."

She pulls back one of the chairs and sits down. Harry notes the red painted lips, high cheekbones, black bobbed hair. Not a classic beauty. A boyish figure. A rare abundance of style. Where has he seen her before?

She removes the glasses—completely unnecessary at this hour—and thrusts out a hand, "Margaret Gautier."

"Harry Douglas." He shakes her outstretched hand. She has a firm grip. And eyes a deep shade of violet.

She smiles broadly at Mick. "Mick and I are old friends. Lots of stories there."

"I can't wait to hear them," says Harry. He makes an effort not to look at his friend. It is then he remembers the scene a long year ago. The purple dress in the owner's box at San Siro. The Polish woman. Mick's hurry to change the subject. Her hair cut short now. Gautier is hardly a Polish name. Not the first hint of Eastern Europe in her aristocratic accent.

"Maggie's got plenty of stories," says Mick. "None of them true." A false grin on his face.

"How are you two?" She taps one cigarette from the pack in her handbag, waits for a light, continues before either Harry or Mick can respond. "The word this afternoon, France will seek an armistice."

"A separate peace?" Harry inclines his head.

"Looks that way." She takes a quick drag. "They've done it. Tanks are rolling into Paris."

"So Britain stands alone. The little man is coming for us. The final assault," Mick says.

"At this hour, he's after French ships and bases, especially those in West Africa," she says.

"Not if we get them first," says Harry.

"What? Send them to join the British fleet? Sail for British ports? You are a naïve one, aren't you?" She stares intently at him.

Mick interrupts. "If the fleet here at Toulon were to sail to North African ports, prepared to resist German attacks . . ."

The martinis arrive. They watch the bartender disappear into a back room. She drains her glass. "Steady my nerves," she says.

Her nerves seem fine to Harry. This revelation, however, he files away. In his experience, people unknowingly expose themselves in small bits of conversation. He remembers an old farmhand's comment from years ago. *Pay attention when people tell you something about themselves. When they give you something, use it.*

"Possible," she says. "I doubt the French will agree. Gallic pride. More likely, we'll demand the fleet disarm and move to neutral ports."

"I'm under the impression the fleet is well dispersed. Alexandria, Casablanca, Bizerte, Beirut," says Harry. "Surely, there'll be recognition of former alliance."

"Britain's in no mood for weakness. A combined Italian-German fleet could dominate the Mediterranean. No more questions of friendship or hurt feelings. France crumbled and is now listed as a *former* ally. The situation is frightfully tense. With increasingly poor communication out of Bordeaux."

Mick and Harry say nothing of their recent experience—the chaos and confusion of impending defeat—in Bordeaux.

"So they won't hand them over," says Mick.

"Handing ships over to a foreign state constitutes treason," she says.

"Gentleman's honor, then?" says Harry.

"Who's the gentleman?" she asks.

"Will they agree to remain in port and immobilize?" asks Mick.

"Not according to my sources. Although Alexandria may move in that direction." She signals for another martini. "They're thinking seizure or destruction."

"They?" asks Harry.

"The War Cabinet. Churchill is extremely worried. His latest remark, 'Kiss Darlan's stern if you have to, but get the French navy.' He's on a bloody tear. Mightily afraid of the consequences should the fleet fall into German hands. Or Italian. Mussolini's bent on controlling the Med."

"So, what's next?" asks Harry. Treason, sabotage? He wonders at the level of information she possesses.

"We've yet to determine locations and capabilities of the largest concentrations of vessels, especially battleships, cruisers, and destroyers." She looks at Mick. "You reported on Toulon, the biggest bunch so far. I've just come from Les Salins-d'Hyére. Only two subs there. In rapid time, we need reports of Séte—Mick, that one's yours—and Ajaccio."

"Where?" interrupts Harry.

"Southwest coast of Corsica. It's a strategic location, though luckily the port is somewhat shallow. No word from there. We don't know what could be coming or going. Mussolini will, of course, have agents investigating." She looks at Harry. "That's your job. Once it's done, proceed straightaway to Algiers to report on Oran and Mers-el-Kébir."

"And what will you be doing?" asks Mick.

"I'll be sitting around watching Garbo films," she says testily.

"It's like that, is it?" says Mick.

"Let's just say I'll give the French navy plenty to talk about."

"Any notions on how to get to Ajaccio?" Harry senses he is interrupting something.

"Last time I looked, it's in the middle of the Mediterranean." Margaret Gautier rises and stubs out the last of her cigarette. She regards Harry with a quizzical gaze, then points a red fingernail at him. "Harry Douglas. Of course. I hardly recognized that pretty face. You're the brave one who pursued the illusive Gabriella." She adds, "Now deceased, so I hear. Your doing?"

Harry starts from his chair. Mick grabs a handful of Harry's jacket and holds on.

She takes a small step back. "My God. Those nasty rumors are true." She glances out the door. "You and Nico have something in common," she muses.

Harry feels the bile rise. He intensely dislikes Margaret Gautier—or whatever the hell her name is. He swallows his anger and says, "Lukas and I have nothing in common."

"Oh dear. Family secrets. How could you know? Nico always was—I should know—in love with Gabriella. Since they were children. Years ago, they set a wedding date. Too bad she's not going to make the ceremony."

With that final bit of unwanted news, she languidly lifts her purse and scarf from a vacant chair, saunters out the front door, and slides into the passenger seat of a waiting red Alfa Romeo.

Chapter Eight

She is a woman apart, a woman one remembers, a woman not to be trusted, a woman who mixes truth and non-truth at the drop of her hat. She doesn't fight clean. She doesn't play by the rules. She makes her own rules.

Lena Dunin is born in 1912 in what was then Poland's northeastern province of Wilno—called Vilnius now—to an aristocratic mother touched with insanity and an absent father who deals in rare and precious jewels. Surrounded by maternal grandparents and doting servants, Lena lives a privileged childhood on a rural family homestead with a barn full of thoroughbred horses and stable ponies. Until 1921, when the Bolsheviks come calling. In a scene of needless violence, her grandfather and three male servants are killed, the horses slaughtered and the family estate set ablaze, the land later is seized by a neighboring Soviet republic. The women move three hundred miles south to where Lena's father's business flourishes on one of Warsaw's most fashionable streets. For the next ten years, they live unwelcome in her father's household, her mother a frequent visitor to a nearby sanitarium, her grandmother a recluse perpetually awash in grief, and Lena, a solitary young girl unable to forget the high-pitched squeals of panicked stallions.

In 1931, in the months after Lena marries Feliks Prus, it becomes clear that hers is not to be a monogamous union nor one destined to bear fruit. Her husband—older than she by fifteen years, a career diplomat with connections, generous to a fault and frequently gone from their home—provides Lena both the freedom and resources to escape gloomy, gray Warsaw and indulge her fondness for hunting, thoroughbred racing, Alpine skiing, the Mediterranean sun, Milanese fashion, and flirtation. She hears from her husband infrequently.

On the first day of September in 1939 when Hitler's aerial assault on Warsaw begins, she has just returned from the turquoise coves of Portofino. For the next week, hour upon hour of bombardment destroys the old city's hospitals, churches and monuments. In the days that follow, German armored units reach the southwestern suburbs where she lives. Not one to hide in her home or exclude herself from the business of war, she and other civilian volunteers erect barricades on the streets and successfully repel a group of German Panzer tanks. In an old warehouse, the civilian fighters uncover a stash of turpentine and cover the streets that lead to the city center. When the enemy tanks approach, Lena and two other women ignite the liquid. The tanks are destroyed and the city is granted one more day of freedom. Until this short-lived success, she has never placed collective interests above her narrow personal ones.

The Warsaw siege lasts until September 28, when the Polish garrison—many of the men starving and sick with dysentery—surrenders. Almost 140,000 Polish soldiers and government officials, including Feliks Prus, are taken by the Wehrmacht. They simply vanish. Two weeks pass, and she receives word that her husband is dead, the result of an accident in a place called Stutthof, a work camp near the city of Danzig. Later, she learns the camp was constructed especially for the imprisonment of Polish intelligentsia, leaving her with no doubt of the lack of truth of the supposed accident.

Thus, Lena Prus holds no affection for either the Russians or the Germans. Given present circumstance, she hates the Germans more. There will be no fear, no concessions, she decides, and swears to do whatever is necessary to rid her country of Hitler's armies. By both nature and choice she is, in a word, consumed with Hitler's fall. She decides she will not be left to pick up the pieces of defeat. She doubts her neighbors will join in her resistance. There are those she knows who will, in small ways, try to humiliate the invaders; but most, she surmises, will keep their heads down, or, at their worst, collaborate.

Emboldened by the shock of her husband's capture and death, she joins the Polish Underground State. She has no husband, no children, nothing to distract her from her vengeance. The following week, she begins smuggling leaflets to her neighbors. One month later in the dead of night, while the Germans busy themselves persecuting the Jews and the gypsies, she traverses a path along the Vistula River, at times crawling flat to the ground in the marshlands, and escapes into the Kampinos Forest. From there, she makes her way—over several days and numerous furtive encounters—to the seventh arrondissement in Paris where old family friends provide a place to rest, passage to London and introductions to the leaders of the Polish Armed Forces in the West.

Within weeks, her upper-class manner and charming personality earn her notoriety on the London cocktail circuit. Subsequently, she becomes acquainted with high-ranking members of British intelligence. Hearing her story and learning she is fluent from an early age in French and Polish and literate in Italian and German, MI6 immerses her in their intensive three-week training course at Beaulieu, the secluded country estate in Hampshire. She establishes herself at the head of the class as the consummate professional. Her private war has begun.

Her face and her facility for languages—she now speaks fluent German and Spanish—allow her to pose as any number of western Europeans. Thus, sealing her fate. As Margaret Gautier, Sophia Falco, and on rare occasion, Lena Nivek—jealously guarded aliases with ingenious cover stories and false documents—she travels to Cairo, Madrid, Istanbul and Rome, and through various means—flirtation, flattery, and divine glamour—makes her way in record time to Berlin, effortlessly infiltrating the Reich. Early on, she learns that German officials are drawn to attractive women who express a certain sexual appetite. They judge her based on her appearance, her cultivated Swiss accent, her comments on fashion and celebrity. Like an exotic pet, they parade her to their private parties. Quite readily, in their desire to impress, they give up classified facts and figures without the slightest discretion. In turn, she feeds them a delicious array of false information. "Totally unsubstantiated," she says, "but a very, very good source, one I trust with my life." She is an incredible liar, a fearless agent and a cold strategist who smuggles numbers on troop movements, convoys, tank exercises, shipping schedules and sailing routes in double-sewn pockets in the fingers of her gloves. In so doing, she has managed to wrangle her way into the good graces of one Winston Churchill.

She quite enjoys the sophisticated games, the power of deceit, but she always feels as if she is walking on a wire. One dreary afternoon, while browsing aimlessly among the shelves of a Charing Cross bookstore, Lena finds a line written years earlier. *"She had the perpetual sense, as she watched the taxi cabs, of being out, out, far out to sea and alone; she always had the feeling that it was very, very, dangerous to live even one day."* Virginia Woolf shared her reality.

16 April 1940. She does much of her work in the dead of night, but early one morning she has arranged to meet two men—one Belgian, one Dutch—at a small hotel six miles from the center of Berlin. At seven o'clock, carefully orchestrated, she arrives by car and enters a door off the main dining salon. Waiters in white aprons move table to table briskly filling cups, delivering plates of wurst and soft-boiled eggs and baskets of brötchen. This area, used as a breakfast room for guests of the hotel, is sufficiently out-of-the-way and suitable for a quiet exchange of information. At least, she thinks so before she arrives. Even at this hour, the room is crowded, abuzz with conversation, and smoke-filled. She guesses, rightly so, that Hitler's new anti-smoking laws have not reached the outskirts of the city. Gossip has it that, in preparation for the ban, Armaments Minister Albert Speer stockpiled cartons of Camels, his favorite brand. The German high command is notorious for small-minded gossip.

She has a way of entering a room that captures attention, and she stops to say a word of greeting to the host. Like her, a displaced Pole navigating an uncertain world. To most guests, he is a kindly entity who shows them to a table, fusses over their coffee, and remembers their names. On the other hand, he is adept at collecting secrets and identifying those who find them useful. Lena and he are well acquainted.

"Fraulein Gautier, how wonderful to see you." The host kisses the top of her glove. "We have quite a lively crowd this morning. I am so sorry to have to say it. As you see, your usual place is occupied."

She, of course, has no usual place, but follows his gaze to a table near the door where a man—his fastidious appearance and severe clothing unmistakably Gestapo—is scanning *Der Stürmer*, Hitler's favorite daily. Every few seconds, he looks up from the page and stares intently at each table of diners. He does not appear to be leaving anytime soon.

The two men she seeks eat at separate tables, like strangers, each careful not to acknowledge the other. She has no wish to draw attention to them, but needs to draw their attention to her. They will have to find another place or cancel the meeting altogether. Something neither she—nor they—can afford to do. The information she intends to provide is timely and critical.

Holding a slim black cigarette holder between her fingers, Lena approaches the table near the door. "Have you a match?"

Gestapo man pushes back from the table and considers her question. He looks her up and down. A predator sizing up his prey. Without a word, he produces a steel lighter from his pocket and presses a thick thumbnail against a small lever. He holds the flame close to his chest so that she has to lean toward him to capture it. His sausage breath nearly causes her to gag. *So early in the day for such odor.* His heavy hand wraps around her wrist. By this time, she is accustomed to Nazi officers' clumsy attempts at sexual flirtation, and thus resists the impulse to pull away.

Holding his eyes with hers—a promise of more to come—she draws several quick breaths until the cigarette's end burns red-hot. She bends even closer, enough that the smoldering ash drops directly into his lap.

"Ach!" The man hops to his feet, the chair tumbling backward.

When others turn to look, she pretends embarrassment. "How utterly stupid of me." She addresses him with a certain formality as if to recognize his high rank. "Allow me to have your trousers cleaned or replaced, whatever is necessary. Forgive me." She places one gloved hand on her heart, apologetic, the other on his arm. "Leave them with the concierge. He will provide another suit of clothing for you today."

Gestapo man assesses her, then brushes the ash from his trousers. She bends to retrieve the fallen chair and quickly makes eye contact with the Dutchman, then the Belgian. A brief shake of her head and the tilt of her chin toward the door tells them to leave and meet her on the outside. At that moment, she knows not where.

For them, she possesses urgent information. *Fall Gelb*—Case Yellow—conceived the previous October, is code name for an aggressive German campaign in the Low Countries with an advance through the middle of Belgium. The attack is imminent. She has details of its timing. In the past, the Dutch were reluctant to take such information seriously. They plan to remain neutral as they did in the Great War and are ill-prepared for such an invasion. The previous week, when Denmark and Norway were surprised by German forces, it became clear that Hitler's strategy for Europe includes the Dutch coastline—another outlet to the North Sea for his U-boats—and Belgium's Ardennes Forest, the logical route for the German offensive into France, north of the fortified Maginot Line. This reality forced both Belgium's King Leopold III and Dutch Queen Wilhelmina to scramble for credible intelligence.

She has been in contact—a brief fervent relationship—with a German intelligence officer, a secret opponent of the Nazi regime, who assured her the invasion, under the code name *Danzig*, is about to begin. In little more than three weeks, bombers, parachutists, and ground divisions will sweep into the Low Countries.

After a bit of confusion, her two contacts find adjacent wooden benches outside in an ancient garden, a solitary place among a stand of trees well hidden from the hotel buildings, a place where guests sit and ponder the gurgling stream, smoke, and pray. She sits on one bench, her coat around her shoulders. The Belgian sits on the other, his long legs draped to one side and crossed at the knee. The Dutchman stands slightly apart, facing away, head down, puffing on a small brown pipe, pretending not to be included. Neutrality intact.

It is news they dread.

"An accumulation of facts," she says, "leading to one conclusion."

"We've heard it before," says the Belgian, "in October, we waited. They never came."

"This time they will come," she says.

"And what are we to do?" the Dutchman asks.

"You have details and the approximate date. The rest is up to your governments."

"We have little time." The Belgian speaks to the Dutchman's back.

She wants to remind them that as recently as January, Churchill had done his best to convince both the Belgians and the Dutch to join the English-French alliance, but they rejected the request, the Dutch refusing to believe the inevitable, the Belgians preferring a diplomatic solution. Before she can speak, she is startled by a sound behind them and turns to look.

A chill of terror grips her, not for her own safety, but for the others. Gestapo man, in a fresh pair of trousers, strides through the trees, his scowl taking her in, then the two men. She rises and reaches out to him, her eyes an invitation. "I was about to give up," she says, the beginnings of a small smile curling her lips. "But here you are. At last." She never makes the mistake of being afraid, and she possesses a huge capacity for invention. The Belgian remains seated, and moves his head slightly away, his gaze giving the impression he is alone in thought, unconnected to her. The Dutchman continues smoking, his back to them, his head tilted to the sky.

Gestapo man stares coldly at her, his lips tight. "Your papers, Fraulein."

"Of course." From her bag, she withdraws Margaret Gautier's identity papers and holds them out, a conscious effort of submission.

"French," he says with disdain.

"My father's name," she says. "As you see, I live in Berlin. Near the Tiergarten. It makes for interesting afternoons." If she keeps him talking, he might ignore the others. At least, the Dutchman can slip away unnoticed.

Gestapo man's approach softens, but he suddenly stiffens, looks past her. "Who are these men?"

"We haven't met. After our unfortunate encounter in the breakfast room, I came here to collect myself." She is correct. The three have not been introduced in any formal way, have not asked for or exchanged names. Better that way. She looks from one to the other, as if in that moment she has just realized their presence. "We simply share this peaceful place among the trees."

The Belgian stands, bows and addresses her in flawless German, "Fraulein, I have no wish to interrupt. Excuse me, if you please." He nods to Gestapo man and smartly clicks his heels.

The Dutchman says nothing, smokes his pipe and, without a backward glance, strolls casually across the narrow footbridge that spans the stream. A morning walk in the woods.

Before Gestapo man can call out to him, she lays her lips against his sausage-stinking ear and whispers, "Promise me you will come to Berlin. You have the address. It is easy to find. I will be waiting."

At such moments, she catches a glimpse of her soul fluttering away. There is not a grain of fact there. She has come to learn that if she is to survive, she must be unencumbered by truth or principle or past.

Two days later, the Dutch government declares a state of emergency, intensely worried they will become the next victim of Hitler's strategic assault. In the early hours of 10 May, residents of Rotterdam awake to distant rolling thunder. The steady roar of aircraft engines follows. The long-feared German offensive has launched. From above, the Luftwaffe bombards the Netherlands, Belgium, and Luxembourg. On the first day of the operation, virtually unopposed, German forces occupy Luxembourg. Poorly equipped and hurriedly assembled Dutch forces suffer more than nine thousand casualties—killed or wounded. Their main force surrenders on 14 May. Queen Wilhelmina flees to England and establishes a government-in-exile. On 28 May, after fierce fighting and exceptional efforts by the Belgian Army, Belgium, too, sub-mits. King Leopold III remains in Belgium in German captivity.

"I have decided to stay. The cause of the Allies is lost," he reluctantly tells his citizens.

The Nazi machine rolls on.

A week later at Cairo's famed Shepheard's Long Bar, Duquesa Sophia Falco of Madrid, dressed in an evening gown cut by a tailor in Paris in the latest Mondrian pattern, sips a Campari and soda in the company of a handsome SS officer who proudly boasts of Himmler's plans to annihilate the population in occupied Poland.

"The Poles are animals. The earth well rid of such scum. We must make room for new German settlers."

She fingers her glass and hoots appreciatively. *How does one explain the existence of such a man?* She adjusts the neckline of her gown and waits for details. His eyes stray to her nearly exposed nipple. A waiter comes and asks if they want something more to drink, and they order a third round of cocktails. The conver-sation and the liquor progress, Sophia Falco murmuring vague flatteries, her voice oozing with the certainty of a wicked sexual encounter. In due time—she understands the need for anticipa-tion—she accompanies her eager companion into the maze of narrow streets in the old city. Eyes vague, snot running from his nose—the gin taking its toll—he fumbles to unbuckle his belt and open the zipper of his pants. In the littered, deserted alley, between breathless whispers of urgency—her need seemingly great—she leans her back against a recessed door. Two delicate fingers and the thumb of her left hand lift the hem of her gown. She wears nothing beneath it. Handsome SS man sways, unsteady in his advance but intent on directing his inflated cock to the black patch between her legs. With her right hand, she finds the pen-sized dagger in the slit seam along the gown's right hip the skillful Parisian tailor camouflaged so perfectly among Mondrian's geometrics. (She frequently has to remind them of her dislike of guns.) For another instant, she hesitates, until she feels his clumsy attempt to enter her, the coolness of the buttons on his chest against her naked belly. One downward motion—the quickness of her gesture escaping his preoccupied notice—drives the dagger deep into his groin.

She moves quickly away as the blood pumps from his artery.

"Filthy bitch," he spits.

Worse things have been said of her.

He slumps forward onto his knees, clawing at the door, black trousers around his knees, dagger protruding from his thigh, polished boots now spotted with blood. His agony lasts no more than a moment. Her sole regret that she did not force him to wallow and grunt like the stuck pig he is.

Slowly, she lowers her gown, careful not to sully her shoes—no telltale evidence to give away. She leaves the body in the door-way and remains in the shadows until she is certain the police have not been called, then retraces her steps to claim a seat on Shepheard's Terrace at a table overlooking the Ezbekiyya Gardens. Notably cool, she orders a gin and lime over ice, and requests the bartender to add a small shot of whiskey on the side. The shot warms her, sending a small wave down her spine, calming the tremor in her hand. An Iranian prince takes the table next to hers, complains about the color of the martini olives, and helpfully points out a spot of red on the toe of her shoe. She blames it on a waiter's clumsiness, a crushed cherry from an earlier Manhattan, she explains.

An hour later, she makes her way to her room, locks the door, and writes a coded message on the inside bodice of her gown. She places the shoes in one cleaning bag, the gown in another, and phones the laundry (the Shepheard famous for its 24-hour personal service) to request the items be cleaned immediately. "To avoid permanent stains from an after-dinner spill," she says. Within seconds, a tall Nubian appears, collects both bags, and hurries down the back basement steps—past the laundry room. The first bag he pitches into the flaming incinerator, the second he delivers to the last door in the hallway where the wireless operator impatiently smokes a cigarillo.

To her surprise, she finds she is crying quietly. Most of the night, she spends expecting to be arrested. Or murdered. In the morning, the bill paid, the Duquesa and her frozen heart board a plane to Berlin.

Chapter Nine

2 3 **June 1940. Ajaccio, Corsica.** Intent on finding and controlling vessels of the French fleet, Mussolini orders the second and third Italian *Squadra Aeree* to Corsica's north coast to bomb and strafe the ports and airfields of Bastia and Calvi.

Staring out the lone window that faces the seafront, Harry sits in a third-floor room at the Hotel de Golfe, feet propped on the sill. A stray dog, head and tail down against the rain, crosses the street below. The room is nothing much, no better than he expected, carpeted in faded crimson, furnished with a single bed, a square wooden table and a brightly painted chair that he now occupies. The walls are stained, the result of a half-remembered storm, the desk clerk explained. More likely—from the potent smell of the linens—an exuberant drunken party. He waits for the rain to stop, time enough to untangle his thoughts, and examine the puzzle running through his head.

Gabriella and Nico to marry? Impossibilities crowd his mind. It doesn't fit. Yes, she was set to move to Nico's apartment, but it was Harry who insisted she go to Switzerland. Harry who feared for her safety. Harry whose heart rose every time he caught sight of her. That she cared for him was understood. Gabriella was beautiful, funny, utterly feminine, fascinating, exasperating. There was always a distance between them. One, admittedly, he sought to maintain. Still, there was a mystery about her—from her—he did not understand. Disconnected somehow. Almost as if the family held some tantalizing secret she dare not share. Why not tell him straight away she had marriage plans?

He has other questions, too. How does Margaret Gautier know such things? She sat with Nico and the family last year at San Siro. Has she seen Nico since? Can it be Gabriella and Nico were betrothed before Gabriella and Harry became lovers, and things had changed between them? Jealousy would go a long way to explain why Alessi was sent to kill him. What of this enigmatic tie in his pocket? Of Signora Terzo's romantic story? There has to be something else she might have told him, but did not.

He knows how close one person can be to another and not know what makes that person's heart pulse. The space between them left uncrossed. "What sort of business are you in?" Gabriella asked him more than once. He wonders when he will let her go, forget the softness of her skin, those sudden bursts of joy. Still, there is this vague notion of betrayal. A notion that will eat away at him if he lets it in. The room is suddenly full. *Stop. Now is not the time.*

The rain has given way to a drenching mist and a beautiful twilight. Beyond the street, a small fishing boat putters quietly into the harbor. The docklands reach out into the inlet. On the far left side is the south quay—home to the main pier and the larger ships. On the right, a citadel perches on the hill above the harbor. A jetty and thick stone walls form a secondary moorage area, a sheltered pier for working boats and pleasure yachts and the mainland ferry on which he arrived. Steps lead up to a walkway that runs atop the seawall.

On the ten-minute walk to the main pier, he observes nothing of importance. Shadows of fishing boats that bob in safe harbor, a sharp smell of the sea, and the soft lapping of waves against the quay. Night falls hard on this island. Layers of clouds block all but a sliver of moonlight. He has counted on the full moon, but now the black space makes it too dark to identify the pier's occupants, let alone take note of crew size or preparations for movement. Walking the main pier's length, he counts the dark silhouettes of at least four naval vessels. There could be more in the basin. The shallow harbor makes it impossible for carriers and battleships to enter, but smaller vessels can moor here.

Harry's surveillance training taught him to gather information quickly, fill in the missing pieces later. But in Britain's current circumstance, the data he transmits must be exact. No room for error, the stakes too high. He planned to scout the wharf areas and be on his way to North Africa on the next southbound ferry, but he has to be certain. There may be other ships he cannot see.

Suddenly hungry—only a stale baguette and cold coffee on the ferry from Marseilles—and unwilling to return to the malodorous bed, he crosses the street and strolls to the end, the inland side, of the port. He passes a few cafés and stores shuttered against the earlier rain. A weathered iron fence guards an old customs house, and he stops at its locked entry gate to listen to the sound of warning bells from the lighthouse tower.

Rounding the corner, the aroma of freshly baked bread alerts him. He spots a light and walks toward it. It is hot, and a door is propped open. Inside, a young man with black closely cropped hair and a deeply tanned face sits at an upright piano playing jazz over a low buzz of conversation. Harry recognizes Count Basie's "One O'clock Jump." The room is packed with what Harry takes to be locals. Four men in a corner reach barehanded into a platter of steaming seafood and pour drinks from almost-empty bottles of wine. Couples stand at the bar holding hands. A lone woman with her elbows on the table bends over a generous plate of mussels. On a bench along one wall, a family of five—mother, father, three children—share a loaf of bread and a wedge of white cheese. The tinkling piano player moves on to Duke Ellington.

Harry wonders where French sailors spend their off-duty evenings. Most certainly, not here.

He sits at a table near the door, the small room's sole source of ventilation. A faint breeze lifts the edge of the tablecloth. On the train to Marseilles, he was thankful to have found a man of similar size who was willing—more than willing to Harry's observation—to exchange his well-worn casual trousers and pull-over shirt for Harry's suit and cuffed shirt. The man's shoes fit a half size too large, but a bit of newspaper in the toe corrected the difference. Thus, to all appearances, Harry arrived in Ajaccio as a simply shod worker, carrying a light travel bag. Better to be taken for a visitor from the French mainland than an agent from the British Isles. At the hotel, he registered as Henri Duget.

A waiter in a soiled white apron approaches the table and speaks rapidly out of the corner of his mouth. "What are you eating?" He asks the question in French rather than the local Corsican Harry expected.

"Soup and bread," says Harry.

"Beans, potatoes, cabbage?"

"That will do."

"Wine?"

Harry points to a bottle of red that sits on an adjoining table.

The departing waiter crosses the room and reaches for an almost empty plate on the table of a fierce-looking man of dark eyes and unruly hair. The big man seizes the waiter's wrist, and without looking up, says, "I haven't finished." He grabs the last bit of bread and stands to leave. The waiter—patient, obedient—gathers the plate and glassware. The man gives the waiter a slap on the back and bids him good night. Both men address the other in Italian. Not their first encounter.

Before he sat down, Harry—in his peripheral vision—caught a glimpse of the large man, enough to note the man's attention. The man glanced at Harry, then looked away. Now, as the man removes the napkin from his collar and tosses it on the table, he steers directly toward Harry on his way out the door, coming within inches of Harry's chair. Purposefully, it seems. No eye contact is made.

Harry works his way through two bowls of soup and a bottle of watered-down wine, and leaves the café in search of an establishment where French sailors are likely to drink their supper. At this hour, tongues will be loose. Enough to provide a choice bit of information. Avoiding the puddles and ruts on the dark side street, he listens for familiar sounds of late-night revelry. There is silence, save the beat of footsteps falling in behind him. Someone taking a walk in the dark. A slight scent of onions and garlic. Barely there. He thinks about stepping aside, allowing that someone to pass, but he keeps walking forward, maintaining his pace.

"I don't know you," says a voice at the rear.

Harry stops, turns. "In the café, you were staring."

"You noticed."

"Are you a policeman?" Harry knows he is not. "I mean no harm, merely looking for a strong drink to pass the night."

"I am not a policeman."

Harry waits for him to go on, but he does not. "What is it you want to know?"

"I want to know who you are."

"Henri Duget. From Marseilles."

"Marseilles? Your accent is not from the south."

"My mother was born in Lille."

"Lille. Soon enough, your mama will have a German lodger and accent. Those Cruccos want only Paris, but must climb over the north to get it." He chuckles, breaking the tension between them. "No wish to serve the Führer?"

Harry ignores the question. "I'm looking for work. I've cleaned a fish or two. Some as big as a shark."

The large man laughs, eyes him carefully. "You speak like no seaman I know. Corsica is not an easy place. We call it a mountain in the sea. A sea that spits you out if it finds your taste is bitter."

"And your name?"

"Ivo Guaneri."

"Italian?"

"The Romans stopped here long before the French."

"So you know of a place where I might find a job?"

"Possible." A long pause. "In Marseilles, do you know a man named Paul Carbone?"

"I've heard the name."

"Françoise Spirito?"

"Friends of yours?"

"Quite the opposite."

Harry's brain connects the two names to a recent case he and Mick investigated. Opium trade routes between Italy and southern France. Paul Carbone and François Spirito run a small criminal empire based on drugs and prostitution. The pair owns brothels along the Riviera and smuggle goods across the border. For the last dozen years, Carbone reputedly has been the most powerful racketeer in Marseilles, closely linked with local politicians, especially the mayor. A man named Simon Sabiani. With Sabiani's blessing, Carbone's thugs control the docks.

The waiter's deferent obedience comes back to him. "Should I know them?"

"Better that you don't."

Harry shrugs. The history is well known. Corsican families wait long and carefully for revenge. He has no time for it now. Uneasily, he thinks of Lorenzo Terzo's promise.

Together, the men wander silently down a desolate narrow street. A gas light fifty feet ahead—obviously the old part of the city—illuminates the ruins of an empty church. Harry would like to know more about Ivo Guaneri and his links to Carbone and Spirito. He suspects there is plenty to learn. At this moment, however, the man's company is a hindrance to his work. He needs an excuse to move along.

"A friend in Marseilles told me there are particular tavernes where one can find a companion for the night."

"Depends what you're after."

"A woman," says Harry.

"In that case, you will want Le Pigale. Pass the cathedral; turn right at the stone wall onto Macchini. When you reach the Avenue de Paris you will hear them long before you arrive."

Harry elbows his way through the dense crowd to the entrance. Le Pigale is wild ground. Raucous singing. Shrieks of pleasure. Stifling heat. Dockworkers two-deep at the bar. French sailors drenched in drink, arm-in-arm with whores in daring dresses. Harry avoids a round-faced woman in red, thin lips parted, a shadow passing over her face when he shakes his head and moves on. He searches for someone sitting alone in a corner, preferably dressed in a striped blue-and-white marinière, fondling only his beer.

"Sad story?" Harry asks.

A thin, pinched-face fellow smiles bleakly. "Sadder than yours."

"Join you for another round?"

"Only if you buy."

Many a story improves with a drink or two. "You are my guest. Name's Duget, Henri Duget. An early night?"

"Lèo Mercier. Duty in an hour, last watch."

"Hate those late watches. Never get used to them." Harry laughs. "I had it, you got it, any questions, I'll be crawling into my rack. Heard that more than once."

Mercier nods, grins—a mouthful of yellowed teeth.

"Which ship?" Harry asks.

"*La-Bayonnaise*, the destroyer. And you?"

"Next to yours."

"The sub *Sirène*? Can't be, I've met most of them. You must be on the trawler, *Borèal*?

"That's the one."

"Didn't figure you for a sous-marinier. Too tall for those racks. Made for midgets."

"Turned down the tin-can service for that very reason. Your crate shoving off soon?"

"I am the last to know such things. Where *Sirène* goes, *La-Bayonnaise* goes. We are sworn to protect the steely eyed killers of the deep." Mercier rolls his eyes. "C'est la vie."

"Two more ships have arrived? Am I right? Didn't pay much attention."

"Just the one. Little sub chaser. Number Three, they call it. It's a shallow port, narrow entry. Not much room for the big ones."

So, four vessels in Ajaccio. Destroyer *La-Bayonnaise*; submarine, *Sirène*; sub chaser Number Three; trawler *Borèal*. None leaving anytime soon.

Mercier finishes his tankard of beer and rises to leave.

"I'll walk with you," says Harry.

"As you wish."

They come to a stop at the end of a street in sight of the pier. "You're on your own now. No reason for you to call it a night," Lèo Mercier says. "There is music. And mademoiselles who love to dance." Mercier winks.

Before turning in, Harry wants to assure himself of the ferry's first departure time, but he cannot very well ask Mercier. The hotel's night manager will have a listing, but Harry does not wish to alert anyone to his plans. The ferry stands between the naval area and the smaller quay. He thinks of retrieving his small bag of possessions and waiting for the night to pass aboard the yellow passenger ship now tied up at the end of the dock. Nothing to breaking a lock and stowing away in a concealed closet. He's slept in worse places. Still, at first light, he has to confirm Mercier's statements.

Somewhere ahead and out of sight, he hears what sounds like a small cough and catches the familiar whiff of Turkish tobacco. An itch at the base of his brain. Something wrong. Harry reacts quickly, turns to retrace his steps. But he has no time to think it through. A figure emerges from the shadows directly in front of him. The figure nods, a brief movement of his head. Harry hears the echo of footfall—of remarkable speed—behind him. A trap. He has walked into it. He winces as the pain catches him at the knees and the back of his head. On his way to the pavement, he inhales, again, the light scent of garlic and onions.

He is aware of two men watching him. Ivo Guaneri, squatting on the pavement, speaks to them in Italian, mistakenly thinking Harry will not understand. "Into the kitchen. There." They pull Harry to his feet and lift him over a high threshold into a room filled with the aromas of spices and fish. Pails filled with brackish water and small sea creatures sit in one corner, a stack of chairs in another. Pots, pans, and cooking utensils are strewn along a counter. The two men push Harry into a wooden straight-back chair. One man holds his chest against it. The other holds a seriously vicious knife. Good soldiers who follow orders. Guaneri edges in the door, pistol leading, angled—Harry notes thankfully—at the floor.

"Why are you here?"

Harry pushes against the man who holds him, manages to rub the back of his head and takes a deep breath to let out slowly, giving himself time to think. One possible answer or another. "We discussed that."

"Where is this female companion? Plenty of opportunities at Le Pigale, my friend. Mademoiselle here. Mademoiselle there. You were not interested. Now here you are. Alone."

"Have me under surveillance, do you?"

"This is my continent. I'll ask once more. Who are you? Why are you here?"

"Get rid of them, and I'll tell you." He meets Guaneri's eyes without blinking and sees the challenge in them.

Guaneri waits the obligatory moment or two, signals the men—a wordless contract—and they leave. Not before giving Harry a final warning appraisal.

Harry smooths his shirt and brushes the dirt from his pants. The decision he makes is deliberate, done with a cool head. "I'm Harry Douglas. British intelligence. Sent to investigate French ships in this harbor."

Guaneri's expression is puzzled, but holds no alarm. "You have no ties to Carbone or Spirito?"

"That's why you nearly broke my bloody skull?"

Guaneri nods. "You knew their names."

"Because I've investigated their operation, their relationship with the Italians. My country has to know their alliances, where their allegiance will be."

"Of course they will side with Pétain and the victors. Whatever keeps their cash flowing."

"And you?"

There is no movement whatsoever from Ivo Guaneri until he lays his gun on the counter and grabs a chef's knife. Harry definitely prefers the gun to the knife, particularly from a man Guaneri's size. In either case, he has not planned to die tonight. Without doubt, he's asked the wrong question. Is Guaneri another of Lorenzo's assassins? Harry's had quite enough of them.

With his free hand, Guaneri pulls a chair off the stack, then sits, legs splayed, within arm's reach directly in front of Harry, no more than two feet of space between them. Harry monitors the knife in Guaneri's hand and tries to conceal his alarm. He sees the strength of Guaneri's grip, bows his head, and steels for the first strike. The man will do what he wishes.

Guaneri leans forward. He is within inches of Harry's face. The odors of onion and garlic—regrettably—may be his last whiff of life.

With the sharp end of the blade, Guaneri draws an oval on the soft wooden floor. He taps it once. "Mussolini wants Corsica. Since 1938, he calls us the bars of his prison." He adds four smaller circles, arranges them strategically and points to each in turn. "We, Malta and Gibraltar, Tunisia and the Suez. These five keep him from controlling the Mediterranean." He passes the knife over his initial shape, now the center of the rendering. "Last week, planes bombed Bastia and Calvia, not two hours north. It is unclear how many Corsicans are dead. It is clear he wants this port." The knife points to Ajaccio. "On the radio we listen to General de Gaulle. Resist, he says. Resist Pétain's armistice. Continue to fight, he says."

Guaneri sighs, surveys the floor map once more, raises searching eyes to Harry's. "In Corsica, we do not surrender. We do not sit quiet while Il Duce takes what he wants. We are free Frenchmen." He drives the knife into the floor. "We fight."

The four men sit in a tight circle in the half-light of the café, drinking dark coffee, smoking Turkish cigarettes.

"You are correct," says Guaneri. "The four French naval vessels in the harbor have been here for some time. The submarine and the destroyer disappear periodically. The sub chaser less frequently. As for the old fishing trawler, I'm unsure of her purpose. She stays close to the harbor."

Harry waits for his coffee to cool. He would have preferred a cup of tea and his pipe, and doesn't much care for the acrid smell of Turkish tobacco. A small sacrifice for the cause. "Smaller trawlers like the *Boréal* are converted to minesweepers. It's a quick way to increase military assets when they're needed. Replace the trawl with a mine sweep. Add depth charge racks on the deck, a three-inch or four-inch gun in the bow. Those trawlers are heavy, built to withstand all types of weather. Now, she's generally used to control approaches to the harbor. That's why she stays put. I'd wager she patrols the perimeter every few days."

Guaneri nods, toes out his cigarette. "What will you do with this information?"

"The French navy has vessels stationed at ports around the Mediterranean. The Germans are busy now, but soon enough they'll realize what they have. We need to know before they do."

"Can we help?"

"Right now, I need a ferry to the mainland."

Guaneri snorts. "A ferry?" He grins at the other men at the table. "A ferry, he says. He needs a ferry." The other men shake their heads and laugh. "Name your destination. We have fishing fleets at your service."

"As close to the north coast of Algeria as I can get. Algiers or the port of Oran."

"We can take you as far as Majorca. Porto Cristo on the eastern side. We often make deliveries there."

"Deliveries?" asks Harry.

Guaneri shrugs. "Cigars, wine. A means to avoid the customs officials."

Harry nods. *Smuggling. Predictable.*

"After that," Guaneri continues, "it is up to you. There are several fishermen who travel south to Algiers."

"How far is Porto Cristo?"

"About two hundred miles. In smooth seas, the journey will take ten hours."

"And rough seas?"

"A little longer."

Chapter Ten

A **moment before**, Nico Lukas had been propped in the over-sized leather chair, his feet crossed at the ankle and resting on an ottoman of soft suede of the same cognac color. Now, he silently rereads the fresh communiqué and casually rises to join Lorenzo at the window. He lifts the shutter to peer at the street below and at the Parco Sempione, a clear view all the way to the Arco della Pace. Nico hands the page to Lorenzo.

They both know what the news means. If Alessi is dead, Douglas is very much alive.

Nico held special affection and admiration for Antonio Alessi. From the early days of their Alpini training, they ate, slept and worked together. Alessi was the first man he'd recommended for Il Duce's covert security services. News of Alessi's death unnerves him immeasurably. His mind travels from one possibility to another. Italy's secret police are unaccustomed to failure, particularly with a man such as Alessi assigned the task.

Lorenzo lights his ninth cigarette of the morning. A smoky haze already fills the room, and Nico imagines the ashtray, within the hour, will overflow with crooked half-smoked stubs. Lorenzo's face is swollen from a night of drinking. "I told you to take care of it."

It is fruitless to argue, but Nico sees the need to defend Alessi, his friend and colleague. "I sent the best man I had. If Alessi couldn't take him, he's—"

Lorenzo interrupts. "He's what? He's done. He's dead. Send someone who can do the job. It's been three days since he left Milan. Where is he now?"

Nico returns to the chair and sits down, sorting through which information to disclose to a noisy man like Lorenzo. Whatever Lorenzo assumes, Nico is not the Terzo family's hired hand. "He caught a ferry from Marseilles, headed for Ajaccio."

"Right under our nose. What's he doing in Corsica?"

"Unknown. He's not there now. Left yesterday at dawn, on a private fishing boat."

"A fishing boat? Going where?"

"Let me finish, and you won't need to ask these questions. I'm told he's on his way to North Africa."

"Why didn't you take him in Corsica?"

"I had no choice. He'd already gone by the time we discovered him. Apparently used another name and passport and changed his appearance. Enough so our men couldn't identify him."

Lorenzo delivers a savage glare. "In other words, your OVRA missed him. Twice. When are you going to do your goddamned job?"

Nico drums his fingers on the arm of the chair. Though he suffers the rebuke in silence, he is weary of Lorenzo's theatrics. And constant criticisms. All the same, Nico knows this is indeed his mistake. He did not anticipate Douglas's talent for evasion.

Unfortunately, he paid the man scant attention at the start. Hardly the mindless playboy Gabriella made him out to be. Obvious now. All the same, Nico's men have more to do than follow Douglas around. The French are a new source of trouble. "What does it matter?"

"What does it matter? For fuck's sake, isn't that how you Corsicans do business? Oaths of vengeance. Kill anyone who disrespects the family. You understand it must be done. You have your social code. I have mine. My father's death must be avenged."

"And Gabriella? Your sister?"

Lorenzo exhales, stubs out the cigarette, half-finished. He walks to a cabinet made of ancient burl wood, lifts a bottle of hard-to-get whiskey from the platinum tray, and pours himself a drink. A generous pour. He waggles the bottle at Nico. "She knew what she was doing."

Nico shakes his head, declines. "What does that mean?"

"Gabby told my mother she suspected Douglas is an agent. British. Swore my mother to silence."

Nico raises an eyebrow. "Doesn't fit their type. Too colorful for the Brits."

"What sort of OVRA chief never inquired or wondered about Douglas's travels? In and out of the country. He shows up in time for this or that, then disappears for days?"

"I am the deputy chief." Nico emphasizes the deputy part of the title.

"At the moment."

"I thought Douglas was exactly who he said he was. A useless pleasure-seeker. A toy hobbyist of whom she would tire quickly. His alliances never crossed my mind. Nor that he was secretly collecting information on your factory locations."

"More than that. Clients. Distributions. Production schedules. Why else would he be here? You are the one who keeps a close eye on these rampant spy networks. British, Russian, German. Norwegians, for Christ's sake."

"There are tens of surveillance spy teams operating in this country. We're aware of them." Nico rises from his chair and walks to the window. The ache in his back screams for attention. "You're convinced she was aware of his deception?"

"Yes." Lorenzo gives Nico a strange look.

"Alessi went out hard. A fierce fight. Killed at close range. Douglas is a man with real talent. A man with capable skills. And not timid about using them."

"Wake up. I told you to get rid of the bastard."

"Do you think Gabriella provided plans, anything of that nature?"

"You mean did she copy specs and hand them over? How would I know? Ask Agnelli."

"She couldn't have known about the bombing raid. Surely she would have warned you."

Lorenzo shakes his head. He avoids the implication. "Surely not. You didn't know her."

"Well enough."

"Well enough to fuck her."

Nico flexes his fist. Some small voice tells him to get a firm hold on his anger. Lorenzo is a gutless shit, but Nico has never laid a hand on him. Nico is accustomed to wearing masks. He cannot afford to lose control. "Well enough to marry her," he says.

"But she wouldn't have you, would she?" Lorenzo finishes his drink, the last drop, stares into the bottom of the glass, smiles. A particularly unpleasant smile.

Over the years, Nico has grown a thick skin when it comes to Lorenzo's unique brand of cruelty. Though Lorenzo is his cousin—step-cousin, in truth, no common blood, thank God—he is not compelled to like him. From an early age, he did not. Nowhere close. Lorenzo's mother and Nico's stepmother are sisters. Years ago, when Nico's father returned to Corsica without them, Rosso Terzo took in Signora Lukas and her stepson, bought them a house in Milan, accepted them as part of his family, assured their position in Milan society. Family is family, after all. Yes, Nico's blood is Corsican, and vendetta is the social code. To any Corsican, vengeance and death are closely related. Lorenzo's notion is the way it is on the island. But Nico has no interest in destructive blood feuds that live on for centuries. "Gabriella was to stay in my flat in Lugano. Indefinitely, she said, when I gave her the keys. I thought she left Milan that same day. If Douglas is who we believe he is, and he cared for her, he told her to go. Why didn't she?"

"My dear Mamma begged her to stay. She wanted her precious girl a few more days. Now Mamma has nothing. No husband. No daughter. Just a son she never cared for. She earned her fate."

Nico looks away. A cruel fate for them all. One Aunt Vivianna did not earn alone. He waits a long moment—collecting himself—before he responds. "I doubt Gabriella was aware of the bombing. Douglas would not have confided it to her. Still, he wanted to be certain she was out of harm's way that night. He thought she was safe enough."

Lorenzo slams his fist down on the cabinet. "So he could destroy my factories with his bombs. My factories. Mine. He knew they were mine."

Chapter Eleven

Before dawn, one of Guaneri's men collects Harry from the hotel. They climb into a small dory at the end of the pier and set out to meet Bethune Nivani. His fishing boat, the *Immaculata*, is moored off a protected beach north of the city in a cove beneath a medieval watchtower, one of many to protect Corsica's coastline.

Built in the sixteenth and seventeenth centuries, the towers served as lookout structures. To gain favor with the Ottomans, Barbary pirates attacked coastal towns and captured Christian slaves. The locals established villages high up in the mountains away from immediate harm, but shepherds, farmers and fishermen worked the low coastal lands, vulnerable to attacks. When hostile ships approached, an alarm warned inhabitants to withdraw with their animals to higher ground. Alarms consisting of smoke, fires or conch shell blasts communicated in turn to the next tower. Within a few hours—plenty of time before the marauders arrived—the whole island knew of an impending assault.

As a rising sun shoots up from behind the peninsula's rocky peaks, the *Immaculata* slips out of the cove and heads west. The morning is hot and dry. Several men on the shore watch the vessel navigate the strait between the tower and the four islets of the Îles Sanguinaires (Bloody Islands), so named for their crimson-colored rock.

Though Nivani's rail-thin frame and cloudy left eye might make Harry believe the man is ill-suited for the two-hundred-mile journey through the large lake called the Mediterranean, Nivani's expression of utter confidence and the scent of raw fish that permeates his sunbaked skin convince Harry that this man and his aged vessel have made their share of runs between Ajaccio and Porto Cristo.

According to Guaneri, the boat is handmade by Nivani himself. As a young man, Nivani worked the docks, a free fisherman, hiring onto this boat or that, whichever required an experienced hand. At the end of each workday, he took up his tools—a crosscut saw, a hand plane, a clawed hammer, and a measuring stick—and walked a short distance to a small slice of forgotten beach where he built, plank by plank, his fishing boat. In a span of four years, Nivani asked for help only once, on the day he called his neighbors together to push his vessel into the sea. For the past twenty years, he and the *Immaculata* have rarely parted. The boat provides sustenance, home, and pride of ownership. Nivani and the *Immaculata* are integral cogs in Guaneri's smuggling empire. What part the ship and its maker will play in the resistance movement remains in question.

Clearing the watchtowers and the red rocks, Nivani opens up to full steam, more than twenty knots over a flat sea. Thankfully, the water is a summer calm, waves no more than a ripple, visibility clear for miles. They pass a number of small islands and tiny sailing vessels that appear like white specks on the horizon.

At the helm, Nivani smokes a wet cigar and says little. When he speaks, it is to murmur some nautical direction that Harry invariably fails to comprehend—partly because Harry knows not the first thing about boats or fishing gear, partly because he is unfamiliar with the provincial language the Corsican uses. On rare occasions, Harry manages to capture a word or two before the wind plucks them away. He tries using gestures, but Nivani squints at him with his good eye and shakes his head, a slight back and forth movement that tells Harry the Corsican judges him to be one thought short of an idiot. After a few long hours, Nivani motions for Harry to take the helm while he goes below deck. Obedient, Harry grips the wheel tightly, feet planted like lead, fearful that an Italian sub, German U-boat or ancient sea creature will suddenly emerge. Ten minutes later, it is Nivani who emerges with an open-mouthed bottle filled with hot coffee, a plate of smoked fish, and a loaf of bread. Nivani retakes the wheel while they eat and drink in silence.

In truth, the hours of silence suit Harry. Hearing nothing but the occasional engine surge and the rhythmic slapping on the hull soothes Harry's personal doubts. Gabriella's death, Lorenzo's threats, and Alessi's attack fade amid the warm salt spray and realization of one man's insignificance in this vast blue sea.

He concentrates on the weight of his mission and its consequences for Britain. He has not the first idea what he will do when he arrives in Majorca nor why he has allowed himself to follow the suggestion of two rough men he barely knows. The Broadway chaps would not know what to make of men like Ivo Guaneri and Bethune Nivani. But here they are. An extraordinary breed. Before this war is over, Britain will require men like them. And be fortunate to have them.

In early evening, the sun still high in the summer sky, the *Immaculata* approaches a long strip of land. The boat runs parallel to the shoreline for a short distance, then rounds a bend and passes between two rock cliffs, silent sentries at Porto Cristo's gate. Nivani drops the stub of his cigar into a puddle on the deck, a sign of increased concentration. The sound of the engine dulls, then quiets as the open sea slips from view. Harry feels the bow of the *Immaculata* lower onto the surface of a tranquil lagoon, a calm extension of the rough sea. Nivani guides her entry into the mouth of a deep grotto. The ceiling presses, dark and close. Thousands of tiny needles reflecting rich greens and blues hang above them. Thick pillars of stone jut up along the shore, and streams of water run in and out of the rocks. The boat's path curves to the right, and the sunlight barely penetrates as they move into a yawning blackness that Harry finds suffocating. The air reeks of rotten eggs. His head begins to throb, an ache creeping up the back of his brain. Struck by a wave of vertigo, he almost loses his balance. The ship's deck shifts like sand beneath his feet.

A guiding light appears on top of the bow, and Nivani—his face now a ghostly presence—glances across at Harry who struggles to tame a budding claustrophobia. He exists in a deep underground hole. Images of cave dragons lurk among the stone forest on either side of the boat. In time, his eyes adjust to the lack of light, and he sees the boat slide into a larger cavern, leaving behind the stifling malodorous air. A thin beam of brightness leaks through the rocks above.

Nivani points to the lines on the rocks, then the watch on his wrist, indicating, Harry assumes, the height to which the water rises at high tide, a signal of Nivani's intention to depart before the water reaches such a level. Harry signals his understanding of the need for haste. The *Immaculata* moves slowly along until they come to a triangular opening narrower, to Harry's perception, than the width of the boat. On the left is another opening. A light—a torch of sorts—has been placed high up on a pillar of rock illuminating the way. The beauty of the crystal-clear water strikes him as the purest he has ever seen. And the most threatening. A man could disappear quite silently into its endless shaft. A sixth sense prompts him to edge away and move to the center of *Immaculata's* deck. Slowly, skillfully, Nivani maneuvers the boat left through the passageway that ends, one hundred yards hence, at a huge crescent-shaped wall. To Harry's recollection, they are now three caverns removed from the opening through which they arrived.

Nivani draws up the boat to a wide dry base, a natural dock of sorts that disappears into a jumble of rocks and pillars. Harry jumps ashore and stretches, easing the tightness in his shoulders. Nivani instructs him to tie the *Immaculata* to a group of stalagmites that jut from the cavern floor. When Nivani is satisfied the boat is secure, he, too, steps ashore. He and Harry stand together, not speaking, arms at their sides, staring into the half-light. In London, they would be two commuters awaiting an early morning tram. Instead of English rain, thousands of tiny needles loom above them.

After a few moments, a faint gleam of light appears at the far end of the passageway. At first, Harry takes it to be a form of subterranean phosphorescence. Until he hears the sound of oars moving through water and sees a rowboat gliding toward them. He makes out the outline of two figures within. As they near, the light grows stronger and he sees that it emanates from torches, one on each side of the boat. Nivani seems to know the men.

He does not smile but his demeanor changes to one of welcome, almost gladness. Or relief. Harry helps him draw in their landing ropes. Nivani extends a hand to help the men ashore. They shake hands and exchange introductions.

"Bethune Nivani."

"Henri Duget."

"Pablo Ruiz."

"Jesus Garza."

The men's features are obscured in shadow, the usual telltale behaviors—body language, the look in the eyes—undiscoverable. Harry judges them neither friend nor foe. They are at least expecting Nivani, and Nivani has got Harry this far, a mild bout of dizzying nausea his only anxiety.

Nivani asks them—in Spanish, Harry notes—where their boat is docked.

"Anchored in the cove at Cala Morta," says Garza. "We unloaded our catch at the Manacor pier, then brought the smaller boat through the underground lake."

"Hay otro corridor?" asks Harry.

"There are many," says Garza. "Follow the underground lake. The caves are interconnected. You are bound to come upon one that leads to the sea."

It takes all of Harry's concentration to translate the conversation. He has not spoken Spanish since 1936 when he landed an assignment studying the socialist trade unions in the Catalan province. After the Confederación Nacional del Trabajo-Federación, the anarchist militia and other anti-fascist groups staged a coup and defeated Nationalist army officers, unions became the most powerful organizations in Barcelona. Harry spent that July and into the fall observing and reporting the initial confusion.

Ruiz looks at him steadily. "One who is unfamiliar with the grottos can easily get lost. You must know where the passages lead. Some are quite narrow. Who knows whether a boat can pass."

Harry sees that Garza, possessed of long lean limbs, is a tall man in fisherman's clothes. Of middle age, his coarse hair contains streaks of gray. Like Nivani, the sun has baked his skin so that lines radiate from eyes and mouth. His face is clean-shaven.

Ruiz—the smaller and younger of the two, not nearly as seasoned as Garza and Nivani—wears his hair cropped on the top and sides. Thin, trimmed mustache, strong jaw, muscled shoulders, face youthfully unlined. His eyes are dark. He wears black pants and a rough linen shirt, a blue patterned scarf around his neck.

"Do you sail south?" Harry wonders how awkward his version of Spanish sounds to the men.

"How far south?" asks Garza.

"West of Algiers."

"It is a long way to go for fish," says Garza.

"How long?" asks Harry.

Ruiz answers his question. "In my boat, maybe six hours. If the sea is good."

Garza gives Ruiz a cold glance. Ruiz stares hard at Garza, a tension between them. So, the boat belongs to Ruiz, not Garza. Harry assumed wrong. Not the first time.

"He is from Marseilles." Harry hears Nivani tell them. Better to be French apparently.

"This is why his language is odd," laughs Garza.

Nivani continues. Harry listens closely as Nivani explains that Harry is traveling to the Oran port of Mers-el-Kébir. That Nivani has brought him this far, but can go no farther. He and his boat must return to Ajaccio. Harry hears Guaneri's name and a phrase he does not recognize.

He can see Ruiz in profile who stands with feet apart and hands clasped behind his back—a soldier at rest, but the tension remains. He shifts his gaze to a spot farther along the lake, then reaches up, smooths his neck scarf, gestures with his hand—a small wave of sorts—and once again clasps both hands behind his back. Subtle, but evident. Of no notice, seemingly, to anyone but Harry. Ruiz's head turns to face Harry's, and he eyes the position of Harry's hands and feet. It is then Harry notices Ruiz's shoes. Hardly those of a young fisherman. More like military issue. When Ruiz meets Harry's eyes, some remote sense warns Harry that this is an ambush. A trap. Orchestrated, synchronized. Ruiz has sized him up and signaled someone ahead. That someone is about to join them, or is waiting at a prearranged spot.

Bandits operate all along the Mediterranean coast. If robbery is the motive, the only visible asset is the boat. Harry wonders if Nivani used this opportunity to transport unregistered cargo and Ruiz and Garza somehow got wind of it. Nivani will, Harry suspects, defend the *Immaculata* at all costs. What can he do if half a dozen bandits surprise them? Aware of the Browning pistol on his ankle, and the knife sheaf against his spine, Harry knows he will not abandon the old man to defend his boat on his own. *Is the old seaman capable of throwing a punch?*

There are, of course, other possibilities. Harry has no clue where Nivani's allegiance lies. Has Nivani arranged this meeting? Are illegal goods being traded today? Has Harry's life been bartered for some greater good of Guaneri's?

He thinks back on the trip from Ajaccio. Mostly silent, but pleasant enough. No hint of malice. No cargo below. No furtive looks or curious detours. No obvious acquaintance of these two men. No, Nivani is clean. For reasons he cannot readily identify, Harry trusts Guaneri. In Ajaccio's dark alleys or in that kitchen full of vicious-looking knives, Guaneri could easily have killed him. No one the wiser. No one to inquire after a brainless agent of the British government. Why take the trouble to arrange with Nivani to transport him hours west to Majorca? He does not figure Guaneri or Nivani for Spanish revolutionaries. Corsican nationalists, yes, but on the side of France's freedom, not Spain's. Betrayal of a British agent would gain them nothing. Indeed, might hinder their cause.

Whatever the case, Harry has a decision to make. Get the hell away from Ruiz and whoever his pals turn out to be, or stick around and see what happens next. He knows he is better off alone, but, again, the old sailor. If they flee, they have two options. Drowning in the bottomless underground lake. Or breaking their necks in the vast black cavern. Neither option appeals.

Harry is unsure what transpired, but when Nivani finishes the conversation, the seaman unties the landing rope, and quickly climbs aboard the *Immaculata*. From the deck, he gives Harry a small salute—his charge has been safely deposited—and without the slightest hesitation, takes the helm. Garza pushes him off. Nivani and the *Immaculata* veer right. In fewer than five minutes, the old seaman and his boat vanish through the cavern passageway.

Thievery is not the game. Nivani and his boat are safe, out to sea before the tide rises. No need to return his favor, after all.

Garza climbs into the rowboat and, without looking back, steps forward into the bow. Ruiz motions for Harry to follow Garza while Ruiz unties the landing rope. Facing the lake, Ruiz bends to his task, intent on steadying himself on the rocks. He shouts something to Garza who, obedient, kneels to adjust one of the oars. Garza gives Harry a quick look, his eyes slide left and right. Then, he averts his eyes.

Sitting in the middle of a rowboat between these two phony fishermen, going God knows where, does not feel right. It is, in fact, all wrong.

With both men's attention otherwise engaged, Harry backs quickly away from the water and slips soundlessly behind the closest pillar of rock. The boat torches manage to throw dim light into two passageways behind the pillar. He runs to the one on the left and keeps running until the light fades, and he is swallowed by darkness. Not dimness, mind you, but total pitch-black. He cannot make out where he has been, cannot see his hand in front of his face. For all he knows, he is standing in a lavish room of Buckingham Palace or within the Arctic Circle inches removed from a half-starved polar bear. He crouches against the wall, breathes hard, and listens for sounds behind him. While he cannot make out the words, there are shouts of derision—at least two voices, then a third, clearly angry. They come nearer to the passageway where he waits. He hears one shot, then another.

These smugglers, or whatever they are, play rough.

A bullet thuds against the wall above his head, another at his feet. Two more shots sound, farther away. The sounds are distorted, echoing off the cave walls. The shots are blind, designed to scare, but he wonders if the boat torches can be removed. If there are three men, two can advance through both the left and right tunnels, leaving one behind with the boat. There are only two torches that he recalls. The third departed with Nivani's boat. Leaving one man without.

Harry ventures farther into the passageway, arms outstretched, striking the sides of the cave so he can orient the placement of his body within the space. He wonders about reptiles or long-distant sea creatures. It is utterly black. Not a glimmer of light penetrates. He does not know how to use the disorienting darkness, knows not whether his eyes are open or closed. Not that it matters. There is no way to be sure of left or right, backward, forward. He has no experience with black caves. Ice caves, yes. Their walls are white or blue. Another challenge altogether.

If he had the least knowledge of cave exploration, Harry would be counting his steps. He would be mindful of turns and dead-end shafts and cautious of a sudden abyss or low ceiling. He would know that caves are sharply cold and wet, and cave explorers are subject to hypothermia. He would know that in pitch-black places, the perception of time becomes indistinct.

He feels the passageway bend to the right and the walls narrow, the walls close enough to touch his shoulders. Harry bends his head slightly to discern the source of a monotonous drip of water. As he inches forward, the floor seems to rise and fall unpredictably, and he stumbles. His leg strikes a hard object and he shoves it forward, hears what he believes to be a tumble of rocks. A long moment later, there comes a splash and an echo at what sounds to be a great distance. He stops, lies down on his stomach and feels with his hands for the ground in front of him. Empty. A great nothingness.

Teetering on the edge of panic, Harry shuffles backward and finds the safety of a cool damp wall of stone. His breath comes in deep gasps. *No cause for alarm, Douglas. Self-control, calm.* In the silent dark, he repeats the words. Clear-headedness is the only way to stay alive.

He sits absolutely still for a while, hears his own heaving and the monotonous drip intensified in the darkness. Nothing more. No pursuit. Not that he can hear, at any rate. He feels his way back from whence he is certain he's come, bearing left where he remembers bearing right, now—lesson learned—counting in his head, kicking a stone ahead of each step, listening through the black silence, aware that his racing heart affects his judgment, his sense of time. In his retreat, the passageway has widened again. The damp seeps through his clothing into his skin, into his bones. He finds he is shivering, the palms of his hands moist and cold. He stops and rubs them together. *Friction, goddamn it, heat, goddamn it, you're in over your head, goddamn it.*

He closes his eyes and inhales the dank smells. He wonders where Mick is. From the day they met, Mick MacLeod has been the one man he trusts. The poor lad from Edinburgh's back-streets made it inside the secret doors of London. No easy feat, that. Mick could figure a way out of this black labyrinth. Mick's brain unleashed, there is no stopping what he comes up with, one idea igniting another. If there is a good man in this world, Mick MacLeod is it. Harry had known it before they were sent to Ethiopia, but that day in Mai Ceu confirmed it. Wave upon wave of men, ordered into action by their Emperor, falling as they ran. Unremitting, as though it would never end. The Ethiopians, ferocious on the attack, could not defend against the tanks and weapons of Badoglio's Italian army. Harry remembers the hot trigger on the tip of his finger, the weight of the rifle on his shoulder, the sounds of men dying. Mick on his right, firing like a mad man, round after round, keeping the Alpini force from them until Harry sent their dispatches. Through that night, they kept each other alive.

He presses the scar on his cheekbone, feels the slight indentation where the bullet struck years ago. Ethiopia. Where unshakeable Mick saved his life. Nothing simple there. It was Harry's first experience with battle. It occurs to him that he may likely have faced Antonio Alessi and Nico Lukas—fighters in the elite Alpini 5th Division—on that day. Four long years ago.

A slight wisp of wind and a faint fluttering—first on his left, then quickly on his right—brings him back from the memory. A series of tiny clicks, a steady scratching noise. He cautiously takes a step forward, knuckles scraping the walls on either side. He hears the sound of water rushing, and then makes out the dimmest bit of light ahead. He blinks. The glow, unmoved, remains. From the light, comes an echo of voices.

He touches the knife sheaf at his spine. He does not intend to die without a fight.

Chapter Twelve

When in a dark hole and two strangers come at you with a torch ablaze and what looks to be a gun in hand, the best course of action is to find a darker hole and hunker down. But Harry has had enough of dark holes. He is desperate to find a way out, too desperate to be cautious, he tells himself, and so he walks toward the men and the light and decides he will deal with whatever risks await.

When he emerges into their sphere of light, the men clearly are startled to see him.

"Dios mio. Qué es esto? Quién es?"

I might ask you the same. Best keep it simple. "I lost my way and my gear."

"You are here in the dark? Alone? How long?" The two men exchange looks of incredulity.

"Hard to know. A few hours. I hit my head. Where am I?"

"You are in the caves of the dragons. Cuervas del Drach. Are you an explorer? A tourist? Are you lost from your group?"

"No, not a tourist. I intended to meet a friend."

"Ah." Nothing else. Again, the men exchange looks.

"I'm not a smuggler, if that's what you're thinking."

They begin to walk. "Where did you lose the equipment?"

Checking my story. "I doubt we'll find it. I was stumbling around. I heard a splash." *True enough.* Harry changes the topic. "You thought I was a tourist? Do they often lose their way?"

"We work the caves, make everything ready. Lights, signs, obstacles in the path. In the summer and fall, people come to the caves. They pay to walk along the path, hear the music, see the underground lake. Sometimes a visitor strays from the path. Not often, but it happens. Sometimes we find them. Sometimes we do not."

"You said music?"

"A concert," they say together. "Chopin. In the amphitheater next to the lake."

At some point in his wanderings, before he stumbled, Harry could have sworn he heard strains of the Royal Philharmonic, but he passed it off as an illusion, an auditory mirage, convinced the darkness had unhinged his mind. "Where is this theatre?"

"It is close. There is a deep cavern that separates us. We must walk around it."

"First, we will check on the bats."

"Bats?"

"Each night, like tonight, we check their location to make sure they have not moved closer to the tourist area. If the bats get restless, we use this air gun to drive them back to their old home."

Harry offers up a silent ode to bats. And Chopin.

Chapter Thirteen

27 **June 1940.** The Royal Navy's First Sea Lord Dudley Pound informs Vice Admiral Sir James Somerville, leader of Force H, that Somerville will command the mission to neutralize the French fleet at Mers-el-Kébir. A strong French squadron has taken refuge there. These ships, a clear and present danger to Britain, cannot be allowed to fall into Axis hands. The entry of Italy into the war prevents the Royal Navy from using its base at Malta. Churchill rejects any idea of evacuating the eastern Mediterranean and places a new naval force at Gibraltar to operate in the west.

This new Force H contains the battle cruiser *Hood*, battleships *Valiant* and *Resolution*, aircraft carrier *Ark Royal*, one cruiser and four destroyers. Somerville, the most able of British admirals, is charming, intelligent, competent, and respected by his French counterparts. When informed of his task, Somerville assumes the French will cede to British demands, even if at the last minute. He and his commanders in Gibraltar share this view.

Harry's rescuers share their dinner and drink and drop him on the road that leads into the village of Porto Cristo. Following his nose and the salty smell of the sea, Harry threads his way through a maze of narrow streets until he comes to a sandy cove where rows of lounge chairs and beach umbrellas are stacked and folded for the night. Along a low seawall, a group of young men smoke cigarettes and ogle the girls who sit at a café table sipping orange soda through straws. Pensive, Harry stands looking at the sea—the moon casting a long straight beam out into the water—thankful for bat caves and tourists and classical music and minds creative enough to put them together. *Without them . . .*

He vows never to befriend, or in any way associate with, so-called cave explorers, the likes of which he does not understand. He walks along the shoreline breathing the fresh night air and glancing at the sky's limitless ceiling of stars. His thoughts turn to his mission. Guaneri got him this far; the rest depends on the winds of fate. Harry wonders again about Guaneri's motives. He will be disappointed if Guaneri turns out to be a fraud. Or worse.

Possibilities for hailing a ride to Tangier are better than going farther east to Oran. He guesses the northern strip of the Spanish protectorate is mighty appealing to Balearic fishermen. Like Majorca, Spanish Morocco allows more political freedom and autonomy than the fascist mainland. From Tangier, he likely can find transport east to Algeria. He does not want to chance running into Garza, Ruiz and friends. He is puzzled as to why they pursued him. It could be that Nivani betrayed him. Or that Nivani had no idea of the fate of his delivery. In any case, he will avoid their like and find another way to fulfill his duty.

Harry is acquainted with Majorca's recent history. For the last four years, he and Mick have kept a close eye on Italy's appetite for Mediterranean acquisitions. Mussolini covets the whole of the Balearics so he can disrupt transportation and communication networks that unite France and North Africa, and British Gibraltar and Malta. In 1936, during Spain's Civil War, when Majorca was vulnerable, Italy's Blackshirts invaded and occupied the big island. They murdered a sizable portion of the population—socialists, communists and criminals—so that Italian real estate investors could acquire lands with the best views of the sea. Italian flags flew over the island until Franco finally won his war. Chances are, Rosso Terzo was advised of a rare opportunity and included himself among those early land investors. Lorenzo is likely familiar with Majorca's famed dragon caves. Indeed, now Harry remembers it, in their moments of small talk at the wedding reception, Signora Terzo lauded Majorca's beautiful waters and told stories about family holidays on the island. A thread that leads him once more to Lorenzo's vengeful declaration.

His speculation is interrupted by a distinctive voice in the distance. Deep and striking. He recognizes the pitch and cadence, lifts his eyes to search the length of a high flat cliff that rises above him, and catches sight of her standing on the elevated seawall. Perfectly elegant, she wears a long strapless cream-colored gown, a conspicuous presence against the violet sky. He has to hand it to her. She knows the Mediterranean glamour spots, and she makes a point of attracting attention. What is Margaret Gautier doing here in Porto Cristo? He imagines her entertaining a group of Italian industrialists on their holiday yachts in Palma's lush and lively harbor. Porto Cristo's small bay does not compare.

She is in conversation with a man dressed in fitted white trousers and navy jacket—one hand in his coat pocket, the other holding a glass of what Harry guesses to be a strong alcoholic beverage. She prattles on about Paris cafés, opening night at the opera house, spring shopping at the Gallería. She cannot be expected, she complains, to live without them—any of them—and trusts that the Germans, when they finally arrive, will be kind enough to allow the Parisians their pleasures. The man laughs and says something clever about French bratwurst. Harry cannot make out the rest because they turn and walk toward a lighted balcony that juts out into the sea where bits of music blend and throngs of dancers swing to Tommy Dorsey. *Porto Cristo may qualify as lush and lively, after all.*

Dressed as shabbily as he is and smelling of dank earth—the least of his noxious odors—he cannot very well arrive upstairs unannounced. Still, he desperately covets an extra dry martini. He decides to establish a position near the edge of the seawall and wait until the party winds to a close. He can keep an eye out, follow Margaret Gautier when she departs and, when the moment comes, inquire after the purpose of her presence. Meanwhile, he imagines a spot of Gilbey's on his palate.

As it turns out, there is no need to wait for the party to fizzle. Within twenty minutes of finding a deserted spot and settling down, he spies her walking along the shoreline, shoes in one hand, cigarette holder in the other. She is alone. From his semi-hidden position, he follows the orange glow of her cigarette. Before she crosses the street, she slips on her shoes and drapes a light shawl over bare shoulders. A scrawny black-and-white kitten slinks across the street in front of her. She picks it up and kisses the top of its head. She continues up the hill toward the end of the street, not looking behind her, where a broad set of steps leads to the double doors of an old church. In a thin circle of light at the entry, she deposits the kitten, extinguishes the cigarette, adjusts the shawl to cover her hair, and disappears inside. According to the sign, the church is Parroquia Nuestra Señora del Carmen. As the clock tower chimes one, Harry opens the door, proceeds down the center aisle, and slips into the fourth pew where she kneels, hands clenched together, murmuring something in Latin. She makes the sign of the cross, sits back in the pew and says, "Here's the situation." She turns to face him. Poised, self-assured, her face expressionless.

"You were expecting me?"

She shrugs. "Who else?"

"What's this about?" he asks.

"All hands to the pumps. You are needed in Gibraltar. It's important."

No unnecessary words, he notes. He isn't sure whether to believe her. "What's the rush?"

"The future of the French Navy. Survival of the British Isles. Fate of the Strait of Gibraltar." Her tone is too matter of fact, too confident, to be a lie.

"How did you find me?"

"You are among many who benefit from Ivo Guaneri's largesse. He has a good understanding with his fishermen. And his smugglers."

He tries to picture the big Corsican consorting with the likes of Margaret Gautier and cannot. "I have a hard time believing what's going on here."

She says nothing.

"Someone tried to shoot me."

"Evidently someone missed."

"Was it you?"

"I don't like guns." She glances at his shirt. "You'll find a change of clothes in the vestry, the door on the left behind the altar. They should fit. Don't know about the shoes. Odds are, I guessed right. You will definitely want to visit the shower."

Determined to get a straight answer from her, he tries again. "I'm surprised to find you here."

"There are too many Nazis in Madrid. Oh, here, in church, you mean?" Her eyes settle on the altar. "It's better to have some kind of faith."

He waits for more, then gives up. "How do we get to Gibraltar?"

"I have friends."

He pictures the two of them atop a donkey cart. "Like the chap upstairs in the snappy sailor suit?"

"Not all Spaniards are fascists. I have a plane."

Things are that easy. "Of course you do."

She was right. Everything fit well, including the shoes. All expensive. He is thankful to be rid of the seaman's odor, and once again dressed in suitable clothing.

She straightens the knot on his tie and stares at his chin. "You'll need a shave before your meeting."

"What's with you and Mick?" he asks.

"You're wondering."

"You might say that."

"He won't mind?"

"Depends on what you say."

"You know your friend."

"Forget it." Harry begins walking toward the door.

She catches up, tucks her arm through his, walks in stride with him. "Mick and I met in Warsaw a couple of years ago. My husband was a diplomat. There are, of course, certain expectations of diplomatic wives. Quite a number of social affairs at different embassies. One's life depends largely on parties and making small talk. One pretends to enjoy oneself, listens to the latest gossip. Who left whom. When so-and-so arrived. That sort of thing. Tiny bits to pass along to the right people."

"That explains it." Harry deadpans. He does remember that Mick made more than a few trips to Poland, as one of few agents fluent in Polish.

She begins again. "There was a party at the British Embassy."

"Ambassador Kennard, our Eton man in Eastern Europe." Harry cannot fathom why he is attempting to impress her with this knowledge.

"I preferred Erskine, his predecessor," she smiles weakly. "Mick and I struck up a conversation, such as it was, his language skills passable at best. Laughable actually. He, of course, was interested, like they all were, in hearing what Hitler's intentions were and what Poland would do. Which side would we choose, if you will. Not that I cared at the time. I wanted the Russians gone. Who would have dreamed what has happened? What is still happening. In any case, Mick and I shared a joke that night and went outside onto the terrace. Believe me when I say those parties put my teeth to sleep. I am a terrible flirt when I'm bored. Mick wasn't having it, so I kissed him and refused to allow him to abandon me until he kissed me back. I embarrassed the poor man."

Harry tries to imagine the situation. Mick red-faced and stammering. Over a kiss. No. It doesn't stack up. He is reminded anew how much he dislikes Margaret Gautier. "I don't believe you."

"Why?"

"It's a stale little story. You strike me as more adventurous than a peck on the cheek. Mick's language skills are fine. I've heard him translate an entire communiqué. Polish to English, vice versa, nothing flat. Most important, the Mick MacLeod I know wouldn't be slobbering on another chap's wife."

They stop at the ancient doors while she rearranges the shawl onto her shoulders. "Shall I tell you another story?"

Harry pushes open one door and waits for her to pass through. "When does our plane leave?"

"Plenty of time."

"All right then." He tries to sound properly interested. "Let's see if you get any closer to the truth."

Silent, they navigate the stone steps and walk down to a seafront bar—closed for the night. Harry finds two chairs and places them facing the sea. From her evening bag, her long slim fingers withdraw two cigarettes. She lights both with a single match, and hands one to him. She inhales until plumes of smoke envelope her.

When it matters, she is all business.

"In 1934, after Hitler rose to power, Poland and Germany signed a mutual non-aggression pact. It was, of course, meant to strengthen Poland's position with allies and neighbors. Since the end of the Great War, Warsaw had prospered under the leadership of Józef Pilsudski. As head of state, Pilsudski maintained Poland's independence on the international scene."

"I'm familiar with Pilsudski and his positions," says Harry.

She smokes again, looks off toward the sea. "Do you want to hear the story or not?"

Harry nods and she continues. "Given our geography, Pilsudski tried to get on with both Germany and the Soviets. He structured informal alliances with France and England and our less powerful neighbors, Romania and Hungary. While on the surface, he appeared to be quite skillful at diplomacies, Pilsudski was very much aware of the instability of these alliances. I remember one conversation he had with my husband, prophetic now. He said that Poland was straddling two stools, and this could not last long. We had to know which stool would tumble first and when."

"And here we are," says Harry.

"And here we are." Her arm sweeps an arc toward the sea.

"Where is your husband?"

"Dead. 1939 September." She continues before Harry can inquire for more. "The Polish people admired Pilsudski because he brought power and respect to us. My husband worked with him until the end."

"Pilsudski died in 1935."

She gives Harry a puzzled look. "Yes. With his death, our country became increasingly divided. Old hard-liners versus the newer moderates. Alliances faded, some dissolving slowly; others eroding almost overnight. As you would guess, it was during this time that Mick MacLeod came calling."

"That fits. I'm listening," says Harry.

"He was quite noticeable at Embassy events and on the street. An Englishman with that red hair and pale skin speaking fluent Polish."

"He's a Scot."

"We all thought of him as English."

Mick's fierce pride will not be pleased at that piece of news. "We all?"

"Those of us who took interest in political goings on. As I said, we were anxious about alliances, particularly with the English. Only five years before, we had sent an ambassador to London. So, relations were new. Many Polish citizens have French lineage, others studied in France. We assumed we could count on the French for protection. The UK was something else. It was common knowledge that Britain thought of us as a buffer—a large expanse of land filled with barbarians—against communism."

Harry is beginning to wonder if there is a point to Margaret Gautier's story. "What did Mick have to do with it?"

"We were, of course, curious. He would come and go. Always concealing a sly grin. We would see him at one party, then another, then not so for weeks. We thought perhaps he was spying on us."

"I thought you all spied on each other."

"Generally true. Though I don't think we considered it in those terms. After all that has happened, it seems we were just playing at our little diplomatic games. Innocents all."

Harry has to agree.

"In any case, one night I had a dreadful headache. We lived in the southwest part of the city, quite a distance from the Embassy party we were attending. My husband called for a car to take me home. It was dark, nothing but faint lights for illumination. Few people on the street. I was sitting in the back seat, anxious to get home to my bed. While we waited for the light to change, I closed my eyes. Later—not more than a moment, or the light would have changed—I heard two shots ring out, then shouting, and running footsteps.

"I saw a man with a gun pointing it at Mick. Mick running toward him as if nothing was happening. He caught the man and threw him to the ground, took the gun away. It was very brave. I admired him for it."

"Who was the man?"

"It was dark, but I thought I recognized him. How would I know?"

"Then what?"

"I told the driver to stop. I rolled down the window and called out. Mick left the man lying in the street, climbed into the car, said everything was fine—just a mugger. I didn't believe a word of it. We dropped Mick at his hotel."

"What happened to the man?"

"He was lying there when we pulled away. I couldn't help thinking I knew the man. And that I didn't know much of anything about Mick MacLeod."

That story, Harry can believe. Most of it. While Mick is not given to vanity, he possesses that healthy sense of self that comes from surviving both the orphan houses of Edinburgh and the cunning conspiracies of the British intelligence service. Mick never said much about his Warsaw assignments, but there was plenty going on in Poland's capital in 1936. None of it as neat and tidy as gossip at Embassy parties. Agents working inside, outside. In Poland's major cities, Broadway was keeping an eye on German gangsters and Russian thugs playing spy games.

"That was the last time you saw Mick?" To Harry's mind, there has to be more to the story. Mick's behavior around Margaret Gautier involves more than a so-called mugging and a timely ride to his hotel.

"No. As I mentioned, he was a frequent guest of the British Embassy. In those days, you couldn't trust anyone."

"Unlike today," Harry interrupts.

She gives him a blank stare. "I was about to say that I finally recognized the man who was shooting at Mick. A high-ranking official from Danzig, a Nazi party member."

"Danzig?"

"I had forgotten his name, but months earlier I had been introduced to him at an informal dinner gathering at Sean Lester's residence in Danzig. Before Lester and the League of Nations were sent packing, that is. I wanted to tell Mick so he would know the source of the violence and take care in dealing with those people."

"Sean Lester, as I recall, was assigned by the League to Danzig to oversee the maintenance of its status as a 'free city.' Lester monitored, or tried to, the balance between German and Polish control."

She nods.

Harry continues. "This dinner guest who was shooting at Mick. What did Mick say when you told him you knew the man?"

"He said there were storm clouds on the horizon. That the League of Nations was incapable of controlling what was happening in Danzig. I asked if he was involved in it. When he wouldn't answer, I assumed the worst."

"Which was?"

She places a cigarette between her lips and lights it, inhaling deeply and tilting her head back, holding it there for a long moment, her eyes narrow. "That he was sent to gather information to undermine Poland's stake in Danzig. That Britain would not support us. I was fearful and indiscreet, and I managed to spread these notions at various parties among my diplomatic and social set. I was, of course, wrong on all counts and later realized I had done serious damage."

To Harry's mind, that explanation goes further in explaining Mick's behavior toward the woman, though he does not fully believe it. "That's when you threw in with Mussolini's fascists and the likes of Nico Lukas and Lorenzo Terzo?"

She laughed. "Oh, there's nothing political in those friendships. I simply enjoy vacationing in the islands. Capri. Corsica. Majorca." It is the first time Harry has seen the woman smile, and surprisingly, he is beginning to be curious. "Of the three, I favor Corsica."

"How so?"

"North of Ajaccio, on a tall bluff overlooking the sea, there's a little village named Cargèse, a beautiful slice of the world. Simple food, peace, sunshine. Fishing nets stretched along the rocks to dry. Each morning, boats set out across the bay to harvest their lobster pots and bring in catches of langouste. Always small, always fresh, meant only for the local people. There is nothing so delicious, or so natural. The Corsicans are a spiritual people. In the village are two Catholic churches that face one another across a small valley. The church on the east side was built by native Corsicans who adopted the Latin rite. On the west side, the church built by Greek colonists, use the Greek rite."

"You prefer the Latin."

She gives him a curious look. "That's where I first encountered Ivo Guaneri."

Guaneri again, more than coincidence. Harry no longer wonders how Guaneri found him in Ajaccio. He still is not sure about either of them, unconvinced of their loyalties. "You were saying about Nico and Lorenzo."

"I met Nico—intense, handsome—at a party in Majorca, then weeks later at the Krupp estate in Capri. He introduced me to his friends in Milan and Rome." Her voice softens. "By that time, my husband was a frequent diplomatic traveler. Our marriage less than satisfying. Warsaw was cold and lonely."

Chapter Fourteen

An hour later, on a darkened corner on the north steps of the church, a black Packard slows and stops. A uniformed driver emerges. Standing stiffly at attention, he opens the door. Before they climb into the back seat, the driver inquires, "Por favor, Duquesa Falco, have you any luggage?"

"No, Roberto. Not tonight."

The driver announces formally, "Your plane will leave as soon as you board at the Palma aeropuerto."

Harry frowns at her, mouths "Duquesa Falco?"

She ignores the question, settles into the seat, reaches into a mirrored compartment for a bottle of Spanish brandy, and pours each of them a shot. Harry senses a strange shift in her mood. It is dark, filled with tension and dismissal.

As it happens, the pilot is an affable American who delivers a steady stream of conversation, even at three in the morning. His black patent-leather hair slicked back under a navy blue cap. A flannel scarf, a lighter shade of blue, wound around the neckline of a dark leather bomber jacket. Harry walks the incline up to the cockpit and introduces himself. The man has small brown eyes and a freshly shaven jaw.

"Clipper Konarski," says the pilot. "Help yourself to coffee. Then come in and look around."

"I'll pass on the coffee. You're from the States."

"How'd ya guess? Chicago, south side, one of those steel mill settlements. You been there?"

"Never. How'd you end up in Majorca?"

"How did I get here from there, you mean? Lemme tell ya. This baby's a Douglas Commercial DC-3. All metal, airframe, really strong. Pratt-Whitney 14-cylinder, air-cooled. Luckiest day of my life when I met this sweetheart. Closest I'll ever get to growing wings. She almost flies herself. On top of that, she's easy to work on. Fix anything with a paper clip."

Harry hates to interrupt Konarski's enthusiasm. "How far to Gibraltar?"

"Top speed is 185, but this trip's gonna be low and slow. Limited visibility tonight, so we're extra careful around the coastal mountains. Flying time about four hours."

"Then what?"

"Lucky this girlie needs a short landing strip. I got eighteen hundred to work with. No room for howlers on that horse track. Brits just finished it last year for those Royal Navy flyboys. That strip's got some rough patches all right. I've seen worse."

"How long have you flown for Señor Falco?" asks Harry.

"You got that wrong, pal. Señor José Herraro bought this baby off the line in '36. I picked her up in California, flew to Chicago, on to Jersey, then the Azores and Majorca. What a dream that was. Been here ever since. Customized the interior two years ago to Señor Herraro's specifications. So the horses will fit."

"Horses?"

"Arabians. In the winter, we carry them to Señor Herraro's ranch in Morocco. The ranch is forty-five minutes north of Casablanca. Nice little landing strip. A cinch to land. We converted the fuselage so two horses can come along on each ride. I have to climb into the flight deck through the windscreen. Fine by me. Their first time, they're spooked, but they get used to it."

Konarski pushes several buttons, fires the engines.

"Señor Herraro must be an interesting character." Harry files away the name and decides to find out how the señor made his money.

The DC-3, now luxuriously carpeted and wood-paneled for its human passengers, leaves the ground so smoothly Harry does not realize what has happened until he sees the field drop away and the faint lights of Palma blink through the fog. Despite the low roar of the DC-3 engines, the hum provides Harry three hours of dreamless sleep, a respite from unexpected events of past days.

Margaret Gautier, aka Duquesa Falco, does not sleep. Rather, she uses the time to change into a summer linen suit of sea green. She prepares a dispatch to the prime minister, to be sent upon their arrival at Force H headquarters, conveying that agent Douglas has been duly delivered to Vice Admiral Somerville's headquarters. She neglects to add that she is returning to a suite in Madrid's Palace Hotel to await a loquacious suitor from Berlin.

When the plane nears Gibraltar, it is almost seven in the morning. Thick fog hangs like a veil over the big rock, visibility severely limited. Harry awakens and hears Konarski on the radio talking to the ground controller.

Everything sounds routine until a sudden backfire startles them. A moment later, black smoke and flames pour from the outer casing of the left engine. A shrill warning sounds in the cockpit. Konarski rushes to shut down the engine and feather the propeller. He twists in the cockpit and summons Harry.

"Push the flame switch. The red panel. Two parallel switches for the left nacelle. And figure a way to get ridda that damned noise."

Harry climbs into the copilot seat and follows Konarski's brusque instructions. Together, they look left at the engine that spits flames and black smoke. The acrid smell of burning oil permeates the cockpit.

Margaret Gautier stations herself at a window where she has a good view of the left engine, front and back. "Flames out the rear."

"Try it again. Both switches."

"The things are jammed," says Harry. He punches the switches again.

"The engine valve is shut down. There shouldn't be any fuel feeding the fire. What the hell is wrong with the extinguisher? Once more. Easy this time. A little finger action."

"How does the extinguisher work?"

Konarski shouts hurriedly. "There should be two separate charges of extinguishant for each nacelle. Bottles of either carbon dioxode or methyl bromide. One backs up the other. A spray ring discharges them into the honeycomb and douses the fire."

"So either the extinguishants are faulty or the spray ring," says Harry.

"Could be that switch you keep punching. Never used it before."

"Can we wait for the fuel to burn off? Will that starve the fire?"

"It should, but she's flying on one. She's going to lose altitude. And the imbalance will limit our turning radius."

"It's out. The fire's out," shouts Margaret Gautier.

"Let's get this baby on the ground before that rock smacks us in the ass. I can't see a damned thing through these clouds."

"On the right side, there's a hole in the clouds. I see water. Land, too. Descend a little, we'll see the runway."

Konarski wrestles the control column and manages to lower the plane a few hundred feet. They see the faint lights of the landing field and the gigantic gray rock called Gibraltar. Konarski attempts a sharp turn for the approach.

"Too rough to turn. We can't line up straight. A few degrees difference, we'll do a dip in the drink. There's a narrow strip off to the right she can line up for. Left aileron cable is shot. Strap in and hang tight." He winks at Harry and grins, clearly relishing the challenge.

Harry is not so inclined.

Konarski focuses on the task and begins the descent. To reduce the chances of cartwheeling, he does not lower the landing gear. "Even when they're up, the DC-3's wheels protrude from underneath and provide a mild buffer. That's what they tell me. We'll find out who the liars are."

Konarski tilts his head toward the ceiling. His voice takes a serious tone. "Over your head, there's an escape hatch."

Harry locates a glass panel between the pilot's and copilot's seat.

"Not that we'll need it," barks Konarski. He keeps both hands on the control column.

An instant before they hit ground, Konarski closes the throttle on the right engine. Racing along the grass at full speed, the plane plows the field, cushioned by clumps of vegetation. The right propeller cuts a swath through the dirt, throwing rocks onto the windscreen, causing the plane to veer right, bouncing the plane's left side off the ground. Finally, the tailwheel makes contact, and they slide slowly to a stop.

The ground crew has heard the plane straining to land and meets them at the end of the track. Two passengers and pilot, shaken but uninjured, clamber out.

One of the crewmen observes, "Helluva bit of flying, lad. Looks like you're stuck awhile. She'll need engine work. We'll straighten out those props. Likely the tailwheel, too."

Konarski surveys his damaged bird, and nervously scratches a knuckle on his left hand. "I want to know what the hell happened. I checked everything before we left Palma. Twice."

"Sabotage?" It is the first thought in Harry's mind.

"Who would do that?"

"Someone who figured you could make it on one engine? Sending a message?" He looks sideways at Margaret Gautier.

Cool and unruffled, she retrieves a bag from the plane and begins to walk unhurriedly in the direction of the hangar. "Package delivered," is all she says.

Harry catches up with her. "The driver called you Duquesa Falco."

She sets down the bag, the unspoken question between them. "In Madrid, a noble bloodline opens doors. Since the revolution, the Spanish are desperate for such reminders. Once you are designated a duchess, people assume there's a duke somewhere."

"People like Señor Herraro?"

"Señor Herraro is not so easily impressed." She looks at the emerald-encrusted watch on her wrist. "I have a plane to catch. By the way, you'll find Mick in North Africa. He arrived there two days ago."

"In Oran?"

"Tangier. An hour across the strait. You'll have a secure radio there."

Harry is confident that Mick's trip from Toulon has been less eventful than Harry's. He picks up her bag and hands it to her. "This may be the last time we meet."

She wears a strange expression of amusement and resignation. "It's going to be a long war, Douglas." She pauses, flashes those sharp violet eyes. "When we do meet again, you need to know something."

"What's that?"

She drops her voice. "I'm not in the betrayal business."

His gut tells him not to trust her. He doesn't trust people who are good liars. And she is, he comes to learn, an exceptional liar.

Chapter Fifteen

His name is **José Herraro**. As a younger man, he belonged to another country and lived another identity. A decade ago, before he grew into a successful businessman and landowner in Majorca and the Spanish Protectorate of Morocco, he was the son of an Italian merchant born into wealth and privilege. A lifetime ago, he was in love with the sound of his wife's voice.

On a glorious day in Rome in early April 1930, stunning nineteen-year-old heiress Maria di Varini wed dashing army lieutenant Ricardo Diatto. After a honeymoon in Venice and the promise of a splendid life ahead, they settled in Rome, in an apartment close to the Via Veneto. One morning in late May, the couple set off for a day at the beach. In the warm sunshine, they traveled in their Lancia on a motorway named the Via del Mare, built at the command of Benito Mussolini. That same day along the same road, the dictator himself sped west in his red Alfa Romeo 8C. Near Ostia, his car overtook the Lancia, blasting his horn as he did. Maria smiled and waved. Pulling over, Mussolini signaled for the Lancia to stop. Maria recognized him and scrambled out to meet him. They talked, and he learned of her daily visits to her family's estate. Later at the beach, Maria told Ricardo she found Mussolini's smile and piercing eyes charming and impressive.

The following day, Il Duce sent his valet to the Varini estate to invite Maria to lunch. When the door to Il Duce's private quarters closed, he pulled her toward him, kissed her, slipped his hand inside her blouse and caressed her breast. He held her tight and said, "Stay with me. I will take care of you." Maria was flattered by the leader's ardent attention. She admired his fascist beliefs and found it incredible to believe that the most powerful man in Italy wanted her as his own. Her mother, Signora Varini, encouraged Maria and counseled her that the dictator's attention would bring honor and credit to their family. Thus, Maria di Varini Diatto began to spend happy afternoons in the company of her country's leader. He lured her to lavish hotels in the mountains. They traveled in private planes and stunning yachts, and toured the countryside in his custom Bugattis and Maseratis.

By reputation, Benito Mussolini was a jealous man. Il Duce's rivals often met with fatal accidents. Fearful and disconsolate, Ricardo Diatto fled. First to Corsica, then to Majorca where Ricardo Diatto became José Herraro. He changed his appearance from handsome young officer with a devilish grin to studious, expensively tailored business entrepreneur. The newly created Señor Herraro lived on his wits. He used a portion of his family's fortune to study copper and zinc mining in northwest Africa. He purchased property in Majorca and Morocco and in a relatively short time established himself as a wealthy and honorable Spanish citizen. By design and necessity, he shunned marriage and politics. Until 22 May 1939. Benito Mussolini's signature on the Pact of Steel aligned Italy's star with Adolf Hitler's. On that day, Señor José Herraro vowed he would use his authority and resources to deflect Italian acts of aggression. Moreover, to crush his wife's lover. In the fall of 1939, he traveled to Czechoslovakia to witness the results of the Nazi invasion. That same year, he visited Poland to observe atrocities wrought by Nazi occupation. Each trip stayed with him. He met others of like mind, and fortified his vow.

His contacts in Corsica put him in touch with the resistance there. Thus began his alliance with Ivo Guaneri and leaders of the guerilla band known as the Maquis. He traveled often to Ajaccio, and one day in April 1940, he was introduced to a woman he first knew as Margaret Gautier.

"Don't do anything foolish," Guaneri warned him.

Chapter Sixteen

"**I want an update**. Your progress." Lorenzo walks in a circle smoking a cigarette, a noisy radio blaring in the background.

My progress, thinks Nico. His cousin—step-cousin—is, at best, an arrogant peacock. At worst, a cold-blooded snake. To hold his anger, Nico moves to the radio and turns it off. "He's been elusive."

"What the hell?"

"There's a war going on."

"One man outsmarts the entire OVRA?"

"He's unthinkably lucky." Nico contemplates the thick Persian carpet at his feet. Indeed, he cannot believe how very fortunate Harry Douglas has been. Until two days ago, that is. "OVRA is committed to larger issues."

Lorenzo flicks the cigarette into the wastebasket, watches a small flame come alive, then die. "You only need one man—a professional killer, a dead shot, a man with guts—to take him. The army of Italy must employ at least one soldier who meets these descriptors. Or have I been needlessly supportive of our militia these many years?"

"I'm doing what I can for you." While he is almost certain of Douglas's death—the description fits precisely—Nico chooses not to tell Lorenzo until he confirms the identification. The body is due in London tonight.

"For me? For me? Have you forgotten who bought your position?"

"For most of my life and his, your father was more than generous. He opened a door. I worked hard to step through it. No one bought my position."

"At least prove you're grateful, for God's sake."

"I've made numerous attempts to do that."

Lorenzo slams his fist on the wall. His hands are solid. "Where is he?"

"For a brief period, we lost track of him, then someone spotted him in Tangier."

"Among the Berber garbage, that would have been simple enough."

"I'll contact you in a day or two. When I know more." Nico must wait for the contact in London to secure the information. He has his own reasons for wanting Douglas dead. Reasons he is not about to share with his cousin. Step-cousin. In any case, the cause of Nico's hostility is difficult to explain, even to himself.

He wonders what Douglas was doing in Tangier.

Chapter Seventeen

Harry climbs the narrow steps to the top floor. The sign next to the door reads Vice Admiral James Somerville, Commander Force H. Harry whistles under his breath, straightens his back, knocks, and waits. Hearing no response, he opens the door and steps inside a small office filled wall-to-wall with filing cabinets. High on one wall, a portrait of King George VI hangs next to the red, white and blue crosslines of the Union Jack. From behind a cluttered desk, a lean pink face and a pair of sharp gray eyes meet his. The man half rises, extends a hand across a typewriter, and nods at the chair opposite. Harry shakes the man's hand and sits down.

"Douglas, is it?"

"Yes sir."

"Michael Townsend, aide to Vice Admiral Somerville. Do you know why you're here?"

"No sir."

Townsend is a man of Harry's age with a brown mop of straight hair and a prominent nose. With rigid posture, he toys with the pencil in his hand and studies Harry's face. Smoke is curling off a forgotten cigarette. Moments pass before he speaks again, his voice low and firm. "I'm led to understand you speak French."

"Yes sir."

"The prime minister has provided Force H the task of neutralizing the main element of the French battle fleet. At this moment, we know the following. Much of the fleet lies in harbor at Mers-el-Kébir, west of Algiers. There is also harbor at Oran. The two are in close proximity, but separate. You must unravel the details. Number and types of ships involved, firepower, capabilities. Most importantly, the exact location of each ship. Exact. You must be clear. We are required to act fast. We have a new adversary in the Mediterranean. The Italian battle fleet. At all costs, we will avert a possible seizure. The consequences are grave. Your job is to acquire the information and relay it to me privately. With all due haste."

Harry notes the rapidity of the tapping pencil and gauges the man's level of anxiety. The enormity of the task is unsettling. "Summarize what you know thus far. That way, I'll know if I'm gathering useful intelligence."

"There are—"

Harry interrupts. "If this material is so urgent, why is it I'm just arriving?"

"The agent before you has been lost."

"Lost? What do you mean, lost?"

"Murdered. Body found a day ago in Tangier."

Harry thinks immediately of Margaret Gautier's comment. Tangier—twelve miles across the Strait—is notorious for violence, bribery, and crime of every sort. A hive of international spies. Harry worries that after that Czechoslovakian business,

Mick has missed a step. Disillusion is a palpable thing. Britain's appeasement was so abhorrent, it threatened to topple him. The pride Mick once carried was bruised immeasurably when Hitler's storm troopers marched into Bohemia. His Majesty's betrayal of a trusting ally became a sharp stick in Mick's heart. Harry fears Mick will never again feel the same about his allegiance to the Crown.

"What is the name?"

Townsend looks puzzled.

"The name of the dead agent. What is it?"

"I'm not familiar with the agent's name. I couldn't give it to you if I were."

"Male or female?"

"The agent was referred to as 'he'."

"Age? Background?"

"I know nothing further about the agent. Can we proceed?" Townsend opens a thick folder on his desk, scans the first few pages, and withdraws two copies of correspondence.

"One more question. Where is the agent now?"

"In all likelihood, the body is on its way to London." The tension in Townsend's face and manner tells Harry discussion on the subject has been exhausted. Townsend begins to read aloud. "On 16 June, the prime minister understood the French had agreed to instruct their fleet to sail to British ports. On 21 June, Admiral Darlan—the French Chief of Naval Staff and Commander in Chief of the French Navy—ordered all French ships currently in British ports should leave for North Africa, a clear contradiction to the initial agreement. On 24 June, Admiral Darlan sent a message that the French fleet was to be kept out of the hands of the Germans, French warships dispatched to the

United States or scuttled if there were no successful means of escape. Later that same day, armistice terms between France and Germany were understood to state that French warships were to demobilize under control of the Germans. Most recently, on 26 June, General de Gaulle, who is opposed to the armistice, feared that the fleet would be delivered intact to Germany." Townsend looked up from the page.

"Confusion," says Harry.

"Precisely."

"What is it you're asking me to do?"

"By 3 July, the prime minister has required a resolution from Vice Admiral Somerville. Credible information is critical. To repeat, number and types of ships, exact locations, firepower and capabilities."

"Resolution? What does that mean?"

"It means an end to the problem, Douglas. A decision acted upon."

"The problem being the French fleet's existence?"

"Quite right. And its governance."

"What about negotiation?"

"The time for negotiation is drawing to a close, the situation rapidly collapsing. The use of force may be necessary."

Harry recalls the conversation in Toulon. What is this? Inflexibility or survival? He does not relish standing in the middle of it. Whatever it turns out to be. "What's next?"

"In Tangier—"

"Why Tangier?" interrupts Harry.

Townsend sighs. "Tangier has a secure wireless."

"Are there not direct links—wireless and landline communications—between the Royal Navy and the French Admiralty?

Why the need for a separate secure radio?" Harry is growing increasingly suspicious of his role.

Townsend does not look up. His voice takes on an edge Harry has not heard before. "The Admiralties on both sides of the channel have extensive landline and wireless communication networks. For purposes of your mission, they will not be used." Townsend continues before Harry can formulate another question. "At a nightclub called The Golden Apple on Rue Portugal, you will meet musician Samy Mokrani. A trumpeter. Mokrani is an Algerian who has lived in Morocco for many years. As an Algerian, he is able to move in and out of France. He will guide you to the right people."

"You've dealt with him before?"

"No."

"It's possible to make a mistake about such contacts," says Harry.

"I can have one of my men act as backup," Townsend suggests.

"Not necessary. How do I communicate my findings?"

"There are secure radios in Tangier and Oran. You will be given the coordinates by your contact. Use whichever is most practical. We have to act quickly. Every moment counts."

A nod of the head, a wordless dismissal. On the surface, it assumes an agreement between two professionals with a common dedication. Townsend is interested in preserving the British Empire. Harry is intent on finding Mick.

At the top of a rise of steep whitewashed steps, a sign outside the Golden Apple advertises a six-piece jazz band, Chinese mint tea, and Irish whiskey. Harry steps inside the chamber and discerns, in the dim light, a slightly elevated wooden stage, its sides adorned with colored lights. Christmas in June. He speculates how six musicians can occupy the small stage simultaneously. He realizes he is in Africa, where reality is a different thing altogether, and all things are possible. He and Mick, in Ethiopia in '36, discovered that truth. Here, once again, is that strange detachment of Arab Africa.

In the center of the room stands a long bar and high stools surrounded by round metal-topped tables, each with two worn-out wooden chairs. The air smells of strong coffee and oranges, the windows flung open to let in the breeze. And the flies. Harry does not expect to see any patrons at this early hour, but there is a man in a white shirt behind the bar. Sleeves rolled to the elbow, he bends over a sink washing glasses. When Harry opened the door, the man looked up and acknowledged him with his eyes, then returned to his work.

From a corner, a man steps forward and gives Harry a long stare, then a polite nod. Harry and the man stand silent. The man is slim with hooded black eyes, a well-trimmed beard on his tapered chin, and deep creases in his forehead. He holds a trumpet down along his side, the bell parallel with the floor. He continues to study Harry. There is a question in his eyes.

"Come." He leads Harry to a table in the darkest corner, pulls out a chair and sits down, and pushes a cigarette pack across the table. The trumpet sits on the table between them. "What can I get for you?" He strikes a match and holds out the flame.

Harry accepts the cigarette and the light, takes a draw, and considers the supposed trumpeter. He wonders how easily Samy Mokrani can be intimidated. Harry exhales the smoke in his lungs. "Information."

Mokrani nods, lights one of his own, points to a chair for Harry.

Harry continues to stand. "Tell me about the man who was found dead yesterday."

"I know the one you mean. What is it you want to know?" There is a hint of French in his accent.

"Name, circumstances."

"I don't know the man's name."

"Description then."

"All right."

Mokrani puts out the cigarette. He's only smoked half of it. "First, let's get something to drink. Coffee, tea, whiskey?"

"Coffee then." Impatient to hear the answers to his inquiry, Harry senses Mokrani has, on the other hand, all the time in the world. Or he is stalling for time.

Mokrani signals to the man in the white shirt who, within a span of two minutes, brings glasses of hot black coffee on a silver tray. He sets the tray on the table next to the trumpet. No one speaks until the man moves away.

Mokrani leans forward, blows gently on the steaming coffee, and takes a contemplative sip. He replaces the glass on the tray and says, "The dead man is an Englishman."

Harry waits.

"Not far from here, he was found. By the open-air kebab, Café Battuta." He sips at his coffee, cocks his head, remembering. "Earlier in the day, I saw the same man at the Fahs Gate leading into the Medina."

"Medina?"

"In Tangier, the medina is the ancient walled section. There are shops, places to eat and drink." Mokrani smiles his humorless smile. "In the narrow streets, there is little room for automobiles. Bicycles and donkey carts carry goods from place to place. The medina is well known by our international spies."

"Go on."

"After the medina, the man stopped here, asked a few questions, drank a cup of tea. I had not before encountered this particular Englishman."

"What sort of questions?"

"How to find a particular place. Which street to travel."

"Which street was he looking for?"

"Somewhere in the French Quartier. He had a strange accent. Not like other Englishmen. Not easy to understand."

Harry feels his stomach churn. "Describe him."

"The fair skin of the North, near in height to you, a muscular man."

The description stuns Harry, and he almost stops, not wanting to know for sure. Still, he presses on. "Hair color?"

"He wore a hat." Mokrani sips the coffee, expressionless, apparently enjoying the one question-one answer game he has created.

Harry grabs Mokrani's wrist. "What color was his hair? Light? Dark?"

"All you Englishmen have dark hair." Mokrani glances at Harry's grip, says nothing. He tries to wrench his arm away, but Harry is not letting go.

"You're certain?"

"Most definitely. Here in the bar, he removed his hat. His hair was almost black. The style, I've heard it called buzz cut."

Harry feels his body relax. He releases his hold on Mokrani. "You don't know the name?"

"No."

There was an agent Harry met in London last year with short close-cropped dark hair. Australian. That would explain Mokrani's comments about the accent. It crosses his mind that others at the time remarked on their resemblance. "What else do you know about the man?"

"A bullet, I believe, to the heart."

"Just one?'

"Presumably so."

Mokrani reaches for the abandoned smoke, relights it. Harry pulls a chair over and straddles it. The two men smoke, neither speaking.

"You'll put me in touch with the right person?"

Mokrani looks toward the wooden stage. "Do you like music?"

"Depends on the music."

"In the Kasbah, there is music for everyone." Mokrani finishes the cigarette and the coffee, presses a coin to the tabletop, and rises. "Stay with me. It is easy to lose your way. You must walk as if you are sure of where you are going. Never let them know you are unsure of the way."

"Who? Never let who know?"

"Anyone on the street. They see advantage in your uncertainty."

Harry files the advice. "First, take me to the place where the so-called Englishman was found."

Mokrani shrugs. "If you wish."

They step onto the Rue Portugal into the blazing sunlight and the crushing crowd of faces. They walk a short way—behind a large, slow-moving man in a white caftan—until they come to a row of loading docks. Mokrani points out a shop he says belongs to his brother, the window filled with broad braided loaves and pastries covered in honey and sesame seeds. The smell of freshly made breads permeates the street. They stop under the awning, out of the sun's glare.

"It is early, and the bread is available. In an hour, it will be gone." Mokrani goes inside, kisses both the man's cheeks, and whispers something in Arabic.

Harry and Mokrani continue around a corner, shoving their way through the crowd that pulses around them. On the edge of the street, shoeless toddlers play with a stick next to dusty mongrel dogs who lie in the shade. Harry is assailed by a group of children, tugging at his pockets. Mokrani shoos them away. A frenzied mix of odors fills the air. The path turns, the street widens. A few steps farther, there is a sign, Café Battuta. Stacked tables and chairs are arranged neatly near the door. At this hour, the café is closed.

"There." Mokrani points to a place across the street. "He lay next to the wall until one of the shopkeepers found him. His body blocked the entrance to the path. Someone wanted to pass."

"How long?"

"Hard to say. As you see, the street is full, even at this hour. Dockworkers, shopkeepers come and go. Goods, animals, dust."

"What time of day was he found?"

"Twilight. The streets were busy with families. There are few lights in the street. Only the dock lamps in the distance."

"So, he could have been lying there most of the day or just a short time."

"No one can say."

"A bullet to the heart, you said."

"That is what I heard."

Every inch of space is taken with goods for sale. There are stalls of cheap trinkets, vegetables, lemons, figs and spices randomly sorted and displayed, sellers loudly bartering with buyers in the narrow spaces. Mokrani points out a man with a brown withered face and tattered clothing watching them. He sits on a stool next to a pile of cages that hold several chickens, a basket of eggs—presumably fresh—for sale on the table. A small black donkey is tethered to one of the cages. Harry makes eye contact with the man who does not look away. For a long moment he stares at Harry, then shifts his eyes to a place where, Harry assumes, the body was found.

"I'd like to buy some eggs," says Harry.

Harry learns what little he can from the egg seller, quickly determining the dead man's belongings had been stolen. One by one or in a single looting, the egg seller could not be certain. He was distracted, he said, having sold a record number of eggs that day.

Harry and Mokrani continue on to an unmarked storefront across from the Kasbah entrance. The tiny space, lined with pillowed benches, is called Les Fils du Detroit, an ancient club for Arab-Andalusian musicians. The men, dressed in white turbans, loose-fitting caftans and flat leather slippers, sit at blue tables strumming their violins and tapping patterns on tubular drums, melding the melodies of Spain and Morocco.

By the third pot of mint tea, Harry has lost patience and the bright geometric tiles close in on him. "I must be gone," he says to Mokani. *With all due haste.* Townsend's phrase of urgency.

"You are in a hurry. They are not," Mokrani says.

Mokrani leans toward one of the drummers—the one with a watery left eye and a stubbed middle finger—and whispers in his ear. The man looks up at the ceiling and stops playing for a beat.

"Thirty minutes," says the drummer.

After whispering once more in the drummer's ear, Mokrani leaves his chair and disappears into the street.

Chapter Eighteen

Harry exits the café, hot and claustrophobic, searching for fresh air. He paces along the crowded Rue de la Kasbah until the drummer emerges, wraps an arm around Harry's shoulders, and steers them north to the Place du Tabor. At the corner, they veer right through a pair of arches toward a sign that reads El Morocco Club.

"Don't be fooled by the modest entrance," says Drummer. Harry chooses to call his contact Drummer because the man does not give his name. "You will understand," he said.

After they enter the club, Drummer's English becomes suddenly flawless, no trace of France, Spain, or the Arab world. Harry discerns a distinctly upper-class clip and cadence. Drummer withdraws a costly cigarette case from a hidden pocket and lights up. "Do you mind?"

Expensive, Harry thinks, down to the way he holds his cigarette. There are hundreds of British expatriates—artists and writers—in Tangier. Drummer takes a few puffs and continues, "The radio. Not surprising to conceal it here. The club has a reputation. Any given night, you'll find every network represented. A rich assembly."

From his work in Milan, Harry knows the statement is not a vast exaggeration. What better place for a spy to hide than among others of the same breed?

Drummer continues, "Along with the usual questionable activities. When you wish to send a message, you will sit at the far end of the bar, order a sweet Rob Roy, no ice, up with a twist. After a bit, when the bartender asks about a refill, you will say you've changed your mind and wish to order a martini. The bartender will nod politely. In a moment, the manager will arrive and remove you to his office."

The possibility of a cocktail brightens Harry's mood considerably. Before he has time to order a lukewarm gin, however, they step outside into the street. Drummer raises his eyes to follow a flock of warblers trilling overhead, then nods at a passerby. He draws Harry to the opposite side of the street—away from the swarms moving past them—into the shade of a weathered awning.

"I'll send a dispatch later. I'm now concerned about transport to Oran," says Harry.

"Your first destination is Rabat."

"Rabat is south. I'm going east."

"The railroads and highways are constructed so you must go first to Rabat. From there, the highway proceeds east to Algeria and takes you to Oran."

"Good lord. How long will that be?"

"Ten hours."

"I can't waste ten hours." Harry is beginning to wonder about the man's competence. "I've heard the trains are notoriously slow, the schedules unreliable."

"There's the plane, but it won't go all the way to Oran."

"What about a boat? It's a straight line from Ceuta to Oran." Given his last nautical adventure, Harry is less than eager for another go at the Mediterranean. Better to gaze at the deep blue sea from above. Considering his last plane excursion was none too safe, he is running out of transport options. "Tell me about the plane."

"Trust me. The safest way is the train, then auto," says Drummer. "Arranging transport is difficult, if not impossible. You are asking too much. You're lucky to get anything with wheels."

"The plane."

Drummer sighs. "There is a small plane that can take you as far as Melilla. From there the road takes you south to Oujda, then across the border and north to Oran."

"A small plane?"

"How much do you weigh?"

"One sixty, thereabout."

Drummer seems to consider Harry's answer. "It's possible. It is, as I said, a small plane."

"A car will be in Melilla?"

"If all goes well."

"What does that mean?"

"I daresay you've got people waiting about at various points of exit."

So, that's the rub. Drummer figures Harry for dead and can't be bothered wasting his time. "Waiting? For me? For what reason?"

"The only reason one man lies in wait for another."

"How do you know this?"

"Two days ago, a man arrived at the port. He was smooth with his questions, but it soon became clear enough he was looking for a British agent, your height and build, your color."

Finally a sign of Mick. "Red hair, light skin, burly chap with a rich Scots accent?"

"No, quite the opposite. This man, I suspect, was Italian. Though he covered his accent well enough. He was insistent, too insistent. No one provided him information. I was concerned hours later, when we found Farrell face down in the dirt, a bullet through his heart."

Harry looks off into the distance, half hearing the rest of it, recalling the sea of black umbrellas, Lorenzo announcing his vendetta. Here is an element Harry has not anticipated. At the time, he thought—foolishly now—Lorenzo was simply making a show of it. But the last few days, Alessi in the mountains, the shooting in the cave, the plane's engine malfunction, now this Italian chap. More than coincidence. More than bad luck.

"I'd be careful," Drummer says.

"Farrell. That was his name?" The idea of it angers him immeasurably.

"Yes, Peter Farrell, a good chap." says Drummer.

"The car in Melilla," says Harry. "Make sure it's there."

All alleyways look alike. He gets to the end of one before discovering he has gone in the wrong direction. It takes him a good hour to find his way back. At the edge of his vision, he is aware of a presence behind him, a steady step, a shadow on the wall. Harry turns his head but sees no one. He stops and checks his pockets, pretending to have forgotten some important item, scanning the colorful disorder of people in the street, those seated at tables or scattered amongst the maze of alleys behind him. Beyond a certain point, the crowd thins. Still, he feels the anonymous presence. He keeps his pace, reaches back and pulls the knife from the sheath, careful to conceal it along his right side.

High, white walls border the twisting alley. The sunlight fades. He walks around a tight corner, bears immediately right into another passageway, and quickens his step. Above him are dark windows, decorative cloths over the openings, the occasional shout from within.

He stops at a recessed alcove, slides through a slatted gate of iron bars, skirts sideways around a layer of reeking garbage, and waits in the shadow of an ancient wall rough with age. The air hangs thick and hot, no hint of breeze, sweat collecting on the collar of his shirt.

From his place of concealment, Harry distinguishes the figure of a man in gray slacks—European from the line of them, certainly not Moroccan—continue past. Through a slim crack in the wall, he sees the back of the man's head look left and right and then disappear, presumably hurrying to the next intersection of alleys. His is not a leisurely afternoon stroll.

Within minutes, Harry hears a sharp unexpected scuff of shoes. The figure reappears, a quick gasp for breath preceding his arrival. Between Harry and his stalker lay the grimy wall and the closed gate. Inhaling slowly—the stench of decay almost overpowering—Harry shrinks back and presses his shoulder against the sheltered wall, knife at the ready. He is careful to control the deep inhalations and the soundless air that escapes his lips. If he can believe Drummer's warnings, this man is here to kill him.

No doubt, the assassin has realized he shot the wrong man. Why else would someone be following him? Perhaps there are two assassins, each on his own, unaware of the other's success or failure. *Don't flatter yourself, Douglas.* A small animal noisily scurries through the trash. The stalker—if he is worth anything—will stop long enough to investigate. Which will mean sure discovery.

A singular hand and the gray muzzle of a gun press forward through the gate slats. Harry inches closer, wraps both hands around the raised knife and waits until the gun in its entirety clears the iron bars, until the anonymous hand and the ensuing thin line of white cuff advance sufficiently. The wrist turns this way and that, the slightest of turns, making it impossible to withdraw in one quick jerk. Harry waits until the hand and the gun pause in position while the stalker listens for another hint of sound and decides whether to dirty his shoes in the garbage at his feet.

Like a hammer, Harry thrusts the knife down hard on the exposed wrist. He hears the flat crack of bone, a sudden bark, a thud as the gun disappears into the space of filthy rubble, and the sound of running footfall.

Chapter Nineteen

Drummer is right about the plane, small definitely an
overstatement. He neglected to mention that the plane is
painfully slow, and there is one solitary seat, occupied, of course,
by the pilot. For two hours, Harry huddles on the pulsating
floor—between a pair of ripe-smelling sheep heads and bags
stuffed with unidentifiable dusty grain.

He emerges stiff and sweating onto a windswept plain surrounded by dry brown hills that overlook the sea. After the
overbearing chaos of Tangier, the air is still and quiet. His hat
and head on fire, he walks for some distance under the relentless
sun to the unpaved road where Drummer told him the car would
be waiting. Here is a hillside with narrow terraces that descend
to the sea, the odd faraway item glinting in the sunlight's glare.
A woman in white stares from a doorway. Her hooded caftan
flutters as the breeze blows through the open door. Farther off,
behind a collection of red mud buildings, there is a cluster of
neat brown houses with flat roofs.

It is an old Renault, a faded blue, scarred by years of use and neglect. The door creaks when he opens it. The worn tires thankfully still have some tread. Harry questions how much petrol is in the tank and how long it will last. Once he sets out, there may be nothing. He spotted a Shell station—Dutch oil obviously still accessible in North Africa—on the first road as he walked from the airfield. Three hundred Moroccan franc notes and three hundred Algerian franc notes are stashed in the glove box. A canteen filled with water sits on the back seat.

He peels off a roll of banknotes and stuffs them in the pocket of his trousers, removes his jacket and lays it on the back seat, loosens his tie and rolls up his shirtsleeves. Someone has laid a map—Arabic characters—on the passenger seat, the route outlined in pencil. If he starts now, and all goes well—a futile assumption, it seems, with this heap and a map he cannot read—he will make it to Oran by eight this evening. Time enough to gather Somerville's information at Mers-el-Kébir and send it to Gibraltar within the twenty-four hours he's been given. He has the address of the church—Cathédrale du Sacré-Cœur d'Oran at Place de la Kahina, on Boulevard Hammou-boutlelis—from where he is to wire Townsend. He will describe himself as an insurance agent, there to settle a claim the church has submitted. The priest will respond with pleasure that someone from the insurance agency has attended so quickly to the claim.

As he checks under the hood, he thinks again about the assignment. He is aware that negotiations with the French Admiralty have gone on for weeks. He wonders if Farrell ever made it to Oran. If he had the intelligence in hand before he was killed. With the assignment so urgent, why has the British Admiralty not arranged for a military transport directly into Oran, or even

Algiers? Instead of expecting him to piece it together. And where in god's name is Mick MacLeod in all this? Margaret Gautier—Duquesa Falco, whoever—said Mick is in Tangier, but neither of Harry's contacts saw or knew of a red-haired Scotsman, even after Harry asked them directly.

He searches the landscape. A low-slung wall surrounds trees laden with what appear to be ripe apricots. Beyond, a grove of olive trees. Harry starts up the car, revs the motor, checks the petrol gauge. Full. All the same, he stops at the station, buys two cans, fills them and stows them in the trunk.

He has not expected this North Africa to look as it does. For an hour he drives east on the narrow coastal road, flanked on his left by stunning cliffs that run down to the sea, on his right, by rich orchards—row upon row—studded with fruit. The sweet scent of tangerine blossoms and a hint of salt fill the air. The road widens and turns south, and he increases his speed. As the sea falls away behind him, the road and the car climb for a brief distance onto an immense flat-topped plateau with a continuous forest of trees. This country, devoid of paved roads, is a series of dirt paths riddled with potholes. For a few hours, he speeds onward over bumps and ruts, through brown stone villages where bearded men—merchants, he supposes—sit in square marketplaces. In one village, he hears the melodious muezzin and sees the men turn to the south and east and knows it must be late afternoon.

The landscape shifts to a wide riverbed, most of it parched save a slight rivulet in the center. The road runs straight through it. As one would expect, a village has been established on the far side, well back from the banks. Likely, to account for the spring overflow. The riverbed gives way to a long straight road—an old caravan trail—that leads to a crossroads where there are no signs, the map no help. The road behind is empty. A fierce glare on the windshield obstructs his view, but he is certain that one dusty road leads to the sea, the other twists east. He chooses east. The angle of the sun tells him he has made the right decision. The glare abates; a cluster of high palms comes into view, a long line of camels rests in their shade. He is thirsty and stops to stretch his legs and relieve himself behind a rock. He gathers a handful of dates fallen from the palms, eats a few, and puts the rest in his pocket. From a respectable distance, he inspects the camels and their white-robed riders. He opens the canteen slowly, drinks, then gazes at the enormity of the desert. The air is thick with haze. Out here, there is nothing. No streets, no lights, few points of orientation in this great emptiness of rocks and sand. No safe haven. In the distance, a plain rises toward the mountains. He pulls his hat down against the sun.

Back in the car, he unfolds the map, follows the pre-drawn line with his fingers—and tries again—unsuccessfully—to decipher the Arabic. He has no idea where he is, but starts up the engine, checks the gauge, and hopes the Dutch are alive and well in Algeria. Given what he guesses is his location, the cans in the boot will not take him as far as Oran. One of those camels could gain an unwilling passenger. He thinks for a moment what he has to do when he arrives in Oran. He desperately needs a bath, the sheep stench ripe in his nostrils.

Over the next few miles, the gradual change in landscape signals the margins of a city. He passes a sign, but his lack of Arabic makes it next to useless. To his great fortune, the next sign reads *Bienvenu à la ville de Oujda*. He realizes Oujda—Morocco's easternmost city—straddles the Algerian border, its population and visitors a mix of Moroccans and Algerians, Arabs and French.

A single winding road takes him through an imposing gate into the town center, and he senses a strong French influence: women in the street, colorful signs and strips of fabric in the trees, a myriad of building designs. An early French occupation, he assumes, the borders changeable and porous over the centuries. He rumbles—the engine mildly protesting its hours of abuse—past shops selling fruits, vegetables and handicrafts. At one point, railroad tracks run parallel, and disappear into a cavernous structure. No exit on the other side tells him the line stops at the border. He recalls the Italian train that refused to enter into France and dropped its anxious passengers in the snow.

Past the main commercial area, he drives up into the mountains. After a point, the road becomes flanked by a deep ditch. A few miles outside the city, an isolated building that looks surprisingly like a military barracks occupies the top of a flat hill. A single guard with a rifle on his shoulder stands watch. The guard seems to be rooted in place—like an undernourished tree—and does not signal for Harry to stop. There is no need. Even the small Renault cannot swerve past the checkpoint without falling into a ditch on either side. Straight ahead, a makeshift gate—three wooden sawhorses and a long pipe—blocks the way, then a barricade of rocks and barbed wire stretches across the landscape. He remembers Drummer's warning about points of exit and checks the knife at his back, the pistol at his ankle. He stops the car well before he reaches the young man in uniform. A donkey stands next to a water trough on one side of the barracks building, matching monochromatic shades of gray. Harry sits behind the wheel.

The guard walks forward a few paces, signals with his rifle for Harry to exit the vehicle, and then circles the small car—deliberately—two and three, now four times, searching for who knows what. Harry steps out of the car but leaves the engine running, reaches into the back seat and retrieves his jacket. He pulls the passport from the pocket, holds it out. The guard, the rifle now on his shoulder, looks to be slowly inspecting each page. He will not let Harry go easily. Harry now understands the purpose of the cash left in the glove box. How much will it take? A gust of wind propels the guard's cap into the sky. The wind is rising; golden dust blows across the hilltop. The guard turns so the wind is at his back and motions Harry to follow him through a door to a small reception area. Inside, another man of similar age and uniform sits behind a table smoking a thick cigarette—hand-rolled, a peculiar scent. In the background, a radio plays music, the same sort as the musicians' club in Tangier.

Solemnly, the guard hands Harry's passport to the man behind the table who—again agonizingly slowly—thumbs page after page, pausing to peer at a stamp or date.

"Where are you going?" The man speaks French with a heavy Arab accent. He draws on the cigarette—the peculiar smell intensifying—and sends a series of smoke rings into the stale air.

"Oran."

"For what purpose?"

"A funeral for my uncle." Aware that Muslim funerals traditionally take place within twenty-four hours of death, Harry quickly adds, "It is a matter of urgency."

"Who is your uncle?"

Harry tries to think of a French name and hits upon the obvious, "Monsieur Gautier. He lived at the port, in Mers-el-Kébir."

"I have no interest in your uncle." Impatience in his voice, the man behind the table rolls his eyes to search a corner of the ceiling. Harry hears the heavy sigh. The guard places the cigarette on the edge of the table, its uneven ash drops to the floor. Saying nothing, Harry reaches into his pocket, extracts a banknote so that the young man can see it clearly. He discreetly extends his hand, and Harry presses the note into it. The young man stares again into Harry's face, eyebrows raised. Harry locates another note. He does not know the protocol for such transactions, and so places it on the table. The guard quickly slips the notes into a hidden drawer.

"Are you a smuggler?" asks the man behind the table.

"No."

"Well then," the man smooths the last page he has examined, closes the passport and holds it out, just enough so that Harry has to strain forward to retrieve it, "since you are not a smuggler." He takes one more draw before he crushes the cigarette on the floor next to his chair. "We have some discretion."

The car is where he left it, still running, and Harry chides himself for wasting the petrol. The sun is falling in the sky and the wind picking up, sending clouds of dust swirling, stinging his eyes. The donkey has taken shelter behind the water trough. Harry considers leading the animal to a place out of the wind, but the donkey's eyes are closed and he lies in the narrow space between the trough and the building with his head against the back of the trough. It is most likely the best place for a donkey.

The guard emerges from the building and hurries through the dust to the makeshift gate. Without the rifle, he looks no more than a teenager. Obviously, lesser in rank than the man behind the table. Harry considers how much the two young men earn in a day of guarding this remote border, and whether they share equally in their appropriation. He figures the take is more different than alike. In any case, the gate now open, the young man waves Harry through.

After a few hundred yards, a small sign indicates he has passed into Algeria. The pavement improves—firm French roads of packed gravel. Nothing about the surrounding terrain has changed. He wonders when this border was marked, which great men decided the exact location of the imaginary line, where it went left and where right, which rock it dissected, whether the line was accomplished peacefully, or if fathers or uncles of those he has just meagerly enriched paid a dear price for it.

When the wind abates and the road flattens—the steep ditches and barbed wire no longer flanking either side—Harry pulls the car to the side of the road, hardly necessary since no other cars come or go, and he sees no motor vehicles in the distance in either direction. He switches off the hot engine. Before the sun goes and the dark night overtakes him, he wants to have a good look around. Were it not for the single highway, it would be easy to get lost in this landscape. The moon will be merely a sliver, well into its last quarter. No help in finding his way. As he empties the last can into the petrol tank, he notices, a hundred yards away, a circle of makeshift tents. Dressed in light-colored caftans and white turbans, six men recline on decorative carpets around a small fire. Young women squat near small pots that hang over the fire. Three dogs race among the tents.

Noisily—no need to have them think he is in any way trying to surprise them—he approaches the group. He feels the knife sheath at his back and the pistol at his ankle. Yes, the pistol is loaded, the knife within reach. He remembers what Mokrani has said about showing certainty of purpose. Thus, he is a busy Frenchman in need of a petrol station and a meal. He does not say that he's eaten nothing but a few dates since early that morning, that the accumulated strain of sleeplessness has hit him, or that he is running out of time.

The men—a family of Berbers going south across the mountains to El Aricha—invite him to sit with them and share their tea. They travel in battered pickup trucks, each flatbed filled with sheep they will use for trading at the local souk. Their tribal French is, curiously, a version of the rural French that Harry picked up in Mont Tremblant's après-ski bars. They move slowly as they sip their tea. They talk of their sheep and the traders they will meet when they arrive in El Aricha. They inquire about Harry's journey and listen—eyes bright with interest—as he tells of the musicians he met in Tangier. They prepare more tea, carefully measure boiling water and mint and sugar. One of the men uses a pocketknife to cut small pieces of meat and hands them in turn to the other men. Harry chews the tough gristle and swallows before he can decide what animal it used to be. After a time, a child—a young boy—carrying a washbasin and towel appears from behind one of the trucks. Each man, including Harry, rinses his hands and dries them. Without hurry, they fold the carpets and the tents and douse the fire.

"Will you travel in the darkness?" asks Harry.

"We have done it many times."

"How far will you go?" asks Harry.

"The wind will carry us."

"The wind can be strong in the mountains," says Harry.

"The wind is the wind. We will stop to let it pass."

The sun is now fully set as Harry makes his way back to the car. The tea has revived him; the men's quiet hospitality and their calm ritual have lifted his spirits. It is their absolute acceptance, their openness that moves him. They do not push against the natural; they pay heed to the darkness and the wind and leave behind a stillness that warms him. Therein, he decides, lies their nobility. Do they have an inkling as to the state of the world just hours away from their camp? Would knowing of it matter?

They and their Berber ancestors have inhabited northwestern Africa for at least 10,000 years. They survived the Romans and the Ottomans. Likely, they will survive a Nazi dictator named Adolf Hitler. Harry imagines himself a Berber shepherd on his way to El Aricha to sell his sheep instead of Harry Douglas, a dairy farmer's son, on his way to Mers-el-Kébir to aid in destroying the French battle fleet.

According to the men's directions, Harry will drive north, then east until he reaches the northern outskirts of Tlemcen where he will find enough petrol to take him into Oran.

Chapter Twenty

Two hours later, the night now fully descended, the Renault and its driver arrive at the top of a steep rise, the faint lights of Oran spread out below. In stages, the city reveals itself. Slightly off to his left, far in the distance, he sees indications of the port. At this hour, distance is deceptive, his own sense of it hampered by his fatigue. He estimates it will take another hour, at the least, to wend his way through the city and find the right highway. He is hungry—there had been no suitable place to eat in Tlemcen—and he searches for a building that might house a food market. Farther on, under a street lamp—its globe covered in a thin layer of dirt, its light a pale shade of gray—stands a weathered sign that announces a café. He cannot tell where the place begins or ends. Off the road sits a series of shacks of mismatched shapes and colors that cascade down the hillside. Through a wide archway, steps lead down to a single open door that signals the entrance.

He does not like the looks of it—Drummer cautioned him about such places—and he is aware he is more than noticeable, a stranger in a strange land, but he is weak with hunger and tired of the road. If he does not eat something soon, his body and mind will be useless. On his first pass, he drives by, scanning left and right. He turns around and approaches from the opposite direction. He parks facing the street some distance away, in an alley between what looks to be an ancient hotel and a carpet store closed for the night. When he opens the car door, the stench of urine and human waste overwhelms him.

He passes through the archway and goes down the steps. There are vacant tables outside and he wonders why anyone, while they eat and drink, would choose to be assailed by such odors. The host—a slight man with a face full of blemishes and a neatly trimmed black beard on his chin—moves his eyes up and down Harry's body and gives him an intense stare. Harry understands the man to say, "Not tonight." But then, he grunts and points to a table along the back wall near a door that looks to lead to the kitchen.

"Good evening. What will you order?" the waiter bows his head and waits.

Harry orders lamb stewed with saffron and dried fruit, cous-cous and bread and a pot of tea. While he waits, he watches the other patrons—mostly men. The men's voices rise and fall, animated conversations in progress. Women dressed neck-to-toe in dark dresses sit silently behind them. Islamic scarves cover their heads.

As Harry finishes and prepares to leave, a gaunt-faced young man—not much older than a boy—wearing a shabby suit, the jacket cuffs frayed, the trousers too long, approaches his table. He gazes at the ground, pulls a cigarette from his jacket pocket, but doesn't light it. He places it on the edge of Harry's table. As the young man talks, he fidgets with the base of his tie. Every few seconds, he hoists up the waist of his trousers, smooths his soiled collar, scratches at his jaw. Harry asks him to sit down, thinking this will put an end to the constant restlessness. But when he does, the young man pushes back the chair, crosses one ankle over his knee and begins to alternately twist and flatten the cuff of his trousers as he eyes the cigarette. Just as Harry thinks the young man suffers from some sort of compulsive disorder, he feels the blow from behind. Multiple hands grab Harry's arms and pull him through a door.

He awakens on the floor, a dim light in the distance illuminating the narrow hallway in which he finds himself. The door next to his chair had not led to the kitchen, but to an alley of sorts. He sits up and rubs his head. He finds his pockets empty, an echo of pain on the back of his neck. Whoever it was has taken his knife, but not the ankle pistol. Undiscovered in their haste perhaps. A ring of thieves. At least two, three maybe. The nervous decoy, the assault from behind, the dark-eyed host who conveniently seated him next to the door. He, the naïve careless foreigner, in a hurry to eat and go. He had been wrong about the young man. Drummer was right to warn him. He searched the floor around him, hoping to find the car keys, then remembered he'd left them, by premonition or pure luck, under the driver's seat.

His identification papers are gone—the passport presumably on its way to a false identification factory, Harry Douglas replicas in process. Papers that will show he is a French citizen, but reveal nothing else. Luckily, there is extra cash in the car's glove box and the address of the church where the wireless exists. A pounding headache starts at the base of his spine and travels to the top of his head. As he approaches the car—thankfully where he left it—he notes movement, a shadow near the passenger door.

Without hesitating, he runs at the figure, grabs him, and slams him against the side of the car. Smaller in stature, the man drops to the ground. Harry forces the man to his feet, Harry's forearm applying pressure at the base of the man's throat, forcing the chin upward. The man staggers, and Harry steps back to get a better look. The café decoy. Harry plants a fist in the man's gut, watches him gasp, and fall to his knees. Harry's knife falls from the man's pocket.

"You're a shade slow, friend. What else have you got that belongs to me?"

The would-be burglar catches his breath and tries to rise. Clutching the door handle, he struggles to his feet and raises his hands, a gesture of surrender. "I have nothing," he mutters in French. "The others took the rest."

Others. At least three then.

"Hoping to get something for yourself here, were you?"

"I take what I find."

Harry picks up the knife from the street. He does not take his eyes off him. "What's your name, thief?"

"Farid."

"Farid." The young man—younger in fact than Harry first assessed—is thin as a matchstick, his clothing soiled, his hair oily and ragged. Harry looks the boy over, pauses before continuing. "There is a certain church I need to find."

"I do not know churches."

"If you know the Cathédrale du Sacré-Cœur on Boulevard Hammou-boutlelis, you can earn an honest wage tonight."

Farid, Harry sees, is reluctant to give anything away, but the boy lowers his eyes and rubs the palm of his hand. "How much?"

"What's a fair price for a travel guide?"

"Five francs," says Farid.

"Ten, if we're there in less than twenty minutes." *Before my head splits apart.* "And a bonus for anything further."

Farid settles uneasily into the passenger seat. Harry walks around the front of the car, slides into the driver's side, reaches under the seat to retrieve the keys and starts the engine, more than eager to put distance between them and this holy hell. He dares not check the glove box to assure the cash is still there, fearful Farid will grab the money and run before he directs them to the cathedral. The old Renault climbs to the crest of the hill. Farid points to a corner up ahead, and they turn left onto a street that leads down toward the lights of the city. "The Old Cathedral is in Hai Yaghmourhassen, near the train station. We must travel this road until we reach the Mosque Abdullah Ben Salem."

"And the cathedral?"

"A block east of the mosque."

For someone who does not know churches, Farid seems certain of the location. "Do you attend this mosque?"

"As a boy." Farid folds his hands in his lap and stares out the window. He is silent for a moment, then adds, "My family lived near the train station. We walked to the mosque for prayer."

In the Muslim faith, the penalty for thievery is harsh—amputation of fingers or hand. How is it that Farid, a seemingly well-educated son of a religious family, does not fear such punishment? "Are you not afraid of being labeled a thief?"

"Muslims may not steal from each other."

"So you only steal from nonbelievers?"

Farid nods. The boy cannot be more than fifteen, Harry calculates.

"There are conditions for punishment," Farid says.

"What conditions?"

"The Hudud specifies many things. The property is taken from a place where it is put away, a place such as a cupboard. The property is not lying about for anyone to see. The theft is proven by the testimony of two witnesses or the confession of the thief, twice. The person who has lost the property asks for its return."

"Two witnesses?"

"Or a confession, stated two times."

"It's no wonder you still have all your fingers," says Harry.

The boy looks down at his hands, nods.

Harry is beginning to wonder about a boy who speaks French easily, quotes text from the Islamic book of punishments, and makes his living—however impoverished it seems—as a thief. "Where is your family?"

"Dead."

"All?"

"All. Father, mother, brothers."

"When did this happen?"

"Months ago."

"How?"

"They were called to evening prayer. My father and two brothers. It was Monday, and I was to help my mother bring the laundry. We lived in an apartment on the third floor. The laundry was heavy and she could not carry it alone. As the youngest son, it was my job to carry for her. And so, I did not accompany my father and brothers. Later, not ten minutes more, when the carrying was done, I ran to join them. When I arrived at the mosque, there was a great cloud of dust—thick and gray—in the street. It was difficult to see. Men were running in and out yelling, carrying others, rushing them away.

There were trails of blood and gray dust. I shoved my way, screaming for them."

"You found them?"

"On the floor. They did not move. A beam had fallen, a support high in the dome. They had been kneeling in prayer when it fell. I could not lift it. I tried but could not."

Farid again looks at his hands, and covers his face.

"And your mother?"

The city is silent, streets deserted, a sliver of a moon high up in the sky.

"Everything stopped for her—eating, sleeping. In two weeks, she died. There is no one left."

You are left, Harry wants to say. "Where do you live now?"

"Near the café in an alley. I sleep in his doorway and eat from his kitchen."

"You sleep in the doorway? Not in a house?"

"I am not permitted to enter. It is a fine house. I may sleep only in the doorway."

"As long as you agree to do what you did this evening?" That explains the boy's odd behaviors.

Farid nods.

"Do you not have an uncle, another relative?"

"He is my uncle."

The boy is one of Fagin's pickpockets, then. Poor children, severed from their families, left to fatten the fat uncle's wallet.

"Here is the mosque," says Farid. "Go to the right, then around the square. The cathedral is there on the left."

It is the better part of a day since Harry departed Tangier. He must notify Townsend of his arrival, inquire about fresh orders. Harry parks the car, opens the glove box, extracts ten Algerian francs, and hands them to Farid. "You've earned your ten," he says, reluctant to let the boy go. God knows where.

"The bonus?"

Remembering his promise, Harry asks, "How far is the port? Mers-el-Kébir?"

"A few minutes more. Back to the main road, then left when you come to the sea. I can take you there." There is an unguarded eagerness in the offer, the unnamed bonus important.

"A distance, then." Harry pretends to consider. "I can return you back to this spot, the cathedral, but not to the café. It will take too long."

Farid shrugs. He looks past Harry into the street.

"Wait here," says Harry. "I don't know how long I'll be. Maybe five minutes, maybe fifty."

Given the French presence in Algeria, Harry pictured a replica of Paris's Sacré Coeur. But this cathedral with its towering doors, mosaic tiles and arched towers—surrounded by proud date palms—is reminiscent of the Moorish style, an urban oasis unaffected by a distant French influence.

Harry figures Farid will either sit and wait or take the rest of the money in the glove box and disappear. The money is unimportant to Harry. Farid is welcome to it. The boy has to survive. All the same, Harry hopes he will see the boy again.

He climbs the endless steps—one's endless pursuit of heaven, he muses—and navigates his way through the canyon-like cathedral. Seemingly vacant, his footsteps echo in the empty space. He has no notion of how many clergymen are housed here nor whom he can trust. As for his cover, insurance claims are not generally settled at this hour. He does not wish to arouse suspicion by declaring such an unlikely occasion, particularly since this transmittal site must be used again. Making his way back to the El Morocco Club in time is out of the question. A Rob Roy may be worth the trip, however. In Algeria, he has yet to come across anything but a strong cup of tea.

Harry proceeds down the center aisle toward the apse, searching left and right. On either side, he counts seven chapels, altars and kneeling benches flanked by sculpted statues of saints and flaming candles. When Harry has almost reached the sanctuary area, a man—pale-skinned, frail of build, streaks of gray in his once-black hair, creases of age in his forehead and cheeks—emerges from a sheltered chapel to Harry's right. He is dressed in a black ankle-length cassock, a white clerical collar at his throat. His eyes search Harry's clothing, head to toe. He nods slightly as if reassuring himself of a decision, then offers his hand, the handshake warm and firm. "I am Father Claverie. Pierre."

Without waiting for Harry to respond in kind, he pivots and leads him past the sanctuary into a larger chapel, a recess behind the altar. There, he kneels as if to pray. Harry follows the priest's lead, lowers his knees to the padded kneeler and steeples his hands in prayer.

"You have come a long way." Father Claverie speaks softly in a flawless French.

"Insurance agents cover great distances. There are hundreds of claims we must attend."

"You have arrived at the right time."

"How is that?" asks Harry.

"At this hour, there are few worshippers and ample time to hear your confession."

"I'm not one for confessions, Father. Will you settle for a few minutes of conversation?"

Father Claverie laughs. "It is a short walk to the confessional."

"I'll need a review on the opening lines."

"No matter."

Father Claverie brushes aside the privacy curtain that covers the penitent's side of the confessional booth, waits for Harry to enter, then takes his place in the center compartment. Through the latticework that separates them, the priest begins the traditional Latin confessional phrase of welcome. Then, in French he adds, "To your left, give the wall panel a gentle push. The narrow opening leads to the room you seek."

The room—closer in size to a coat closet—smells of myrrh and sandalwood. Unbidden, remnants of gray Sunday mornings in St. Charles come to mind. His mother bends over her rosary murmuring frenzied prayers that do not include her only son. Until old enough to contribute to the farm's labors, Harry was nothing more than an uninvited guest. He shivers at the memory.

Pierre Claverie sits at the wireless machine and transmits Harry's message to Gibraltar. Within minutes, a return communication clicks in. URGENT. REQUIRED BEFORE DAWN. ALL DUE HASTE.

"Marching orders," says Harry. "Will you be here when I return?"

"Oui. I will sleep for a few hours. It is wise to secure your information and return quickly. The wireless goes down frequently. Sometimes, we must wait."

"Point me in the right direction," says Harry.

"Go back through the door panel and exit through the confessional curtain. Kneel for a few moments in prayer. Do not be hasty. You have spent a bit of time, mind you, confessing your sins. Wait until I genuflect at the sanctuary, make the sign of the cross and leave."

"There's no one here, Father. I'm in search of ships, not absolution."

"What harm will it do? A moment of prayer can change the world."

Not this world.

Claverie rises from the chair and turns toward the door panel. "Do you know where you are going?"

"I have a guide. At least I'm counting on it."

Father Claverie raises his eyebrows in surprise. "It is unwise to trust anyone in Oran. There are those who are quite ruthless. You must use caution."

Chapter Twenty-One

The car is empty. Harry chastises himself for expecting the boy to remain, to place a promise over a sure means of survival. Still, he is disappointed. He opens the glove box and is surprised to find the money envelopes full, untouched. Perhaps he guessed right after all.

The boy's directions had been clear enough. Take the main highway to the sea. Turn left. Twenty minutes. Harry starts the engine and turns the car around in the direction from which they had come, skirting the square on the opposite side, the lights of the mosque and the highway visible ahead.

He sees him standing in the abandoned structure staring up at the injured dome. Harry pulls over and idles the engine until Farid finishes whatever thoughts are in his head, opens the door and slides into the passenger seat. They do not speak until the highway stops and they smell the sea. The road branches left or right.

"Left," says Farid.

The Renault obeys.

"You all right?" asks Harry.

"It is three months."

"Why do you stay with your uncle?"

"It is all I know."

"What about a job? A real job?"

"It is difficult for young men to find work. I have no skills."

"I can vouch for you as a travel guide."

Farid turns his face toward Harry. He has an openness of expression that only children manage. "Yes, that is something."

"You told me you carry laundry."

At this, Farid gives a small chuckle. "It is not my favorite job."

"Seriously, Farid, you are educated. You speak French. You know the Quran. And, truth be told, you're not much of a thief."

"No." Harry sees the boy is more comfortable now.

"What do you want to do?"

"I would like to play the piano."

"The piano," says Harry. It is, of course, not what he was expecting. "You should learn."

"I know how to play. I know how to make the jazz."

Harry laughs. "You need to go to a city called Ajaccio in Corsica. There are places there to play the jazz."

Farid is silent, but Harry senses he has something more to say.

"I can drive this car," says Farid.

"Where did you learn to drive?"

"My brothers."

"Your family owned a car?"

"No. A man who attended the mosque owned a car very like this one. A different color, older, but the same. His wife died. He did not have a woman to cook for him. In return for my mother's cooking, he allowed my brothers and me to ride in this car and then, after many months of eating," Farid smiles, "he taught us to drive. My mother's couscous drove us many miles, and many more for her bagita." Farid puffs out his cheeks and pats his belly in imitation of the man's growing girth.

Harry laughs. The boy is a natural comic. Despite everything that has happened to him, he is able to find humor. Harry is glad for his company. "Your mother was a good cook?"

"An excellent cook," corrects Farid.

"Driving is a rare ability. Add that to your list of employment skills."

"What are these employment skills?" He asks it with childlike curiosity.

"Things you can do well. A talent not everyone can claim. A talent that will cause others to want to hire you. Playing the piano. Driving a car."

"Which of these talents do you have?" asks Farid.

"I'm no piano player. I can speak and listen in a couple of languages. I know how to ski."

"And how to drive a car," adds Farid. "You ski in the snow or on the water?"

"In the snow," says Harry.

"Can I show you how I drive this car?" Farid is warming to the idea of legitimate employment and independence. Harry has no wish to discourage him.

"Another night, Farid. If anything happens to this car, I won't be able to complete my job. Many people are counting on me."

"Nothing will happen to this car. I will make certain. You have helped me. It is what I can do to help you."

They pass a row of docks. "This is the port of Oran," Farid announces.

The light, though meager, is enough to illuminate vessels moored in the harbor.

They enter an open gate and drive the length of the pier. Seven destroyers. Oran is the shallower port, thus, no carriers or battleships. How many at Mers-el-Kébir? Both ports are within easy reach of the Italian, particularly the Sicilian, coast.

As they approach the end of the pier, Harry lifts his foot off the brake and cuts the headlights. He takes note of a group of men in French naval uniforms who have come from the port authority building. Odd for this hour. A late meeting. Harry sits and watches them walk in the direction, he assumes, of their respective ships. The men stop and gather, obviously in serious discussion. In the face of France's surrender, these commanders have no choice. If the Italians or the Germans demand it, they are obliged to turn over their ships. The action will most likely be sudden.

"What are they saying?" Farid asks.

"If it were my ship and my men, I'd be thinking up ways to stay out of Hitler's navy."

"What can they do?"

"They wish they knew. It's not their call."

"Who will make this call?"

"Their commander."

"When?"

"Very soon, Farid."

"Is it possible they will be permitted to go to their families?" It is an honest question, asked with open-eyed simplicity. A question with obvious meaning to Farid.

"No. That is clearly not going to happen." Harry does not want Farid thinking there is any good to come from the French surrender, least of all for the French. He counts the men. Eleven. Four more vessels somewhere about. The men disperse. Four cross a short bridge to a concrete bunker-like structure. Of course, submarines. Harry wants no part of that duty. In the Great War, more than five thousand German submariners lost their lives. Drowning has always been last on Harry's list of desirable ways to leave this world. Given his recent experience in a black cave, his list is due for revision.

Once the officers depart and Harry is certain the pier is deserted, he leaves Farid and goes off to inspect the location of each vessel and prepare a detailed map. None looks to be going anywhere soon. In the early morning, on his way back from Mers-el-Kébir, he will station himself on a site above the pier and count again, double-check the locations. The submarines will be difficult; coordinates for the bunker will have to do.

When Harry returns, Farid has shifted to the driver's seat. Harry does not protest. He will give the boy a chance. From the passenger seat, he has time to record the port of Oran information. The little Renault speeds its way west on the unlit road, first running inland from the port, then curving north and west along the coast. Farid drives awkwardly, both hands gripping the wheel, one foot pressing the accelerator, the other hovering in the air over the clutch. Within ten minutes, in the bend of the long curved highway, Harry instructs Farid to pull over. Farid hits the brakes hard, and they skid to a screeching stop.

"You need a bit of practice on the brake," says Harry.

The lights of the Mers-el-Kébir port shine bright. Harry catches sight of the largest naval squadron in the Mediterranean, an impressive fleet of warships of every sort. Son of a bitch. Two modern battleships, the *Dunkerque* and *Strasbourg*. Townsend had specifically named them. Two older battleships, *Bretagne* and *Provence*. Then, the monstrous carrier, *Commandante Teste*. Mick spotted it in Toulon and speculated it was on the move. A flotilla of destroyers, all larger than the smaller ones in Oran, and countless other vessels—sloops and trawlers and patrol boats.

Harry almost gasps at the dramatic image. No photograph could capture the dreadful reality. He understands—as he had not before—the extent of Britain's peril. With this armada, Mussolini and Hitler will control entry and exit to the western Mediterranean and the seacoast of every European, African, and Middle Eastern country. Britain will come tumbling down.

Chapter Twenty-Two

Genoa

At one in the morning, Lorenzo hears the steady rumble of engines, the scream of accelerating bombs. He knows before he leaves his bed and summons his driver. The factories are gone.

Hours later, he stands, drink in hand, mouth clenched tight. He tosses the liquor down and drops the glass into the wreckage at his feet, his anger, once hot and sharp, replaced by quiet resignation. The once stunningly beautiful buildings are unrecognizable, entire back walls destroyed, their fronts open to the street, thick cracks in their foundations, curtains shredded, priceless Murano glass blown out, centuries-old furnishings in rubble. One lone cabinet—the cupboard from which he poured one last glass of American bourbon—is left standing, under a slice of mirror hanging frameless on the side wall. He stares at his fractured image, impressed with his own good looks, striking amidst the gray background of ruin.

The second production wing is demolished, parts and models blasted into the sea. No means of replacing them. No chance of another loan. The bank already wary. Farber Manufacturing's finances precarious even before the bombings began. He hesitated to tell the old man. Now, he has no choice.

"Bastards." He lights a cigarette, sucks at it hard, and reconsiders his plans.

His mother is well cared for. A relief. His father rightly saw to his wife's continuing comfort, knowing full well the son lacked the talents of the father. For the time being, the Terzo factories will be all right. Plenty of contracts already in reserve. But the Farber fortune changed direction a year ago immediately after the Gran Premio. Recklessly, he had wagered the lion's share of Farber's annual profits on the outcome of that race. On Romano's assurance, he had counted on Apelle's victory, paid the idiot a king's ransom to fuel the rumor about the jockey's illness. A word here, a word there, a sudden shift in the odds to drive up the payout. Romano had located the ultimate hopper, best on the circuit, so he claimed, injected right under the skin, undetectable by the saliva test. The prize purse and the payout would set up Lorenzo for years, enough to sit out this European conflict on a beach in Majorca, pretending he cared about serving his power-hungry leader, sending the occasional invented "intelligence report" to Nico at OVRA headquarters.

Out of the gate, Apelle had taken the lead, broken the record for the first thousand meters. Confident, Lorenzo counted his winnings. On the backstretch, the horse faltered. Romano's refreshment had not delivered the promised results.

"What the hell happened?" Lorenzo stormed at the jockey. Unresponsive, punch-drunk, was how the jockey described the thoroughbred.

After the race, Lorenzo was desperate. He begged his father for cash to replenish Farber's accounts. Grim-faced, his father obliged. Farber was none the wiser, Lorenzo in the clear.

Later that summer, Rosso invited the family and guests to the Milan estate for a long weekend. A big gathering for a big announcement, his father had said. Buckets of champagne, a small orchestra for dancing, picnics on the lawn. Afternoon became evening. Fireworks boomed over the lake. Everyone gathered round for the highly anticipated declaration. Laughing, drinks in hand, drum rolls, the music stilled.

Rosso Terzo commanded the moment. "I've made a decision," he stated solemnly. "After great deliberation, it is a decision that will preserve our company's legacy of innovation and accomplishment."

Rosso had altered his will. Lorenzo was stunned. Gabriella—now primary heir—was to inherit the engineering firm and the whole of the Terzo factories. As executor, Nico would manage everything. Everything. Gabriella and Nico. Lorenzo, intentionally and publicly disgraced. Left nothing but the Franciacorta vineyard and the villa on Lago d'Iseo. His father could have called him for a quiet conversation, informed him privately. Why choose a public debasement? He had felt the tightness in his body, the disbelief, the hot rage on his face, the bottomless hatred in his gut at the image of his father.

For that humiliation, Romano would pay. He would live under Lorenzo's foul thumb, forever in his debt, made to carry out all manner of schemes until Lorenzo tired of him. There were angry words, accusations, murderous glances. With Gabriella, he'd been out of control. One afternoon, she'd visited the Farber factory and challenged him on some small issue, openly disagreed with a directive he had given the staff. He remembered the pleasure he felt as he gripped her throat, slammed her back against the wall in his office, his knuckles under her chin, squeezing her windpipe. She was powerless to stop him. If not for a timely knock on the door, he might have kept squeezing. Gabriella left his office, never returned, and barely spoke thereafter, even at family gatherings.

But he had the last word, as it were. He prevailed. He was patient. Hardly his nature. To get what he wanted, he had to be patient. Not much in this world—good or evil—gets done without patience, he told himself. He waited. His father never expected it. Came the perfect opportunity, both of them together, neatly packaged, gone in one spectacular instant, the tire disengaged— undone—on that curved unlit highway. One more secret into the family pool. Who could know? The car unrecognizable. The blame shifted. Who would guess the British bombs would fall that very night? Collateral damage, they said. No one the wiser. No other conclusion even considered. Afterward, he had played it right, vowing revenge, railing against the Royal Air Force, accusing Douglas and his like, pressuring Nico to put a target on Douglas's back.

Now, all of it belongs to him. Except that damned clause that cites Nico as executor. Controller of everything. No matter. Nico is off in the south, preoccupied with Il Duce's wars, seizing French ships for Mussolini's new Holy Empire. In war, there is always a chance that Nico may not return. Lorenzo stops, wonders why that particular thought has not before occurred to him.

There is one last chore. The trip to Monaco. Breaking it to Farber. Afterward, he will charm one—or two—of the old man's beautiful companions for a languorous holiday in Majorca. Settled by the pool, he will have ample time to decide about the factories. More importantly, Nico's fate in this oh-so dangerous war.

"On the way to Milan," he tells the driver, "stop at the Romano residence."

Chapter Twenty-Three

Harry has a chill of premonition. He sits in the passenger seat, recovering the last details of the Oran moorings and sketching the map, filling in names and distances. In the driver's seat, Farid points downhill to the Mers-el-Kébir harbor, eager to describe the layout of the docks below.

"There, at the end, you see the big ones. What do you call a ship such as that?"

"A battleship," says Harry.

"I would like to guide such a battleship," says Farid. "I think I can do that."

He urges Harry to finish his notes so they can get out of the car, so Harry can explain to Farid about the other ships and their roles in the sea. Farid's hand is on the door handle, anxious to pull it up or push it down—whichever direction will cause the door to open. A vague instinct warns Harry to tell Farid to remain in the car, to wait for Harry to lead the way. From behind, a distant light—a light absent an instant ago—reflects off the windshield, a single beam that does not belong on the road at this hour. Harry

lowers his pencil and turns to watch through the rear window.
The light is coming up fast—too fast. Farid is leaning away from
Harry, putting his weight against the door, adjusting his feet as
people do when they prepare to step out of a car. Before Harry
can say anything, before he can grab the boy's arm, the door is
open, the seat beside him vacant, the boy out of the car and out
of sight, the light and the roar of a motorcycle engine suddenly
upon them.

There is a shriek of brakes, the dull thud of gravel spraying
against the car as the motorcycle turns abruptly, the beam of light
now facing away. The area surrounding the car suddenly dark.
Harry hears two quick pops. He crouches in the seat, reaches for
his gun, then pushes his own door open and drops to the ground.
The sound of the engine fades as it speeds away. Farid's ashen
face appears before him, lips white, mumbling an indecipherable
word as his eyes empty. Harry kneels in the gravel, holds him
close, whispers as a father would do to his child. "You're all right
now. I'm here. You're going to be all right," he lies. A dull rage
rises within him.

Harry lowers his head, curses silently. Carefully, he gathers
the boy's body and lays it on the back seat, marveling at the
lightness of the boy's bones. A boy should not be so weightless,
so excruciatingly thin. He wonders what garbage the boy was
permitted to eat. He folds the boy's arms across his chest and
closes the eyelids, arranges his legs so the feet are placed together.
It is then Harry notices the shoes are too big for Farid's feet, the
socks ragged and torn. In that moment, Harry wants to kill the
uncle, the man who prides himself on his cleverness in swindling
foreigners. The man who grows rich but provides nothing, not
even a proper pair of shoes or socks for his nephew, who expects

his sister's child to sleep in doorways and eat from discarded plates. This boy who would command a battleship. This boy who wished to make jazz.

When Harry completes his reconnaissance, he will carry Farid's body to Pierre Claverie. Surely, the church will know the proper burial rites for a young Muslim boy. After, he will go and find this uncle. This uncle who must be taught how to care for an orphaned boy. This uncle who lined his own pockets with a boy's innocence. This uncle who stole a boy's honor. It is the least and the most that Harry can do—the only difference he can make for Farid.

For the remainder of the night, Harry walks back and forth over the damp piers and seawalls of the Mers-el-Kébir port, checking the ships' positions, figuring their coordinates, an urgency now buried deep within him. It is two minutes before four when Harry catches sight of what he assumes to be the pier guards changing gate shifts. He takes a moment to orient his position and heads toward the T-shaped dock that leads to the exit gate. Satisfied that what he has recorded is accurate and precise, he inches toward the dock, intending to slip out without notice. He must drive the car to the cathedral and transmit the information in time to meet Townsend's deadline. He ignores the bone-deep weariness that washes over him. Duty does not stop because one's body and soul are exhausted. It is a lesson he learned at the end of his father's strap. Resting and laying about are punishable things.

He approaches a wood plank that serves as a temporary connector from one dock to the next. When he hears a scraping of metal, he looks to his left. In the distance, a uniformed man moves silently toward him. He assumes the man is a guard who will ask to examine his credentials or, worse, search him. To avoid the possible ruinous consequences, he folds his notes and tucks them inside a loose board that juts out from the dock. Quickly, he works out a convincing story about his presence at this early hour. He is an overworked inspector getting an early start, checking on moorage availability for his shipping company. Of course, he had no inkling the area is restricted.

The distance between Harry and the guard closes. When their eyes meet, Harry realizes he's been all wrong in his presumption. He reels backward into the water, shoved off the narrow dock by a pair of muscled hands. His clothing and shoes pull him down. Cold water rushes into his nose and mouth. He tastes oil and salt. He forces his eyes open, finally touches the hard stones on the bottom, and pushes off toward the surface to fill his lungs with air. Two strong hands force his head back. Before he is plunged down again, he sees the shadowy silhouette of his kneeling assailant.

Entangled in his jacket, he twists around to find bottom. He struggles to loosen the sleeves and slams his head against a protruding piling. Still, he manages to right himself, grab hold of the piling and heave his body out of the water. He chokes in one gasp of air before he is thrust down again. Each time he resurfaces—over and again, it seems—the assailant knocks him under.

There is no escape. Doomed to drown. Death by suffocation. His brain half-remembers the training lecture. The average person holds a breath for thirty to sixty seconds. Once he runs out of breath, his chances are slim. Water fills the lungs and windpipe. Odds of making it to the surface sink dramatically.

For that fraction of a second it takes to suddenly see the world clear, it crosses Harry's mind that his assailant has followed him,

watched him, patiently searched for and chosen the perfect
spot—the perfect hour of Harry's fatigue and inattention—to
kill him. The space between the two narrow docks prevents
Harry moving left or right, and the plank on which he had been
crossing is directly above. His attacker has simply to wait until
he surfaces in order to push him down again. *A fish in a barrel.*
Indeed, a fine bit of surveillance and planning.

It is obvious who will be the first to tire of this game. The clock
is running down, Harry running out of air, his oxygen depleting
rapidly, his muscles all but spent. Soon, he will be unable to fight
his way to the surface. Blackness will claim him.

He swears he hears a familiar voice call his name. An echo a
long way off, his brain playing tricks, an auditory mirage, a last
vestige of life, the water muffling and distorting the sound. Air is
what he needs. He wills his panic away. If he can situate himself
opposite the plank, he has energy enough to swim underwater
a few meters, time enough to surface and take in a few breaths
before the assailant finds him in the semi-darkness. He touches
bottom, flips himself around to catch the faint light of the street
lamp at the surface, and kicks furiously.

The hard pain in his chest—he pictures an elephant's rump
sitting square in the middle of it—and the realization that he lies
on solid ground tell him he is almost alive. There is a warmth on
his face, a blinding light that drags him halfway to consciousness.
He tastes salt on his tongue and feels cold seawater leaking from
his nose and mouth. Still, the weight bears down on his chest. In
vain, he tries to sit up, sputtering, but a powerful hand presses
down. Another stiff push causes a new flood of fluid from his
lungs. He coughs and two arms prompt him to sit up while he
spews oil and waste and water.

"Jolly Christ. You're a regular spigot, you are."

Who is this voice? Who called his name as he tried to escape his watery deathtrap? He cannot remember how or when someone pulled him from the water and laid him out. A gash on his forehead throbs. A heavy hand holds a cloth in place.

"A few more inches, that pretty nose would be flat."

Harry has not yet opened his eyes. "Where the hell have you been?"

"I'm right here, laddie. Saving your arse again."

"Who asked you? I had it handled."

Mick cuffs him on the chin. "Aye. Stand up then and hold this against your bloody head. We need to get out of here before the guards find your friend."

"My notes." Harry points to the loose board and retrieves the precious packet.

In the dim light, he recognizes the spotted face of the man who seated him at the restaurant. His eyes stare at the stars, his throat and chest red with blood.

Chapter Twenty-Four

Harry's report dispatches directly to the Prime Minister.

To the Attention of Prime Minister Sir Winston Churchill,

*As requested, find herein the report on port and vessel specif-
ics—including name, type and location—regarding elements
of the French Fleet located in the port of Mers-el-Kébir (MEK),
Oran Province, Algeria.*

> *PORT COORDINATES. 35° 44' North; 0° 43' West*
> *PORT AREA SIZE. 10. 98 km² (approx. 4 sq. mi.)*
> *PORT PROMONTORY. Lighthouse, Fort MEK*

> *CONTEXT. Of the entirety of the fleet of vessels in the
> French Admiralty, the ships now standing in the MEK port
> constitute the biggest single concentration—the strength—of*

the fleet. In addition, there exist eleven (seven destroyers and four submarines, plus a number of smaller vessels) moored in the nearby port of Oran which is eight kilometers east of MEK, an air travel distance equal to 5 miles. North coordinates are approximately the same, 1° west.

STRUCTURES. The following capital ships are anchored at MEK, moored stern to the mole, in the following order, from northwest to southeast—Dunkerque, Provence, Strasbourg, Bretagne, Commandant Teste (aviation transport). Six light cruisers are moored on the south side of the harbour. Remaining smaller ships (patrol boats, trawlers) are scattered along the pier east of the smaller cruisers.

SHORE DEFENSES. On a hill to the west of the harbour is a battery of six 6-inch guns, to the hard south of the harbour is another battery of four 4.7-inch guns. To the east in the vicinity of Oran are batteries of three 6-inch guns, and four 4.7-inch guns. Harbour entrance is protected by anti-torpedo boat and anti-submarine booms. A mine net stretches from Cape Falcon to a point north at Point Canastel. Both the breakwater (30 feet high) and Fort Mers-el-Kébir (100 feet high) protect the side armor of ships inside the harbour.

LOCATIONS. Attached find a detailed map of the MEK harbour noting anchorage and shore defenses.

INTERFERENCE. Low possibility of Italian submarine presence. On two occasions, agents of the Italian government (presumably OVRA) conducting surveillance were encountered.

CONSIDERATIONS. Approximately 200 civilians work in and around the MEK port. The city of Oran, eight kilometers to the east, records a population of 195,000.

TIME ACCURATE. 500 hours on 3 July for MEK infor-
mation. 200 hours on 3 July for port of Oran.

I remain,
Harrison J. Douglas, Field Agent
Military Intelligence, Section 6, His Majesty's Service

Following the transmittal, Mick and Harry settle Farid's body in a room in the cathedral's basement. Claverie dresses and bandages the gash on Harry's forehead after Harry showers and changes into dry clothes—the black slacks and white shirt of Claverie's religious order. It has been a seemingly endless day, and now the three men sit on separate chairs in the small reception area of Claverie's living quarters. Mick and Harry puff on thick cigars, Claverie on a French cigarillo. They sip warm brandy from gold-leafed altar cups. It is quiet, the light muted, the sun's golden rays climbing a bank of tall windows. A courtyard garden emerges—purple and pink in the dawn's light. A small patch of orange trees and rows of lavender fill the space behind a ceramic saint who holds a child in one arm, a lamb in the other.

Claverie speaks first. "The Algerian belief is that everyone is born with a destiny—a time to be born and a time to die. There is a resignation about death. Grief over the dead is seen as a denial of Allah's will. It is also believed that a man is not fully a man until the age of forty. Thus, a woman grieves less for those who die younger. Tears of grief are considered weakness among men. Women are permitted these tears, but not men."

"You believe in these customs?"

"No, these are Sunni customs, descended from the ancient Berbers."

"Based on what he told me, Farid has no close family. Only an uncle—his mother's distant brother—who, from his description, saw him as an apprentice to his criminal circle."

"We know members of Farid's community who will care for him. They will wash the body and drape it in linen before burial. There is a cemetery where a hole is dug."

"What about a coffin?"

"Coffins are forbidden. Part of this belief is simple geography. There are few trees from which coffins can be made. Thus, the bodies are wrapped in linen and placed in the ground. Many graves are unmarked, but I will inquire as to where Farid's family is placed. Someone will know."

"A service?"

"There is a simple prayer before burial. Nothing elaborate. Out of respect for the dead, the burial is to occur within 24 hours of death. We will assure everything is done properly for Farid."

"I liked the kid," says Harry. "He deserved better."

"Tell me what happened," Claverie says.

"We stopped the car on a high plateau above the Mers-el-Kébir port to get a bird's-eye view of the layout. There was a sheer bank down to the sea. The road curved around and down. Farid got out of the car, the driver door, and I lost sight of him."

"The driver door?"

"He wanted to drive," says Harry. "To show me he could. I saw no harm in it. At that hour, there were no vehicles on the road. It gave me time to transfer my notes."

"Then?"

"Immediately after we stopped, Farid was anxious to rush out. He wanted me to explain the ships in the port. By that time, he had told me about his family and how he came to be living with this uncle. As I said, I liked the kid and . . ." Harry trails off and sits silent, scratches his chin. "I was finishing a few drawings, so I told him to wait. I was abrupt, and I could see he was impatient. I saw a light in the rear window. A single light reflected off the mirror. I remember thinking it was odd for the hour. And for our location. With just the one light, I assumed it was a motorcycle. It was coming up fast—too fast—for that curve we were sitting on. I remember thinking at that speed the driver won't see the turn in time to slow down. Before I could say anything, Farid was out of the car. I saw the light swerve and thought I'd been right about the speed, that whoever was driving that cycle wasn't going to make the curve. It flashed through my mind the cycle was going to hit the car, and we needed to get out of the way. Not an instant later, I heard a brake screech, a spray of gravel hit the car, and two quick pops. Pop pop. I understood then what was happening, and I reached for my gun. I crouched in the seat and rolled out the side door. The cycle engine revved and sped away, in the direction from where it came. I called out for Farid. I found him on the ground."

"Could be OVRA. Sounds like their op," says Mick. "They're all along the coast. Given France's recent surrender and Mussolini's intense interest in acquiring the fleet, it's easy to assume the Italian secret service is in play. The ports of Algiers and Oran are a short ride from Sicily."

"No. OVRA didn't kill him."

"How do you know?"

On the drive back to the cathedral, Harry thought through the reasons, but in the presence of the priest, he is not willing to disclose them. "On the outskirts of Oran, I stopped at a café. Not my best decision, but I was hungry and tired and needed a break. Before I walked in the door, I had a feeling about the place. In any case, before I got out of there, my identification—passport, license—all stolen. Plain careless on my part. Farid played the role of decoy. He sidetracked my attention so the thieves could do their work. The IDs were fraudulent and identified me as a French citizen, so there wasn't much to give away. They're changing hands out there now, I suspect, putting a few francs in the thieves' pockets."

"Someone killed him for these false identities?" asks Claverie.

"Nothing like that. The thieves already had what they wanted. After leaving the café, I encountered Farid on the street and realized he was just a boy." Harry sees no purpose in exposing more of Farid's sins. "I couldn't afford to drive around for hours looking for this place." Harry spreads his arms to encompass the room. "I offered him a few quid to act as my guide, and he directed me straight here. It's possible someone saw him get into my car, didn't like the idea, and followed us."

Harry doubts the logic of his own scenario—if Farid were the target, the killer had any number of opportunities to shoot him before that bend in the road—but it is a plausible story for the priest. It could be true. Except for the small detail about the man who tried to drown him.

"You're saying Farid was involved in thievery?"

"The kid was a pawn used by his uncle and, I gathered, a few others. If Farid didn't do what they wanted, he had no place to sleep and nothing to eat."

Harry hesitates to mention the next piece of the story, but he needs to know if and how Claverie is involved. Only the priest and Townsend knew where Harry was going. And Claverie had issued that strange warning before Harry left the cathedral. "Before he died, Farid mumbled something. I didn't get it at first. He said it again, and I heard it plainly. 'Corsican.' Why would he say that?"

Plenty of Corsicans travel to and from North Africa. As French subjects, Algerians and Corsicans move easily to and from the mainland of Europe and Africa. In the back of his mind, Harry has an inkling that Ivo Guaneri is involved, but he resists the idea. There was something in Guaneri that inspired Harry's confidence—a sheer force of will—and Harry is reluctant to abandon it. But evidence is mounting.

Claverie's next comment stuns him.

"For two years, since Hitler decided to take Austria and Czechoslovakia and Poland, our church is torn by politics. One day, we have a trusted ally. The next day, we are enemies. Algiers and Oran are, of course, situated on the coast, within sailing distance of Sicily and Italy. We require information, contacts in the Mediterranean we can trust. We turn to those we know in Corsica."

"Guaneri?"

The priest nods. "Ivo and his group. We see them often enough. Also a man named Lukas."

"Lukas. Nico Lukas?" asks Mick.

Pierre Claverie takes a long slow puff on the small cigar. He draws in deeply before exhaling. For a while, Harry thinks he has nothing more to say. "Ivo Guaneri and Nico Lukas were childhood playmates. I was a young priest, my first year, at the

Eglise du Sacré-Coeur in Ajaccio. They were altar boys, if you can believe it. Good boys who wanted to do right. Mischievous, of course, but they took their duties seriously."

Another sacred heart.

Harry tries to picture the two men as angelic boys in their blessed black-and-white garments—fetching and carrying for the priests. "The question remains, why would Farid's last words be 'The Corsican'?"

"What do you think it means?" asks Claverie. An evasion if ever Harry heard one.

Mick leans forward. He has been listening—thoughtfully—to Harry's exchange with the priest. "The obvious answer is that he recognized who killed him. A man he knew to be Corsican. Until three months ago, you said Farid lived and traveled in the neighborhood, from his home to the mosque, passing the cathedral several times a day. The boy did not travel far from home. You knew him and his family, by sight and by name. From what Harry tells me, he was an observant boy, curious about his surroundings. Likely, he met this man, or heard of him, and knew him to be Corsican. It could be this man attended the mosque, lived or visited in the neighborhood. Do you know anyone like that? Did you see anyone in the cathedral or on the street last night when Harry left?"

Mick knows there is another possibility. That Farid was caught up with people and things that involve killing, things that others call assassination. Visitors to his uncle's home. Visitors he knew to be Corsican.

Claverie's face stiffens and goes dark. He checks the clock on the wall. On his feet, he stubs out the cigarillo and downs the last gulp of brandy. He rubs his hands together. "I will give these questions a great deal of thought. Meanwhile, I must speak to the imam about Farid's burial. Remain here as long as you like, wherever you are comfortable. When I return, I will check the wireless for messages."

After Claverie hurries out, Mick turns to Harry, "What was that all about?"

"Suitably vague. Didn't want to answer outright. Better to ignore. Unpriestly to lie." Harry pauses. "He's going to give your questions a great deal of thought."

"Do you trust him?"

"He's a priest."

"Look who's being evasive."

"On the surface, Vatican City—as a separate state—maintains a formal policy of neutrality, but last time I checked, it's surrounded by Mussolini and his henchmen. As we learned in Milan, the Church excels at avoidance. Competing loyalties. Who knows the real story about the head chap's bedtime arrangements with these characters? There are hundreds of churches that make their own decisions about which side of the bed they wake up on." Harry finishes his brandy and walks to the window.

"Where you stand depends on where you sleep, is that it?"

"You know how it goes."

"Better than most. German sympathizers disguised as loyal British lords and ladies."

"This connection with Guaneri and Lukas. How does that fit with what we know about Lukas?"

"We know Lukas is OVRA deputy, one step down from the top. We know Broadway has had him in sights for at least a year, maybe longer. We know he's related to the Terzos by marriage, not blood—his stepmother Teresa is a sister of Vivianna—and that Rosso Terzo took them in when Nico's father left them and returned to Corsica. *Corsica again.* Nico was born in Ajaccio, mother died when he was nine, father remarried within two years and the family moved to Milan to be close to stepmother's family. Hence, the Terzo connection. For whatever reason, the father went back to Corsica and left son Nico—then thirteen years old—with stepmother Teresa."

"What's the father's name?" Harry asks.

"Karol Lukas."

"Where is he now?"

"Unknown. Assumption is he lives somewhere on the island," says Mick.

"Corsican. The spelling of the last name puzzles me. Lukas with a 'k'. The common spelling is 'c.'"

"The 'k' implies eastern European origin. Czech, Polish, Hungarian, Georgian," says Mick. "The Poles are experts in underground work."

"Sounds Czech to me. Karol. Lukas with a 'k'. Polish and Hungarian have a few extra letters. The name Karol is definitely Czech. If my math is correct, he'd be close to fifty."

"What are you thinking?" asks Mick.

"I'm thinking Karol Lukas, if he is Czech, was none too pleased with Hitler in March 1939. I'm thinking young Father Claverie is well acquainted with Karol Lukas and son Nico." An image of Laura Savic—the Czech resistance fighter—breaks in unexpectedly and sends him back to Budapest. Almost two years ago. He hopes—but doubts—her colleagues survived the German occupation.

"You're thinking the Lukas who Claverie referred to with Guaneri was not Nico Lukas, but Karol, the father?"

"Right. Claverie just said Lukas. You supplied the first name. He told a story about altar boys. We made the wrong assumption."

"Not the first time," says Mick. "That's why he left in an anxious hurry."

"Could it be father and son play for opposing teams?" asks Harry.

"Purely possible. In the '20s, there was a serious independence movement in Corsica. Corsicans wanted to be rid of France, to be independent, but Mussolini was wielding power in Italy and he had eyes on Corsica. Karol Lukas may have left Milan to become involved in the separatist movement. Wouldn't surprise anyone if Claverie was in it, too. Mother Church disagreed, but an idealist young priest sided with his parishioners and risked his life for a free Corsica."

"Enough reason for a father to leave his son in the care of a wealthy stepmother. If the senior Lukas was involved in treasonous activities, he wanted the boy to be safe."

"Better find out why Claverie left Ajaccio," says Mick. "And which Lukas we're talking about." He twists the burning end of the cigar into the ashtray and looks up at Harry. "Speaking of Nico Lukas, I'm almost sure I saw him in Casablanca."

"When?"

"Townsend sent me to count ships. After I gathered the intel, I stopped for a drink at a bodega called Omar's near the Central Market. I sat at a table in the corner. Wasn't there two minutes when I noticed a familiar face at the bar hunched over a Negroni."

"You're sure?"

"No. As soon as I saw him, I left. Wanted to avoid conversation."

"What do you suppose he was doing there?"

"Same reason I was. Checking out the French fleet."

"Any activity?"

"Casablanca is busy. Ships coming and going at a steady pace. Day one, I posted twenty—destroyers, supply ships, sloops, a couple of subs. The next day, two more destroyers, but the subs were gone. One of the Norwegians told me there are sixteen subs there, but they're always on the move in and out of the Atlantic. I didn't see that many. Told Townsend it was hearsay, but likely true."

"Tough for the Italians to grab anything outside the Strait." Harry puffs on the cigar. "So you didn't see Lukas again?"

"Not in Casablanca. When I got to Tangier per instructions, I made straight for the El Morocco. Quite the scene. Packed with bird-watchers and expats. Who's perched at the bar but Margaret Gautier and Nico Lukas."

"Fascinating. She told me she was on her way to Madrid. Did she see you?"

"Glanced my way, then ignored me. I took the signal."

"Did you get a good look at Lukas?"

"Across the room."

"Did he, by any stretch, have a bandage or sling on his wrist?"

Mick thinks for a minute, reconstructs the scene. "Not that I saw. Both arms, hands were in sight, on the bar. Why do you ask?"

"I had a run-in with someone in Tangier. I damaged a wrist. Not mine. His. You're sure there were no bandages?"

"Can't say outright. Nothing I noticed."

"You plan to tell me the story of Margaret Gautier?"

"Another time," says Mick.

"Is she compromised?" asks Harry.

"Not likely. She reports directly to the prime minister. Knows her way around, but something's brewing."

"Why would she be with Lukas?"

"Why is anybody with anybody in Tangier? Shifting winds now that France has fallen. As our evasive priest pointed out, yesterday you were an ally, today you are an enemy."

"Lukas has always been the enemy," says Harry.

"Has he?"

Harry moves away from the window, stubs out the cigar, and walks toward the door. "I'm going out for a while. Will you be here when I get back?"

"Depends. Where are you going?"

"Unfinished business."

"You want company?"

"Not this time."

Chapter Twenty-Five

Nico Lukas again finds himself in Tangier. For the last forty-eight hours, he has been constantly on the move. After a brief meeting with Il Duce in Rome, he caught a military plane to a meeting in Casablanca. Then, a slow train crowded with local workers carried him from Casablanca to Tangier. Lately, his missions run together. Breakfast in Marsala, lunch in Olbia, dinner in Algiers. All of dire importance to one official or another. Lack of sleep, an overabundance of nicotine, and alcohol are taking a toll on body and mind. He has to focus, get hold of himself. This next meeting is unexpected. He must take care that personal resentments do not play a role in what he has to do. He must tamp down his feelings and get on with the business of war.

The sun is warm on his back, the street alive with commerce and the smell of roasting goat. Stalls sell argan oils and dried saffron, red hats and yellow slippers. Hawkers offer almonds and plums. In front of a tobacconist shop, a woman—a dirty scarf pulled low over her eyes so he cannot tell her age—holds a small cup. Her feet are clubbed, and she uses one hand to scoot back and forth across the stones. He hears the clink when the coin he drops into her cup hits bottom. She looks up from beneath the scarf. Her eyes lock into his. She says something he does not understand.

His instructions lead him to a narrow twisting backstreet and a plain, whitewashed building with steps up from the street. Inside the outer gate is a high courtyard, a terraced patio half covered by a linen awning. Beyond is a small cluster of trees, the smell of jasmine sweet and strong. He opens the gate, turns into the courtyard, follows the walkway to a towering door of aromatic wood, and rings the bell. After too many minutes of waiting, he thinks about walking through the trees to the other side of the building. Finally, a young woman in the traditional flowing blue djellaba arrives at the door.

"You had better come inside," she says.

Away from the sun, it is cool in the darkened interior. There is no sign of the man he is to meet. Not that he would recognize him. At one time, he carried the image vivid in his mind, but over the years, the memory slipped away and dissolved into vagueness, so that he no longer remembers his father's face.

He stands a few paces from the door in the center of the reception room wondering what compelled him to come, wondering why Lena insisted that he be the emissary, wondering what she has to do with it. He watches a dark silhouette move toward him and emerge into the light until they come face-to-face. The man is equal in height to Nico, but his body is leaner, his shoulders stronger, his face tanned and leathery from a constant sun, his watchful eyes hooded by a prominent brow. It strikes Nico that he does not recall any part of this man except the long-forgotten smell of him. The scent that takes him to a crowded room on a narrow street in Ajaccio, the day his mother died, the day his father hugged him to his chest and wept. And to another room in Milan, the last time his father loved him, the last time he laid eyes on this man.

Why has he come? His duties await in Oran—meeting with Tanasi's network, piecing together the strategy for Mers-el-Kébir. Now the French have surrendered, the Sicilians are keeping watch, anticipating a command to forge ahead with Il Duce's plans for seizure of the French vessels. Mussolini made it clear. They must not allow the British to negotiate away the fleet Il Duce covets. Nico should be on his way to Oran, not here in a strange house in Tangier.

"You have your mother's face," says Karol Lukas. His voice is deep and rough.

Nico swallows hard, finds his voice, the buried anger of his youth. "Teresa believed you would return. For many years, I believed it too. Until one day I stopped believing it."

"You were wrong to think I could return."

"Why?"

A beat. A sigh. "In those days, it was considered an honor to support the resistance. Our compatriots were generous with food and shelter. People gave us everything they had without accepting payment. The mosquitoes, the heat, the uncertainty. No life for a boy. My instinct was to protect you from it."

"And afterward? More than fifteen years?"

"More than a hundred years."

"Save the regrets."

"Rosso was a wealthy man. He promised to look after you."

"Rosso kept his promise. I was well educated in the Milanese life. Today, I own flats in Rome and Lugano. I have a responsible

position. Rosso was indeed a rich man. And a good man." Nico
stares at some distant spot on the wall. "I would have preferred
a poor father."

"I was a fighter. I could not be a father."

"You chose not to be a father."

"The cause was important to me. And just. I wanted to have
purpose. We fighters lived a different life."

"And later? After the separatists surrendered and you found
yourself still living?"

"A fisherman."

"Where?"

"I have a house in Cargése. A village on the coast, north of
Ajaccio. The fishing is at least good."

"Cargése. I've heard of it." He recalls Lena's story. The connection explained. "There are two churches, are there not?"

Karol frowns, then an almost imperceptible nod. "Two
churches, one Greek, one Latin. They sit across the chasm from
one another."

"What are you are doing in Tangier?"

"Once again, I am a fighter. An old fighter, but one who
understands."

"What is it you understand?" asks Nico.

"The world cannot be ruled by men like Hitler and Mussolini.
I have been in Prague and Warsaw. I have seen what they did.
What they will do again."

"So you don't live in Cargése?"

"Only a fool tells the OVRA deputy where he lives." A swift
grin.

A nod of understanding. "A wise man. What do you want?"
asks Nico.

"The channel between Sardinia and Corsica is narrow. Guaneri wants you to know he and his men are there. He wants you to know they are Free French. He wants you to know they will resist. As long as it takes, they will resist. Fascists will never rule Corsica."

"How is Ivo?"

"Staying alive. Railing against tyrants."

"And you are with him?"

"At times, I am."

"And other times, you are where?"

"It would be a betrayal to say."

Nico considers the floor for a long moment. "Sometimes I am just a son. Nothing else. Just a son who wonders about his father."

It is Karol's turn to stare at the floor. "You remember Claverie?"

"Of course."

"He is at the Sacré-Cour in Oran."

"I know it," says Nico.

"You've been there?"

Nico pauses before he answers. "Oran is a strategic city, an important listening post. We have people—agents, such as they are—in many places. It is a dangerous place."

"Unlike Tangier?"

"It is best to take extra care in Oran, particularly now that France has surrendered."

"Mussolini can't want the whole of Algeria, can he?" asks Karol. "I understand his desire for the coast. But all that sand in the south? Berbers and their camels? Is that what he's after?"

"I cannot say."

"You cannot say. Such is this world. To know and not to know. To say and not to say."

"Is there something else?" asks Nico, his voice slipping at the end.

Karol Lukas looks away. Almost undetectably, he shakes his head. "No, nothing."

Nico turns away. He pauses in the doorway. The boy in him waits for his father to invite him to sit at his table, to eat and drink, to talk into the night. To ask how his son has spent fifteen years. The boy in him wants to understand his disappointments, to hear the reasons his father did not come for him. Was he not worthy? Was he not loved? The boy in him longs to close his eyes, to put his head on his father's chest and feel the warmth in his father's heart.

The man—servant of Il Duce, deputy head of Mussolini's OVRA—must forget this place, must blot out the face of the woman who met him at this door, the clothing she wore, the sound of her voice. He must forget what he now knows of Guaneri, of resistance fighters, of Claverie's connection and the name of his father's village. The man must leave before he wilts under the steady gaze his father casts upon him, before his resolve crumbles, before he begs on his knees to remain with this man he did not recognize, save for the smell of him.

Nico offers his hand, and Karol Lukas steps forward to take it in both of his. The grip is strong, the hands rough. The boy's breath quivers. The boy's heart beats faster. The man, without speaking, without looking again into his father's eyes, disengages his hand, opens the door, descends quickly to the street, and disappears into the crowd.

Chapter Twenty-Six

Harry parks the car adjacent to the carpet store, the shop door now unlocked and somewhat ajar. The morning's heat has not yet permeated the store's interior, and as he passes, a faint rush of cool air emanates from the narrow opening. Across the street, the faded café sign hangs from the roof by a single link of rusted chain. Odors of stale garbage and fresh animal waste—made more pungent by the heat of the sun—assault his nose. In the light of day, the cascade of squalid shacks takes on a less menacing look, and Harry envisions the lot of them tumbling down at the slightest burst of air. Last night in the dark, he could not immediately find the entrance, but today he locates the widest archway and follows the steps down to the single door. As he walks, he notes movement at one of the outdoor tables and stops to observe a woman in a long dress and headscarf kneeling in the sand beneath the tables. Her back is to him, but he sees that she is picking up scraps of food and stuffing them into a bag. She does not look up from her task, but he understands that he is watched.

According to Farid, the uncle lives in a house on the far side of the café, away from the constant smells and noise, and Harry finds his way to the door that last night he assumed led to the kitchen, to the table where the now-dead host, the man of the intense stare, seated him. He hears a distant din of voices, but within the maze of small rooms, it is impossible to determine their location. On first try, the door does not budge—apparently locked—but he rattles it several times and the lock disengages. He steps into the alleyway outside, leaving the door open. There are six arched alcoves with windows above lining both sides of the alley. He walks past each one, listens intently, peruses the threshold and searches for signs of ownership. At the last alcove, he stops, turns, and glimpses a pair of sandals in the doorway to his left.

"What do you want?" The questioner stands inside, his upper body and face obscured in the darkness.

"I'm looking for the owner of the café."

"For what reason?"

"I have business with him."

"What kind of business?"

"It regards his nephew, Farid."

The questioner grunts and points around the corner. "Nephew? Pshaw. He has no nephew that I know. He lives in the private house, but you won't find him at home. He went looking for his brother."

"His brother?"

"They live there together. He went out last night and did not come home."

Harry follows a hunch. "Is the motorcycle here? That's what I'm calling about."

"I heard the engine late last night, after the café closed. I cannot help you." The sandals step away from the alcove and the door closes.

Harry pivots and walks to the corner. Set back from the street inside a white gate, there is a broad patio of gray tile, a balcony above with two shuttered windows on either side. At the end of the patio, three steps lead up to an arched door of cedarwood. Over the door hang two symbols that, to Harry's mind, are out of place in this French territory. The Italian flag and a likeness of Il Duce himself.

The house is larger and finer than those around it. Well maintained, freshly swept, no trace of sand or dirt on the stones. The steps, the doorway are clean.

"I sleep in his doorway," Farid had said. "I am not permitted in the house."

Why not allow Farid inside this fine house? Surely there is an unoccupied corner, a blanket to cover him. Who affords such a house from the proceeds of one dilapidated café? Someone who sells false identity papers? Someone who harbors secrets? Someone who signals one's allegiance with a flag and a photograph?

Harry inspects the perimeter for spots of grease or the faint scent of gasoline. A motorcycle's resting place. Where is it now? He and Mick saw no outward sign of it at the port. Of course, they had scant time to get away before the port gendarme arrived. Who would give no notice to a Canadian who looked like a wet dog and a Scotsman with Algerian blood on his knife?

The sound of an automobile approaches. Harry retraces his steps, disappears around the corner, and waits for the moving gearshift, the idling engine. A car door opens, the gate creaks, a car door slams, the gear re-engages, the engine starts again, then stops and shuts down. The car door opens again and slams shut again. There are footsteps on the patio stones. Harry slips through the gate. His left arm tightens around a scrawny neck. His gun presses hard into a kidney. He shoves the man toward the passenger door of the car.

"Open it."

The man is shaking now. "What do you want? I have nothing."

"Get in the car." Harry releases his hold and raises the gun to the back of the man's head.

"Slide over. Start the car and ease slowly through the gate." Harry climbs in, the gun now at the man's temple.

"Take my wallet. There is money."

"Keep your money. At the corner, turn left. Drive until I tell you to stop."

Harry remembers, on the outskirts of the city, a deserted stretch of road where houses and buildings thin out. They travel south and then west until Harry spots what he's looking for. "Pull over and stop. Get out." The man hesitates. Harry motions with the gun. "In this direction."

"I tell you, I have nothing you want."

"You're wrong about that." He directs the man to walk to the isolated shepherd's hut some seventy paces from the road. It is a crude hut. In front, there is one window with no glass and a low outer wall of rocks that have fallen away. The door tilts on its hinges. "Inside."

"No." The man stops and refuses to enter. "I don't know what you want from me."

He is a thin man of average height with black glistening hair and a weak mustache. The likeness to his brother is startling. If Harry had not seen the other man dead, he would swear he is the same man. The man's shoulders shake, but Harry recalls the strength with which his brother repeatedly pushed his head underwater and held it. It strikes Harry that Farid mentioned more than one man. "They are all bad men, all of them."

"Inside before this gun goes off. You'll wonder where your balls landed."

The man sneers one last time, then shrugs and pushes through the rotten door. The uneven earthen floor holds a bench under the lone window, a filthy blanket in the corner. The smell of sheep pervades the space.

"Empty your pockets." The man is dressed in European-style clothing, dark gray slacks and a white dress shirt, unbuttoned at the collar, rolled at the sleeves, no jacket. From the pants pockets, he withdraws a wallet, a key—presumably to the house or the café—and a sheaf of papers.

"Sit down and roll up the slacks." Harry suspects there will be an occupied knife sheath at one ankle. He is not wrong. Nor is he surprised to find an Italian four-shot derringer .22 pistol in the right ankle holster. He pockets the derringer and drops the knife out the window. He is now certain these men are connected to the Italian network of spies that Drummer warned him about. "Remove your shoes and socks. Throw them out the window. A good heave, if you please. Then off with the slacks and shirt."

While the man unbuttons his shirt, Harry flips open the wallet and finds it stuffed with Italian lire. There is no indication of the man's identity. "Now, unroll that sheaf of papers you're carrying."

The man is hesitant, but he—now dressed only in white underclothing—slowly unfurls the documents. Inside are three detailed maps—one, the most direct sea route from the Sicilian port of Mazaro del Vallo to Algiers; two, a detailed map of the port of Oran; and the last, the port buildings at Mers-el-Kébir. The fourth sheet shows one grainy photograph, a passport version of one Harry Douglas.

Harry examines the photograph and frowns. "Handsome chap. The nose off a bit."

The man is now seated, and Harry presses the muzzle of the gun up until it rests under the man's chin. The pistol jerks. "You're going to tell me your name and how you've come by these documents. Then you're going to tell me about your young colleague Farid and why you had him killed."

Chapter Twenty-Seven

The luxury motor yacht *Vivianna*—forty-nine meters in length and custom built in the classic style at the Benetti Darsena Lucca shipyard in 1927—slides from its berth at the smallest and most private marina in Palma de Majorca. With its massive salons, bar, and lavish staterooms, the ship is no ordinary pleasure yacht. Over the past dozen years, it has traveled the world entertaining a host of celebrities, business moguls, lords and ladies. At capacity, the ship can accommodate eleven guests and five crew members. The hull, constructed of oak and pine, boasts a cruising speed of eighteen knots.

At the helm, Captain Italo Cali motors past the black-and-white-striped lighthouse of Punta de Cala Figuera that sits atop the cliff marking entry into the Bay of Palma. Today, the captain transports only one passenger, bound some hundred nautical miles to the west and south to the port of Málaga on the east coast of Spain. There, a second passenger will come aboard and they will continue past the Strait of Gibraltar to the port of Tangier.

Beyond being informed of this destination, Captain Cali has not been consulted. It is a matter of contention between him and the owner.

Earlier in the day, Captain Cali—impeccably dressed in white uniform—stood on the teak sundeck, anxious to discuss the route and timeline he'd been given. "There is an abundance of ship traffic to the south."

"Why are you telling me this?"

"The traffic is not all friendly."

"It's a big lake. Avoid it."

"This avoidance is not easy. By the time we reach Málaga it will be dusk and difficult to navigate."

"You're paid to navigate. That's all you're paid to do. You transport my guests wherever I tell you, whenever I tell you."

Cali swallows his antagonism. Swallowing one's anger is not a natural trait for a Sicilian, particularly not for a Catanian. Again, Cali attempts to express his hesitation. "In the past month, there is an increase in underwater traffic by the Greeks, the Italians, and German U-boats. Especially in Tunisia and along the Libyan shore near Tripoli. At night, it is more dangerous. They attack the mercantile ships, particularly the British vessels. From Málaga to Tangier, we must be extremely careful. We will pass the British naval base at Gibraltar. Their destroyers patrol the area."

"British ships are not my concern. You're not suggesting we take a ferry between Málaga and Tangier?"

Cali shakes his head. "No. I simply wish to emphasize the danger."

"Send word when we dock in Málaga." Lorenzo settles back on the lounge chair and closes his eyes. "You are dismissed, Captain."

Italo Cali is a responsible man, a careful man, meticulous in his attention to the ship he commands, a man who knows every ripple in the coastal waters of Spain, a man who values a worthy crew member, a man who appreciates the power of the sea. Cali counts his new employer among his least favorite of human beings. He understands what sort of man he is and often ponders how a father the like of Rosso Terzo begot a son the likes of Lorenzo Terzo. Cali has captained the *Vivianna* since the day she was completed, and he holds the woman for whom the yacht is named in high regard, but the time has come to search the marinas for another ship to command. When he returns to Majorca, he will encourage his crew to do the same. Perhaps there is an owner in Porto Cristo on whose word he can rely.

Pascal Romano stands in the stern—one foot on a polished brass footrest, the other on the thick plank of deck—surveying the receding dockside as the *Vivianna* eases unnoticed from the pier. Málaga's lights twinkle on the water until the ship reaches the mouth of the harbor and moves into the open sea. Here, the light emanates from the flashing buoys and the faint lighthouse beam some miles up the coast. His hands clutch the rail. Darkness has fallen, and he is anxious about traveling under a moon hidden by clouds, the ship's running lights no match, in his mind, for the black night and the swells of the Mediterranean. When he arrived from the airfield an hour ago, the captain showed him to his cabin and informed him of their prompt departure. Romano would have preferred to make the journey to Tangier in the glare of day. He is aware of the intense U-boat activity in this part of the Mediterranean as well as the deadly squalls that erupt without notice.

He hears the footsteps on the deck behind him and smells the familiar scent of Silvestri pine and amber aftershave. Lorenzo—dressed in finely creased white slacks and a light navy sweater—is fresh from the shower, his dark hair oiled flat. In one hand, he holds a glass of the aged bourbon on which Lorenzo has grown increasingly dependent. There is no offer of refreshment, and Romano is reminded of the change in the way he is treated since that fiasco with the Gran Premio. A servant meets with more courtesy. That said, Romano prefers to remain within Lorenzo's tight circle. Contacts like his do not come along every day. Such is life in Milano.

Lorenzo is insultingly drunk.

"About time you arrived. I told you to meet me in Palma."

"By the time I got your message, Málaga was the closest I could manage. Glad to see you too. Why the rush?"

"Limited window." Lorenzo takes another gulp from his drink and smiles.

"Where are we going on this black night? I thought we were sailing to Porto Cristo. You told me this was playtime in Porto Cristo."

The smile shrivels. "That was a lie."

"Which part?"

"We're meeting someone."

"Anyone I know?"

"Nico."

"Why the rush to see Nico?"

"He's only in Tangier another day or two. And Tangier is the perfect place."

"For what?"

"For what you're going to do."

"What do you want from me now?"

"You brought the revolver?"

"What the fuck do you want with the revolver?"

"He can't see it coming," growls Lorenzo.

Chapter Twenty-Eight

An unnatural quiet hangs over the cathedral. Transmissions received from Gibraltar indicate that the French have refused to comply with British conditions regarding disposition of their fleet. Yesterday, the British Admiralty sent the following message to Vice Admiral Somerville: "You are charged with one of the most disagreeable and difficult tasks that a British admiral has ever been faced with, but we have complete confidence in you and rely on you to carry it out relentlessly."

Somerville commands the bridge of the HMS *Hood*, flanked by the HMS *Valiant* and HMS *Resolution*, and escorted by the carrier HMS *Ark Royal* and a dozen cruisers and destroyers. Somerville receives a second message from the British Admiralty. "Before dark, the French ships must comply with our terms, sink themselves, or be sunk by you."

With some urgency, Somerville sends a messenger to Admiral Marcel Gensoul, the French commander at Mers-el-Kébir, offering three options:

- Bring out your ships and join the Royal Navy.

- With a reduced crew, sail your fleet to a British port, from which the crew will be repatriated.

- Sail your fleet to French, West Indian, or American ports and decommission there.

Gensoul vacillates. A fourth option is added.

- Scuttle your ships where they lie.

In the afternoon, a little after one o'clock, the boom gate to the Mers-el-Kébir harbor opens. To prevent the French ships from sailing, Swordfish planes from the carrier *Ark Royal* mine the harbor entrance. Still, Gensoul takes no action, and the French Admiralty fails to respond. Somerville waits.

At half past four o'clock, Harry and Mick leave the cathedral's transmission room, and drive resolutely and silently along the coastal road toward Cap Falcon. They park on the bluff that overlooks the port. Up a dirt trail, they climb a distance to the old Fort Mers-el-Kébir that stands solid at the tip of the promontory. It is a steep ascent and provides for clear observation of the port and surrounding areas. The sun sits behind them as they fix their field glasses on the French ships that lie at anchor in the harbor. Surely, the French Admiralty will send a peaceful solution before Somerville must act. History tells them that, given time, initial French refusals often come around to acquiescence or agreement.

They want to believe the French Admiralty will not risk the destruction of their ships. Nor place their sailors in grave danger.

They scan the horizon. From the northwest, they mark the progress of the British flotilla, the battleship *Hood* pushing forward along the coast. In disbelief, they watch as British ships close to within a few miles of the harbor. Harry and Mick hear the French buglers sound Action Stations. Decks come alive. Ships chatter. Shouts, curses arise from the distance. Crew members stand at their guns, ready. Incredibly, it appears the French intend to make a determined resistance.

It is nearly six o'clock. In a matter of minutes, the sun will set. The French Admiralty has not complied. The *Hood*'s two forward gun turrets—as well as those of the *Valiant* and *Resolution*—rotate into position. Soon thereafter comes the order to open fire. The first fireworks—a sound like distant thunder—from the *Hood*'s guns smash the side of the *Bretagne*. A mammoth column of water splits the sky. The earth shakes. In slow motion, it seems, a section of bulwark pilings crumbles into the sea. Slabs of concrete and huge chunks of railing shoot up and then fall to earth, showering the French ships. Alarm whistles shatter the air. Port workers, like screaming flocks of birds, scurry for safety.

The coast-defense batteries answer force with force. Someone gives the order to fire. From the shore, artillery guns—French 75 mms—open up. The second salvo rattles the sky and scores a direct hit on the *Bretagne*. A deafening barrage of shells whistles toward the other French ships. Then comes the high pitch of nervous voices. Sailors drop onto the docks or jump into the now-flaming sea.

The *Dunkerque*, badly mauled, prepares to unmoor and cast off, but three heavy shells bombard the big battle cruiser, followed in quick succession by ear-splitting explosions and orange fires on deck. Sailors climb into the water, down the cargo nets that line the sides of the ship. Opaque clouds of black obscure the bridge.

The brutalized *Provence*, unable to move more than five hundred yards from its berth, takes multiple volleys and bursts into flames fore and aft. Again, the *Bretagne* takes fire. Its stern disappears. At 6:09 p.m., the old ship capsizes, sea churning around it, hundreds of officers and sailors stranded in her interior.

A hundred yards off the breakwater, near the harbor entrance, a shell strikes the destroyer *Mogador*, detonating its depth charges. An unrecognizable slab of hot metal is swallowed by the sea. Not one sailor has time to abandon ship.

Through the haze, Harry and Mick can see nothing, but they hear a whispering drone, a hum that grows louder and stronger. Blackburn Skua fighters, escorting a squadron of Swordfish bombers from the *Ark Royal*, roar in low, dropping air torpedoes into the sea. Whistled shrieks pierce the heavens. At least one torpedo finds the *Dunkerque*, another strikes the patrol boat *Terre-Neuve* moored alongside. The *Dunkerque* floods quickly. To prevent it sinking, the crew, before abandoning ship, rushes to run the ship aground.

Another screaming pass from the Blackburn Skuas sends massive columns of black smoke rising from the harbor. Shore defenses no longer return fire. The French ships are still. Somerville and his Force H cease the offensive. Each of the three British battleships has fired twelve salvos, 144 rounds.

Harry checks his watch. The naval and air bombardments occupied a mere thirteen minutes to realize mass destruction. The celebrated French fleet is now in silent submission.

A smoky haze and the pink glow of the setting sun lend a dreamlike quality to the astonishing scene. The battleship *Bretagne*, majestic moments before, has simply disappeared. The other ships are engulfed in flames, half submerged in the harbor, or collapsed into themselves. Jagged pieces of metal point to the sky. Everywhere the air is pungent with oil, gasoline, and the sweet smell of burning flesh. *Dunkerque* and *Provence* are beached and abandoned, flaps of water banging against their hulls. The once-steadfast lighthouse stands ruined, truncated, beyond repair, without function.

Bodies of the dead and their severed limbs fill the harbor. Corpses, face down—some aflame—float languidly on the water. Mick points to a sailor pulling himself onto the shore. His body moves as if he were whole, but he has but one arm—the other wrenched from his shoulder. The skin on his face has melted.

The sight sends a shiver through them.

"Bloody hell."

Three deadly syllables. Bloody hell.

Chapter Twenty-Nine

ownsend instructs them to report within twenty-four hours to Gibraltar. Representatives from the British Admiralty will arrive for a debriefing. A transport plane waits in Algiers.

"I have business in Tangier," says Harry.

"It will have to wait," says Townsend. "You're ordered to Gib."

"Mick will do the briefing," says Harry.

It doesn't matter who does the briefing, he reasons. They'll hear what they want to hear, make their way to the same conclusions, congratulate themselves.

There is static on the line, but Harry hears Townsend's voice raise a level. Harry drops the receiver into its cradle and walks to Claverie's quarters. From another phone, Harry places a quiet call to the El Morocco in Tangier. The line is crowded, and it takes a minute before the operator establishes the connection. He asks for the bartender, describes the person he is looking for, and waits.

"Hello, who is calling?"

"Hello Margaret. I knew you'd be around."

"And why is that, Harry?"

"I need a favor."

"I trust this is not going to be a habit. What is it this time?"

"A piece of information."

"Just a piece of information, he says."

"Is Nico Lukas in Tangier?"

"Last I heard, he was on his way to Oran. In light of recent events, I'm not sure that's necessary."

"In light of recent events, is he still in Tangier?"

"I'd say it's likely."

"One more question before you hang up on me. Is he sporting a damaged wrist, his arm in a sling maybe?"

"I hadn't noticed. It hasn't affected his activities."

"Glad you're having a party. I'll take that as a no." Harry pauses. "I thought you had business in Madrid."

"Finished." A prolonged silence on the line makes Harry think the connection has been lost. Then she adds, "If you're looking for a man with an arm in a sling, try Sami Mokrani." An instant later, the line goes dead.

Harry is not surprised.

He thinks back on his interactions with Mokrani. In Tangier, the man had every opportunity to keep a close eye on him. Mokrani didn't have to go looking for him. It was Harry who showed up at The Golden Apple. At Harry's request, Mokrani led him to the alley where Peter Farrell's body was found. Harry asked a few pointed questions about the manner of killing. Mokrani answered. A single bullet to the heart, he said. He would know. At the supposed site of Farrell's killing, Mokrani nudged Harry in the direction of the old chicken seller. Bad advice.

The chicken seller shared next to nothing save vague notions of time. Totally unaware, the old man had said, of any theft that had occurred. Now, as Harry reconstructs it, he sees the story is all wrong. At the time, he was in a rush to assure himself the murdered agent was not Mick McLeod. He failed to see the story for what it was. A pack of improbable lies.

At the musician's club, Mokrani disappeared without a word of explanation. No matter. At the time, Harry thought Mokrani nothing more than a runner, a messenger. He is, of course, more than that. Townsend said he had not worked with Mokrani before. So, Townsend didn't know. It made no real sense why Mokrani would want to kill Harry. Until. Until Harry's conversation—interrogation, to be accurate—in that rugged little shepherd's hut outside Oran.

Mokrani works both sides.

Not exactly a double agent. Too low-life for that. Just a chap who takes orders.

Harry recalls how hard Mokrani stared at him when he arrived at The Golden Apple. As if he didn't believe his eyes. Of course, Mokrani thought it was Harry he had killed in that alley. Mokrani knew Farrell's movements, enumerated them as if he had been following Farrell that day. The medina, the nightclub, the street in the French Quartier. Mokrani didn't know Harry by name—or Farrell either, for that matter—but he possessed that grainy photograph dug out of Broadway's photo collection and passed through hands assigned to dispose of its subject. When Harry walked into the nightclub, Mokrani realized he had killed the wrong man, and he had to set it right. Had to set it right before his handler learned the truth.

Does Mokrani take his orders from Nico Lukas? Mokrani and his two colleagues in Oran must be small cogs—assassins—in the OVRA network that thrives along the north coast of Africa, most especially in Tangier, Tunis, Algiers and Tripoli. Mussolini is eager to grab the region for his new empire.

Yes, that explains a few things. Four times, Lukas tried to have him killed. If Mokrani had not mistakenly killed Farrell and his pal mistakenly killed Farid, if Claverie had not disclosed his connection to Lukas, Harry would never have made the connections, never known where to place blame. At this moment, one Mokrani pal is dead, the other bound to a chair in a putrid-smelling shepherd's hut.

There are scores to settle in Tangier.

Chapter Thirty

I t is long after noon when the *Vivianna* eases into her assigned slot in the old port. Quite rightly, Captain Cali has waited off-shore until given official approval for docking. In his experience, Tangier officials give priority to commercial craft, those paying hefty fees for the privilege of loading or unloading their goods. Luxury liners and pleasure yachts must wait interminably for the more profitable harbor traffic to clear. Thus, some time ago his two passengers departed on the small-motorized tender. When he saw them off, they neglected to tell him when they would return or why they were suddenly in a rush, after so many hours at sea, to reach the city.

Cali closes down the engine. The crew ties up and quickly lowers the gangplank; they have no wish to waste time. After a wave of approval from their captain, they depart—passports in hand—for a few precious hours of shore leave in the nearest Spanish-speaking taberna. The younger Majorcans of Cali's crew have not experienced Tangier. It is new. He tried to tell them something of the ancient city, of the walled fortresses and the ancient trade routes, of the Phoenicians and the Carthaginians and the Romans. He wants them to love, as he does, the shabby old city, to wander aimlessly in the cool tunnels of the magnificent medina, to sit still on a curb in the shade of a palm listening to warblers' singsongs, to marvel at the view from the terraced cliffs high above the sea. But they are more interested in drink and loose girls than in history and beautiful seascapes. They will spend this time in battered chairs drinking bad whiskey, smoking the local kif, and testing their adolescent charms. As he did at their age. In a few hours, they will return, never having perched on the rocks gazing out at the dazzling sea.

After he completes the docking routine and does what he can to prepare for the next departure—whenever that may be—Cali leaves the yacht, walks along the seaside boulevard and climbs the crumbling steps to the Café Hafa located along the cliff top overlooking the Bay of Tangier and the Strait of Gibraltar. It is a simple place—best known for the view and the unique shade of blue that graces its walls. Its whitewashed balconies tumble down a steep hillside to the Mediterranean. He sits and sips the café's special brew of mint tea and listens to the local crowd socialize at the tables nearby. After a while, he orders bread and soup, lingering over every spoonful as he stares across the strait at the Sierra Morena peaks on the Spanish side. Every now and again, he sighs at the pleasure of it.

Every time he returns to this tip of Africa, he feels its freedom. In this land of Hercules, he is a small part of history, one piece of earth. For a time, he can forget Lorenzo Terzo and his childish demands. He can forget the ships and submarines that threaten the sea he loves. He can forget the fascists who have come to pillage Majorca's gifts. For a few hours, he can be a careless man.

The peaceful Italo Cali wraps his hand around a second glass of tea—the warmth of it invading the inelegant bones of his fingers. He closes his eyes, inhales the fresh scent of crushed mint, and wishes he could remain here until the sun drops through a purple western sky into the Atlantic, until twilight passes into night, and the night becomes dark and deep. But, alas, he must return to his ship before his employer decides it is time to set sail. Perhaps Lorenzo is on the bridge already, anxious to depart, fuming at his captain's discourtesy. Nay, his captain's insubordination.

What Cali cannot know is that when he again assumes his role and duties as captain of the *Vivianna*, he will depart the port of Tangier with a list of passengers unlike those who disembarked hours ago, a list that will include two lifeless bodies and a third who is very much alive and utterly without conscience.

Chapter Thirty-One

They tie up the small tender in one of the harbor slips inside the Royal Yacht Club. Across the small stretch of water, the semicircular beach of rocks and fine golden sand are dotted with bathers. In the fifteen years since its inception, Lorenzo has visited the club many times. He is more than familiar with its layout, and he smoothly guides Romano through the intimate Admirals Lounge to the Grande Terrace. It is Tangier's most lucrative place of business, a club for diplomats and politicians and men of industry. International yachtsmen who sip pink gin and enjoy leisurely lunches overlooking the Strait of Gibraltar as they buy and sell expensive information.

Lorenzo proposes that they order lunch and drinks. When the sun burns hot, they will cross the street and seek the shade of the covered passageways that lead into the Kasbah. From there they will take the backstreets—avoiding beggars and peddlers selling their parakeets and roasted chestnuts—to the brothels of the Zoco Chico where they will pass the afternoon.

He assumes Nico is registered—like many others on this terrace—at the Hotel Continental. Its views of bobbing boats in the harbor, ornate parlors, Moroccan arches and mosaic tile present an exotic appeal. As the sun sets, he and Romano will settle in the Continental's lounge—eyes on the door—to await Nico's arrival. Romano will disappear into the street. Lorenzo and Nico will emerge, ostensibly looking for a small café for dinner. The absence of light in the medina's blind alleys will serve as perfect cover. Lorenzo will retire to the clean linens of his yacht to anticipate Romano's report.

Sami Mokrani orders another dish of pastille.

"You don't eat for free," the proprietor yells at him from the kitchen.

He made a terrible mistake, linking up his young colleagues with the likes of Nico Lukas. Though more than capable of cruelty and violence, they are mere street gangsters, inexperienced in games of war. Now one of them is dead, the other missing. He should have known not to involve them, no matter the payments they were promised. It is one thing for him to risk his life, but their lives were not his to give. He thought he was clever, predicting France's surrender, working in secret with the fascist conquerors.

In a few minutes, he must meet with Deputy Lukas himself. Mokrani is not anxious to recount his failures. They had one assignment. Capture and kill the British agent. Mokrani could sidestep, push the blame onto the others. He has never felt remorse about lying. Especially to protect himself. If he tells the truth, the OVRA deputy will surely have him jailed or worse. *First, I stalk and kill the wrong man. (In truth, the picture was unclear, but I dare not offer such excuse.) Then, Allah sends a gift. The very man himself passes straight through the door of The Golden Apple and inquires for me. Now I am sure he is the one. When opportunity arises, when I know he is unfamiliar with the Kasbah's streets, when I am certain he cannot escape, I draw my gun and prepare to fulfill my order. Instead, I suffer a broken wrist and lose my gun in the filthy rubble. All is well once more when, with information from my contacts in Oran, we track him in the night to the highway that runs from Oran to Mers-el-Kébir. This time, we are certain he cannot escape, and we can shoot him dead. Now Nassim is dead on the dock at Mers-el-Kébir, his throat slashed. His brother missing—presumed to have met a similar fate.*

These mistakes are not forgivable. He knows Lukas too well. The ruthless OVRA care nothing for excuses. Cold justice waits for him. Mokrani was given an assignment. A simple assassination. It still may be possible to convince Lukas that his trust is not misplaced. That the deed can be done. If only he knew where Harry Douglas might be.

Ahead, Nico smells alien cooking spices and resolves, before his rendezvous with Mokrani, to stop and fill his stomach with whatever is offered. There is no guarantee he will have the opportunity again. He finds an empty table. The waiter takes his order. It is late, but the waiter assures him the cook will prepare something for him.

The air is dry and clear, the night sky filled with stars. He looks into that shimmering distance, remembering his father's face, his voice, replaying what happened an hour ago. He cannot shake the encounter and struggles with the words his father spoke. Indeed, the words he did not speak. It is impossible to erase the words he hoped Karol Lukas would utter. The words that did not come.

Nico resists the inescapable. Uncrushed by guilt, his father came simply to deliver a message. The two men could well have been two strangers exchanging polite conversation, each one careful to disclose nothing of value, nothing of affection or devotion.

Guaneri will resist, he said. His father told him these things deliberately. Guaneri. Nico knows it is not Ivo Guaneri who leads the Corsican resistance. It is Karol Lukas who witnessed the carnage in Warsaw and the surrender in Prague. It is Karol Lukas who directs the guerillas—the Maquis—in the Corsican hills. Ivo and his men are with him. Free Frenchmen. Free Corsicans. Tough sons of bitches. The old lion has found a new war. He is a Gaullist now. Leader of the Corsican resistance. When Il Duce is ready to take Corsica, Karol Lukas will be ready for Il Duce.

This is what Lena wanted him to know.

The immediate question Nico must answer is whether to dispatch agents to Cargése. It is possible Cargése is as his father described, a quiet fishing village with two groups of worshippers who stare at each other on Sunday mornings across a deep chasm. Two priests who, in the evening twilight, stroll across the abyss to share a glass of wine and the village gossip.

Or, the old man unknowingly let slip the truth. That Cargése is the center. And Oran's Sacre Coeur an active branch of the resistance. Claverie makes sense. Nico remembers Claverie's allegiances. A month ago, Mokrani informed Nico that his colleagues suspected the Sacré Coeur acts as a major transmission center. Until today, he did not know Pierre Claverie serves there as priest. His father told the truth about Claverie.

Nico is not surprised. The relationship with the Church in Rome is a curious alliance. Mussolini, of course, realizes the importance of the Church's support. His rallies, by design, begin with a morning Mass. The pope and the Church benefit from such complicity. Mussolini earns credibility with the people. In turn, the pope's position is protected, and the fascists serve as a safeguard against the Church-destroying communists.

Nico is more than aware, too, that what happens outside the confines of Rome is another story. Certain Catholics in Poland, Czechoslovakia, the Balkans, and now the French will resist this clerical-fascist coalition. Some will be fearful and submit. Still others will greatly benefit from the new Nazi rule, like Jozef Tiso, the priest who was appointed leader of Slovakia.

In any case, it is not Nico's intent to judge the Church or its clerics. He collects secrets. Military, political, domestic, foreign. The intelligence he receives may be genuine or false. He must consider and judge it without regard to its affiliation. Of course, clerics are sometimes involved in political maneuvering. Through political and financial alliances, the Church has maintained its power for centuries, its clerics not without guile or guilt.

It strikes Nico that his father, his dearest childhood friend Ivo Guaneri, and the priest they served as children exist on one side of this war. He on the other. So be it.

His senses, honed and heightened, scan the perimeter of the square. Instinctively, he takes in the sound of dishes clattering, voices rising—an argument of sorts inside the café—then farther away, a distant foghorn. Though the night shadows have dulled the clarity of images, he sees a man pushing a cart along the street, something not quite right about his effort. From his seat against the wall, Nico lifts the Beretta from its holster, holds it under the well-worn table, checks the chamber. All the while he keeps his eyes on the cart and the silhouette. In this part of the city, there is a risk of being robbed, but that is not what concerns him.

The man and the cart pass. Nico sees there are small cages piled haphazardly on the cart. Birds—parakeets by the sound of them—packed within. A constant flutter of wings. Hence, the suspicious awkwardness as the man moves to steady the teetering cages.

Nico stands and slips the gun into the waistband of his trousers.

He walks the last kilometer into the heart of Tangier, naming the players in his mind, setting the pieces in place. He realizes, in his reverie, he has paid no attention to the route, given no notice to those around him, and he chides himself for such carelessness. Tangier is never the city to let down one's guard. He lays a hand on the weapon. The Beretta is loaded. Ready if the need is here.

Margaret Gautier awakens from a nap at the Hotel El Minzah in a suite overlooking the stunning Bay of Tangier. Leisurely, she bathes, dresses, locks and stows her small valise, deposits the pen-sized knife in the seam of her flowing caftan and enters the brightly lit corridor. The door closes. She locks it behind her and proceeds in the direction of the stairwell. Though the reception salon is four floors below, for reasons of safety and secrecy, she prefers the stairs to the caged elevator. As she turns the corner she hears the scuff of shoes on marble and perceives a single shadow—an unmistakable profile—on the wall. When she draws nearer, she distinguishes an officer in Nazi uniform descending the stairs. She stops and presses back against the wall, her breath quickening. She knows him, and she takes a moment to calm herself. She has no wish to encounter him again. He is a high-ranking medical man. In Berlin, she had masqueraded as an actress out of Vienna, and spent a good deal of sexual energy and creativity extracting information about rumors of rampant drug use, particularly methamphetamines, among German officers. She remembers her thoughts as she left the so-called doctor. A thin veneer of sophistication covers a brutal core. There is something evil about the man.

When she delivered the drug information to London, the prime minister was intrigued. Some of her finest work, he said. *If only he knew the half of it.* It was he who recommended Tangier and this hotel as the perfect place to gather intelligence. In search of sun and isolation from London's affairs of state, Churchill himself had wintered here in 1935. He predicted—correctly, it seems—the German high command would favor it. Built in 1930 at the behest of a British aristocrat with extensive interests in Morocco, the hotel is constructed in a Moorish style while adding the comforts of an English gentleman's club. Of all the hotels in Tangier, El Minzah is without doubt the most extravagant, reigning supreme in Andalusian good taste. Guests can survey the Bay of Tangier, the Gibraltar strait, the Rif Mountains, and the hotel's abundant gardens of roses, gerania, lilies, and hibiscus. The carefully tended lawns are shaded by palm, the air sweet with orange blossoms and eucalyptus. Situated where Europe and Africa almost touch, the hotel hosts international diplomats and political supermen, a welcome respite from Hitler's Europe.

Strolling through the lobby, Margaret pulls her shawl over her head and acts the part of one of Hollywood's stars. Before the pitiless doctor spies her, she quickly disappears into the dark street and trusts Nico does not arrive before she returns.

The bartender pours a measure of tonic, adds a jigger of gin and a fresh slice of lime and carries it to the end of the bar where

Harry stands, one foot on the rail. *At last, a drop of alcohol one can boast about.* Harry raises the glass. "To absent friends."

In the mirror, he notes the door behind him open and close. Night has arrived. Three men walk in. They check their hats, pocket the token the coat clerk provides. Harry recognizes the man in the middle. Tall and trim. French. Almost a year ago in Milan, they exchanged information about the Italian military withdrawal from Majorca. Word was, Spain's Generalissimo got what he needed from the Italians and no longer wanted them around. Early in the civil war, Mussolini's proconsul, Arconovaldo Bonaccursi, and his execution squads rid the island of the Nationalists' enemies—three thousand communists had staked a claim to the island and used it as a gathering spot—and cleaned out its prisons by shooting all the occupants.

Harry is inclined to believe the more practical explanation for the military's exit from the island: Mussolini needs his troops for the eastern front. Given the Italian occupation, Albania now requires more round-the-clock supervision and so-called guidance, and Hitler's sudden invasion of Czechoslovakia has motivated Il Duce to demonstrate an active presence in Eastern Europe.

The familiar Frenchman is in the company of two men Harry does not know. New friends, perhaps. As of 22 June. The three are escorted away from the sea of noise to a table in the back. In the mirror, Harry manages to make eye contact with the Frenchman who stares back at him with what Harry can only interpret as a question in his eyes. No shame of defeat. Rather, how could you goddamned bloody Brits do such a thing?

I'm asking myself the same question, Frenchie.

The bartender appears again. Another drink? Harry says, "I hear Mokrani and his group are here tonight."

Puzzled, the bartender asks, "Where'd you hear that?"

"The entertainment news. Where else? I'm asking because I saw he's laid up for a while. A bad arm."

The barman wipes the counter around Harry's glass and does not look at Harry. He mumbles, "Haven't seen Mokrani in a day or so. If I do, I'll tell him you're looking for him."

"No bother. Just asking."

The man standing next to Harry stirs his drink with a finger and takes a sip, then smokes his cigarette down to the stub—puffing furiously—and crushes it on the floor. Nothing left but a trace of tobacco. His hands are disproportionately large and Harry notes the tips of the man's index finger and thumb are stained an ocher shade of yellow. He remembers a chap in Milan who studied the differences in the manner men and women hold their cigarettes. They had a lengthy discussion about it.

The man inclines his head at Harry and seems to smile an apology. He wears a gray double-breasted soft-shouldered jacket and a pair of two-toned wingtips that only style-conscious Italians dare to show off in a place as blistering as Tangier. He brings out a money clip, lays a bill on the bar, and returns the clip—an ornamental Italian coin—to his pocket. Beneath his jacket, on his waist, is a small pistol in a black leather holster. Before he goes, he looks Harry up and down. Harry stares calmly back, then turns toward the mirror and savors his gin and tonic. The door closes behind the man, and Harry realizes the man's drink is unfinished, half-full in fact.

"What's that chap drinking?" Harry asks.

"Gin, campari, vermouth. A Negroni, they call it. He's not happy. No oranges. Who would guess a Moroccan bar runs out of oranges?"

"Mmm. How long was he here?"

"Walked in five minutes before you did."

"Familiar?"

"First-timer."

There is an undercurrent of tension among those at the bar. Harry thinks about sitting. The man's quick departure tells Harry that within the hour someone of Italian persuasion will come looking for him. Better to locate an inconspicuous table with a clear view front and back. Standing at the bar with his back exposed will serve no purpose.

So it is, on the evening of 5 July, they are assembled in disparate places in old Tangier. Sami Mokrani in The Golden Apple's dining room preparing a fairy tale that could save his life. Nico Lukas in an outdoor café on the Rue Portugal deciding between love for and betrayal of a man he once called Papa. Lorenzo Terzo and Pascal Romano in the Kasbah's poshest watering hole awaiting their prey. Margaret Gautier, aka Lena Prus, on the narrow steps of the medina eluding a brutal lover. Harry Douglas in a neatly positioned alcove of the El Morocco Club seeking retribution—justice—for a young man condemned by circumstance. A young man he hardly knew.

Chapter Thirty-Two

Out of patience in the bar, they step outside onto the balcony. Lorenzo stares at the cigarette he holds. Romano leans over the railing and hollers at a group of beggar children below. In the last two hours, Lorenzo and Romano have consumed a bottle of the Hotel Continental's most expensive whiskey.

"Shut up, you idiot."

"It's long past dinner. Why are we waiting? He's not going to show."

"Forget your stomach. We have one shot at this," says Lorenzo.

"*We,* he says. What he means is *you*, Pascal." The liquor has loosened Romano's tongue. Lorenzo stands four inches taller than Romano. He reaches down and taps Romano's chest with the cigarette. Romano slaps it away. "What the hell. Stay away from me."

"Pull yourself together. No arguments. It has to be tonight. He's registered at this hotel. He'll walk in that door sooner or later."

"*Later* is my guess." Romano starts toward the balcony steps, falters, begins again. He can barely stand. "Your little café plan is not going to work."

"We'll persuade him to go out for a drink."

"Strong-arm him, you mean?"

"There are other ways to persuade."

"That posh club of yours? That should be quite the shoot-out. A little mob of tanned yachtsman shaking their heads, whispering 'Tut, tut.'"

"The El Morocco."

"Witnesses?"

"He'll never make it there, will he?"

"Then what? How are we going to convince anyone he was murdered by a stranger in the street?"

"We'll be long gone. Back on the *Vivianna*. Underway before anyone finds the body."

"Out to sea in the dead of night? Cali won't like that." Nor I, worries Romano.

"He'll do what he's told."

"Someone murders OVRA's deputy chief, and no one investigates?"

"The man has enemies. He's a spy. This is Tangier, the city of spies. Where else would someone shoot him? Just aim the goddamned gun and pull the trigger."

"Easy for you to say, Lorenzo."

"And for you to do, Pascal. Come. Sober up. We'll walk in the street."

Outside the archway on the Place du Tabor, Mokrani smokes and waits. Lukas is late. Why he changed their meeting place, Mokrani does not know. He must decide how much to disclose to Lukas. He cannot afford to make an enemy of a powerful man in Mussolini's government. Algeria will soon be under its control.

Algerians no longer French, but property of Italy's fascists or the Reich's Nazis. Though the chance to seize the French ships in Mers-el-Kébir is lost, Mokrani knows of other ships in Oran's harbor. A trading chip, perhaps.

While he observes the crowd of visitors who enter and exit the doors of the El Morocco, he repeats the phrases in his head. *Give me a few days. I will repair the situation. I can learn where Douglas is. I have reasons for wanting him dead.*

A man he does not recognize exits the door, looks left and right, and heads toward the archway where Mokrani waits. The man wears an expensive European suit. *A newcomer. Italian or Spanish. Certainly not Scandinavian. Not Austrian or German. Could be French, but Frenchmen do not dress so smartly. There are a few Americans around, but they have their own odd mannerisms.*

Before Mokrani can speculate further, the man approaches and asks the direction of the Hotel Continental. He inquires in French, but an Italian accent underlies the question. Wealthy Italians prefer the Continental to avoid the German high command who reside at the El Minzah. Mokrani holds the cigarette in his good hand. He uses the injured one—the bandage evident—to point out the appropriate direction. The man thanks him and begins to move down the street, but stops abruptly and turns.

"By odd chance, is your name Mokrani?"

"Who's asking?"

"A man at the bar." He points to the door of the El Morocco. "He asked the bartender if your group was playing tonight. Said he'd heard you were—how did he put it—laid up with a bad arm."

"Do you know this man?"

"No."

"What did the bartender say?"

"That he had not seen you in days. That, if he did, he would tell you this man was looking for you."

"And what did the man say to that?"

"He told him to forget it."

"Ah, a fickle music fan. They are everywhere."

Mokrani tries to control the emotion in his voice. There are few people who know of the condition of his arm, fewer who know how it came to be. Can Douglas be on the other side of that door? Standing at the bar, the man said. Mokrani has seen no one who looks like Douglas go in or out. Of course, in the crush of patrons, he could have missed someone. *If the man is indeed Douglas, why is he asking for me? Douglas cannot know the extent of my involvement with OVRA. He cannot possibly know of my tightly woven deception. The last time I conversed with Douglas, it was strictly business—navigation, passing one spy off to another. No hint of treachery. In that dim alleyway, Douglas cannot have known me. I made sure of it. A change of clothing, a hidden face. No. He could not have known me.*

The stranger moves away and Mokrani resumes his place. If the inquirer is Douglas, Mokrani has the advantage, the element of surprise. When Lukas arrives, he can tell him he knows where Douglas is, that he is waiting for Douglas to come through that door. This time, he will not fail. *Though handling a gun with one arm requires a certain skill. If I miss with one shot, I will not be blessed with another. The dagger will be more useful.*

She lowers her head and reaches out to touch the wall, feeling her way down the worn steps, mindful she does not catch her sandal on a loose stone. Her body is beginning to relax, sure now she will not encounter the dreaded man of medicine. She hears the light tinkling of bells behind her and moves aside to see a child run past. *Where is a solitary child with bells on her slippers going at this hour?* The child flies down the steps and stops at the bottom, seemingly bewildered. A finger to her lips—deciding which way to go—she rushes off to the right. Margaret's steps become more rapid as she nears the bottom. When she reaches the last step, she searches the street, but the twisting passageway and the dark night have swallowed the child. She wonders then if the girl was real or illusion, a creation of her imagination, a reminder of the innocence that left her long ago. She has become expert in the nature of illusion—false impressions, misdirection, sleights of hand. One day she is Margaret Gautier, the gregarious and stylish socialite who resides in Berlin's most fashionable neighborhood. Another day she is Spanish royalty, the spirited Duquesa Sophia Falco of Madrid. On rare occasions, she is Lena Nivek, the sexually adventurous and manipulative Viennese actress. Never again, she vowed, would she be Lena Dunin, the eleven-year-old girl who, helpless and distraught, listened as her perfect white stallions were slaughtered in the night.

Nor will she ever again be called Lena Prus. For reasons known to few, she has not used that name in more than a year. Nico knows her as the widow of slain Polish diplomat Feliks Prus. By chance, she and Nico met in Majorca four years ago. Seeking refuge from cold Warsaw winters, she alternated holidays among Capri, Corsica and Majorca. One evening, she and Nico—cocktails in hand—found themselves standing together on the high balcony of the opulent Terzo home, enjoying the views, awaiting the ten o'clock dinner bell. They introduced themselves. Through dinner, they talked of hunting partridge in Spain, snorkeling Red Sea reefs, and skiing Austria's ice-blue glaciers.

Rosso Terzo, famous for gathering up winter visitors, filled them with Spanish wine and told stories of war, including how he built his now expansive estate. When Mussolini abruptly recalled his troops and abandoned acres of unused and untitled land on the Spanish isle, Rosso Terzo, the consummate opportunist, claimed an exquisite slice of it. Lena became a regular guest at Rosso's soirees, sailed the Balearic Islands aboard his yachts, and eventually joined the Terzos in Milan for special holidays. She was at once attracted to Nico Lukas. Polished conversationalist, handsome escort, influential public servant. Try as she did to seduce him, it was clear enough that he was enamored with cousin Gabriella. There were rumors of their betrothal, rumors she chose not to believe.

Lena was not dismayed to discover that she and Nico occupied opposite positions in this European war. Hers, the result of Hitler's atrocities and a firm belief in the values of those who opposed him. His, the product of an affluent upbringing and the security that comes from knowing powerful men. In Milanese high society, there is much to gain as Il Duce's loyal soldier.

Months ago, when she was dispatched to Corsica to scout probable sites for clandestine surveillance of Italian naval maneuvers, she was put in contact with Ivo Guaneri. In their search for suitable ground, she crossed paths with a handsome fisherman from a secluded village on Corsica's west coast. Instantly—without a hint as to the fisherman's name—she noted a striking resemblance to Nico. Color, build, cadence of speech, even the way he tilted his head as he listened. In time, she learned the name and real business of Karol Lukas. She judged him a hard man, given to passion and violence and a solitary life. She learned to value his many talents, and discovered one day, to her surprise, that she held genuine affection for him.

From Karol's village, they established two key surveillance networks for the Crown. One based in a hand-tooled local church, the other in a cavernous cathedral in Oran.

She recalls an early conversation between them, brief and pointed.

"Killing isn't part of what I do," she had told him.

"Of course it is. Why else would you be here?"

It is nearing midnight, the streets still bustling, though slower than at midday. Nico wonders if Mokrani has waited. He doesn't really want to see the man. Or anyone else, truth be told. He'd rather find his bed at the Continental and sleep off his depression. But it has to be done. Despite Mokrani's inabilities to finish the simplest of tasks—*he's an Arab, after all*—he deserves to know his so-called colleagues in Oran are dead. Nico never wasted a care on either of them, but their intelligence was useful. With France's surrender, the Algerian underground has surfaced in Oran and Algiers, particularly among young Jews and French army officers. Already, they've distributed anti-fascist leaflets. There is word they have purchased weapons and acquired Italian army uniforms and false identifications. To stay informed, OVRA must count on locals like Mokrani's gangsters. At that loathsome little café in Oran, he met with them several times. Didn't trust them one whit. Without them, Nico is hard-pressed to penetrate the resistance groups. He has no easy means of recruiting. Although he has no use for Mokrani, he must keep him alive. At least until he finds another like him.

"You've come." Mokrani flips the cigarette aside and straightens, standing away from the wall on which he had leaned most of the night. He is wary. Lukas is hesitant. Or is it weariness? Mokrani has not lasted this long, or served two masters, without useful instincts. He stands in place, keeps a distance, waits for a group of men to pass.

"It's late. I'm tired," says Nico. "Let's go inside and sit down." He starts toward the door of the El Morocco.

"There are too many to talk comfortably." Mokrani remains where he is.

"As you wish." Nico moves into the shadow of the arch, lights a cigarette, hands it to Mokrani. "Your colleagues are dead."

"Both?"

Nico nods. "One on the docks at Mers-el-Kébir. The second in a hut south of the city. My people found them yesterday."

"Was it Nassim on the docks?"

"Not sure who is who. Throat slashed. Nasty business."

"And the hut?"

"Hard to say. He'd been dead for several hours. When they found him, he was close to naked, tied to a chair. From the looks of it, he fell backwards and hit his head."

"Tortured?"

"Doesn't appear so. A few abrasions on his face. Nothing else."

"Douglas?" Mokrani has to wonder what his so-called pals revealed. *Why else would Douglas be in Tangier?*

"My guess."

"He's inside," Mokrani nods toward the El Morocco.

"You're sure?"

Mokrani draws hard on the cigarette, shrugs, exhales a circle of smoke.

"So, now you have your own reasons," says Nico.

"He must come this way."

"Then you can't miss, can you." Nico almost smiles. "Let me know when it's done. Leave word at the desk. The Continental." Nico steps closer. "By now, he knows you are disloyal to his cause. Let us hope he has not spread that word to his superiors or to his contacts in Oran."

He turns away from Mokrani's pitiful face, anxious to leave and make his way to the hotel. He waits for a woman to pass through the archway. She is alone. She wears a colorful flowing caftan, a shawl loose around her head. Jewels from a small evening bag glitter in her left hand. Though she is close enough for him to smell the familiar perfume, she stares straight ahead toward the open door of the El Morocco. Hidden in shadow, she has not noticed him.

"Lena," whispers Nico. "Lena." Louder this time until she stops. Her head swivels.

"Nico?"

She hears the shot and sees his body jerk back against the wall. For an instant, nothing registers. Then, even in the darkness, she watches his face drain of expression. Nico clutches his left shoulder and gasps, "Behind you, Lena. Get down." He reaches for her shawl.

Mokrani does not move. *Was that bullet meant for me?* Lukas slumps and eases to the ground, the wall above stained with color. He slouches against the wall and lets out a sharp gasp. Mokrani crouches with him, keeps his head down and his body in the deep shadow.

Lena turns and runs. It is dark and she does not see the step. She falls, catches herself before she hits the street, and rushes forward. She cannot lose the shooter in the dark. She hears the footfall ahead and hears him struggling for breath. She runs. It is a race through the labyrinth of narrow passageways. Her fingers find the switchblade in her pocket. She is getting closer. When she gets close enough, she will use it on the man who shot Nico. She runs swiftly, quietly, her hands touching the side of the buildings. She stops, steps out of sight into a closed doorway. Against the whitewashed buildings, there are two silhouettes. Two. One taller. They turn to look back, then continue on. The shorter man holds a gun. The shooter. The other's hands, she cannot see. She keeps to the shadows, tries to control her breathing so she can listen to their talk. Up ahead, she sees them stop. Their voices are muffled. She cannot distinguish their words.

She considers her chances. Were there only one, she would take him in an instant. One thrust to the ribcage, then upwards to the heart. But two. If she separates them, there is a chance. She pulls out the knife, releases the safety so the single stiletto blade extends to a needle point. Sharp steel penetrates deeply. She has used it before. With devastating results. She must be quick and quiet. She holds the blade in her right hand. She will isolate the shooter, the shorter one with the gun. Fair is fair. Perhaps the other man is innocent. They are yelling at one another, the taller man more aggressive. His voice rises and falls, rises again. She catches bits of the conversation. *Hurry. The boat. Police.* He jabs a finger at the shorter one's chest. The taller man walks away, the movement of his body distantly familiar. He is climbing a set of steps. She watches his hands. He has no gun. It is the shorter man she must pursue. The man who shot Nico. The man who does not know these are the last moments of his life.

There is a sound, and she presses the length of her body against the doorway. A group of men passes by. She falls in behind them.

They talk loudly in French and turn down an alley off to the right. She stands exposed in the darkness, not ten feet from the man with the gun in his hand. He is alone, the taller man nearing the top of the steps. When the tall one reaches the top, she thinks, he will turn and wait for the other, call out to him. She must do it now before he climbs the last step, pivots and looks down. She strides closer to the man with the gun, steadies the knife in her hand, brushes against him.

"What do you want?" he asks.

She smells the strong scent of whiskey and decides, once and for all, he is a dead man. She brings her right hand around to his stomach and drives the point of the stiletto in and up. A startled look—surprise—spreads out on his face. Before his legs give way, she withdraws the knife and quickly sidesteps into the shadow, hiding herself under an awning.

Before he falls into the dirt, she hears him call out. "Lorenzo."

It is Lorenzo Terzo's silhouette she recognized. *Oh dear God. Why on earth does he want Nico Lukas dead?* What has she missed?

Nico gasps for breath. "Get me a towel. A shot of whiskey. A bottle of whiskey."

Mokrani braves a glance left, then right. *Where is the shooter? If I move, am I dead?*

"Go, you fool. Go." Nico clenches his teeth and groans. If he could reach his gun, he would shoot the man. He is bleeding heavily, his hands stained with blood. He wraps her shawl tightly around his shoulder and holds it in place with a stiff knot. He has passed into that state of muffled sounds and blurred images. He tells himself he must remain conscious, get to the hotel, find the doctor. Where is Lena?

Harry sits at a table across from a stairway that goes up to the second floor. When he checks the entry door, he sees Mokrani rush in and run to the near end of the bar. He yells, demands something of the bartender. His mouth is open, and patrons stop their conversations to stare in his direction. He points to a bottle on the shelf. The bartender shakes his head, but Mokrani insists. He grabs the bartender's arm and holds on, urging the bartender to hand him the bottle. There is something frantic in his behavior, a wild animal in need. When the bartender stands firm, Mokrani shoves his way in, seizes the bottle and a stack of towels, and runs for the door. The bartender hollers after him. Those standing at the bar exchange shrugs and return to their drinks.

Though the scene holds no more interest for others, Harry drops several bills on the table, and follows Mokrani. After Harry clears the door, he draws his pistol, pulls the hammer back, and hears the bullet fall into place. Inside the archway, he sees Mokrani kneel. Another man sits on the ground, legs splayed. Harry creeps along the wall until his eyes adjust to the night, and he is close enough to get a better look. The man on the ground is bleeding. Mokrani pours whiskey onto a towel. When he presses the towel against the man's shoulder, the man lets out a low growl and spits into the dirt. With his good hand, the man on the ground grabs the bottle and gulps it down. Whiskey rolls over his chin. He slumps forward, head on his chest. "Help me up." The man grunts with effort and puts out an arm for Mokrani to lift him upright against the wall. Again, the man raises the bottle and drinks what is left.

Thus occupied, the men are unaware of Harry's presence. He levels the pistol at Mokrani's middle. "Turn around slow. Hands out front."

Mokrani straightens, holds out one hand. "The other is ruined. I cannot extend it."

Two days ago, Harry decided Mokrani was going to die. It was a fixed decision, and he returned to Tangier with one purpose. He considers killing Mokrani then and there, but—fortunate for Mokrani—he appears to be unarmed. Harry is not in the habit of killing infirmed, unarmed men.

"Who is that you're nursing?" asks Harry.

The other man speaks. "Come to finish me off, have you, Douglas?"

"It wasn't me who shot you, Lukas. I followed your nurse from the club. He grabbed that bottle of whiskey from the barman and those towels. Isn't that right, Samy?"

Mokrani lowers his hand.

"Keep it out front," says Harry.

Mokrani seems to obey, but Harry notices the other hand—the so-called injured hand—make a swift move to his pocket. Not quite infirmed. Definitely not unarmed. Harry's finger closes on the trigger. The sound echoes along the passageway. Mokrani opens his mouth. No sound comes forth. Two shots. Harry wants more, but Mokrani's eyes tell Harry he knows he is gone, the bullets lodged deep in his gut.

With some effort, Nico heaves himself away from the wall so that he faces Harry. "It's good riddance." The whiskey bottle drops at Nico's feet. Harry lowers his gun.

Nico's look is direct, challenging. "So, now we're pals."

"Not likely. I'm forced to admit I have no good reason to shoot you. At the moment, you're in no shape, in no position, to shoot me." The two men stare at each other, a measuring look. Each balancing the possibilities. Nico blinks first. Harry adds, "Much as you'd like to."

With a towel, Nico wipes his face, now glistening with sweat.

"Who is it shot you?" asks Harry.

"Don't know. Lena went after him."

"Lena?" Margaret Gautier. Harry almost says her name, but catches himself. Lukas likely is unaware of the seemingly infinite number of personages she inhabits. Harry guesses, with good reason, she has not shared her work, particularly since it involves the opposite side of his allegiance. "What do you mean, she went after him?"

"I wanted to shield her. I told her to get down. I grabbed for her." His hands pull at the shawl. "But she started running. She's out there."

"I'll find her."

Lorenzo has not imagined the ascent would be so steep on the ancient steps. It is hard to breathe. He looks down from the top and sees a dark mass on the ground below. *What the hell? Drunk in the dirt? Idiot.* "Get up here." Romano does not move. Annoyed, Lorenzo descends halfway—he sees no pleasure in repeating the climb—and calls out. "C'mon. We must get to the boat." Romano's body is still. Lorenzo moves farther down. He is anxious to depart. The light is dim, but he senses something is seriously wrong. Romano lays face up, eyes wide, both arms outstretched, a dark circle on his shirt. Stunned, Lorenzo turns and struggles up the stairway, panting with fear. He loses his footing and crawls to the top. He does not stop, but stumbles headlong down the other side, onto the beach where the tender bobs next to the pier.

Harry sees her standing in the shallows, staring out across the water. She turns toward him. There are great splotches of blood on her gown.

Lorenzo Terzo lays at her feet, palms open to the sky, half in-half out of the water, one leg bent awkwardly, a wound cut deep into the flesh of his belly. He wears white slacks, a dark sweater rolled up on his chest and one shoe. The other floats nearby.

"He tried to kill Nico."

"Why would he do that?"

She takes a breath, and he can see her try to pull herself together. He has not imagined her in this state. Eyes closed. Hands trembling. "He always was a worthless sort." She presses three fingers to her temple. "We have to move him. This tender belongs to the Terzo yacht. The yacht must be moored somewhere in the harbor. I'll recognize it."

"In the dark?"

"When the sky shows a bit of light. The crew will get him aboard. No local authorities need know." She steps toward the body. There is something frantic about her, and she almost slips in the rocks and sand.

Harry reaches out to steady her.

She turns her head slightly and looks away. "There's another one."

"Another what?"

"Another dead. Back there. At the bottom of the steps."

Harry wonders what she has done. "Who?"

"I don't know his name. He shot the gun." She sits down on the rocks, then quickly stands, unable to decide where she should be. She turns toward Harry. "Why would Lorenzo want to kill Nico?"

"Knowing Lorenzo, it has everything to do with money. You should know. You're the one with the family ties."

"Family ties," she almost laughs. "I'm a Polish widow who, by happenstance, chooses to gather information for the British cause." She stares down at Lorenzo's body. Eventually, she says, "And by some appalling fate, I am in desperate love with the enemy." She says it with what Harry would describe as extraordinary bitterness.

He is uncertain what to say. "He calls you Lena."

"He has no knowledge of Margaret Gautier, Sophia Falco or the others. You must not tell him." As if she has just realized their presence, she touches the splotches of blood on her gown. "I must go. I have to be sure he's all right. That he's alive."

Harry shakes his head. "You can't do that." He points to her bare feet, ignores the bloody gown. "He's been escorted to his hotel. He'll see a doctor and be out cold in an hour." Harry does not mention that he told a man in an expensive Italian suit to call the doctor at the Continental. And paid another to take Nico there. "I'll bring the other body. Find your shoes and anything else identifiable as yours. Board the tender. Find the yacht before the sun comes up. Can you manage it?"

She nods.

"Tell the captain to get out of here. And stay the hell away."

Chapter Thirty-Three

Harry secures air transport out of Tangier. Not an easy thing, but he begs, and from Gibraltar, Townsend unhappily obliges. The plane is filled with soldiers—uniforms with the insignia of Churchill's new Special Service Brigade—on their way home from God knows where. A commando unit, at least twenty sitting along both sides of the fuselage, shoulder to shoulder, weary heads nodding. Harry squeezes into a space between two smaller men and hunches in. The smells of diesel fuel and tired men envelop him, and he fills his lungs. He is grateful for the cold hard floor and the men beside him. He studies the shadowed, unshaven faces that line the opposite side. It does not matter who they are, only that they are whole—with limbs that move and stretch, faces that frown and smile.

It is night, and Harry senses they are passing over the tiny villages scattered along the African coast, heading north across the narrow channel that separates Tangier and Gibraltar. In a few hours, he will stand on the damp shores of England, far from the screams of men on fire, nowhere near the lonely limbs that float in a distant harbor. The images cling. He does not try to shake them loose.

Can he excuse his part in the carnage? Can he justify being an accessory to slaughter? He wills his brain to find some meaning in it, but there is no clarity, save the hackneyed term: political necessity. The words chafe. The England he knows is not capable of such violence. In his years of service to the Crown, Harry has never questioned his purpose. Who gave permission to destroy or disfigure those young men—erstwhile allies, former partners in war and peace—who will never reach home, who paid a tragic price for French indecision? The greater good? The moral accountant who tallies the Crown's deeds will have a devil of a time with this one.

He wants to ask what has happened to the world. The answer will not, in any way, satisfy him.

He considers the men in this cold, gray space. He wonders what they have seen and how they will sort and register their memories. Their faces give nothing away. One soldier meets Harry's gaze. The soldier sits forward, elbows on his knees, slowly rubbing his hands together. It is a forlorn pose. He nods in weary acknowledgment. Harry nods in return. Then, this man does a curious thing. He rises in place and grabs the strap handle above his head. Swaying slightly, in a clear voice—above the roar of the engine—he begins to sing.

We're going to hang out the washing on the Siegfried Line.
Have you any dirty washing, mother dear?
We're going to hang out the washing on the Siegfried Line
'Cause the washing day is here.

The others—seated—begin to clap and laugh. Every man joins in until the final verse is sung, and the voices fade. The soldier nods in Harry's direction and takes back his seat. There is a small smile upon his face as he leans against the hard wall of the fuselage, hands flat on his thighs, eyes closed, able at last to rest.

Harry knows *here* is the core of war. Men such as these, men whose limbs float in the sea, women such as Margaret Gautier. Her words come back to him. "It's better to have some kind of faith." At the time, he found it inconceivable that a woman the likes of Margaret Gautier possessed such conviction.

Unsummoned, an ice-laden crevice of rock and shivering gusts of wind crowd his thoughts. There was little chance of survival. He remembers his helplessness, the certainty of near death. Gabriella's golden ghost stepped forward, enveloped him, warmed him, held him, saved him. *You must not give up,* she had whispered. The next instant, the storm died. The moon rose full. The stars shone brilliant in a coal-black sky. Her shining image, much as he bade her stay, melted into the night. Only the echo of her whisper remained. He hears it now.

It floods his mind, this notion of faith. This inconstant notion of faith.

Historical Notes and Further Reading

The raids on the ports of **Mers-el-Kébir** and Oran (three miles to the east) are regarded as critically important to Britain's survival. On 22 June 1940, when the French signed the Franco-German armistice, Britain stood alone in Europe. At that time, the British Royal Navy (15 battleships and battlecruisers, 7 aircraft carriers, 66 cruisers, 164 destroyers and 66 submarines) was the largest in the world. Italy and Germany ranked a distant fifth and sixth in number of vessels. The French Navy, fourth in size behind the United States and Japan, boasted dozens of powerful battleships, cruisers, and destroyers. These were scattered in English and French ports. The British Admiralty feared that if the French ships, particularly the larger vessels, fell into German or Italian hands, the whole of the Mediterranean Sea would come under Axis control, effectively closing the Strait of Gibraltar and the Suez Canal to British commerce and supply lines.

According to minutes of his War Cabinet meetings, Churchill—though he did not wish to add further misery to a former ally—foresaw looming danger in allowing the French fleet to remain intact. Certain cabinet members were strongly opposed to attacking the French ships. However, after days of fruitless negotiation with the French Admiralty, all agreed that use of force might be necessary. Vice Admiral Sir James Somerville, selected to command the naval squadron at Gibraltar named Force H, expressed great reluctance and regret in executing his orders on 3 July. Thirteen hundred French sailors lost their lives. After delivering news of the mission's success to the House of Commons, it was reported that Winston Churchill wept.

In preparing this novel, I found the following resources immensely useful.

- Brown, David. *The Road to Oran*. London: Routledge 2013.

- Larson, Erik. *The Splendid and the Vile*. New York: Crown Publishing 2020.

- Mangold, Peter. *Britain and the Defeated French*. London: I. B. Tauris 2012.

- Milton, Giles. *Churchill's Ministry of Ungentlemanly Warfare*. NY: Picador 2016.

- Mulley, Clare. *The Spy Who Loved*. London: Macmillan Pan Books 2012.

- Ohler, Norman. *Blitzed, Drugs in the Third Reich*. Boston NY: Houghton Mifflin Harcourt 2017.

- Wharton, Edith. *In Morocco*. 1920.

- National Archives of the United Kingdom. Kew, England: War Cabinet minutes, June-July 1940.

Acknowledgments

For the past fifteen years, I have been fortunate to study the craft of writing with extraordinary instructors and renowned writers Michael Koryta, Laura Lippman, Stewart O'Nan, Debra Dean, Sterling Watson, John Searles, Ann Hood, Andre Dubus III, Les Standiford, Dennis Lehane, and Margaret McMullan. Their unusual talents have enriched my life.

To classmates in the Writers in Paradise writing institutes (Eckerd College, Saint Petersburg, Florida), my thanks for your vivid imaginations, astonishing originality, and thoughtful evaluations that add light, joy and renewed resolve to my own writing.

I am indebted to those—generous with time, knowledge, and support—who endured and provided guidance to early iterations of this manuscript, including Justus Doenecke, Carol Doenecke, Frank Samponaro, Nancy Teets, Marilyn Wittner and Grace Albritton.

My deepest gratitude and love belong to my husband John Belohlavek—professor, researcher, writer of history, first listener and final reader—who unfailingly brings a willing ear and a keen eye to our nightly critiques. Icy gimlets ease the sting of his thorough appraisals as I march off to revise yet again.

To those who read my work, I am more than grateful.

About the Author

Writer and illustrator Susan C. Turner's recent work concentrates in the crime/mystery arena. She prefers to set her narratives in Europe in the pre- and postwar periods of the 1930s and 1940s. *Assignment in Oran* is the third in a series featuring characters Harry Douglas and Mick MacLeod. The first and second books in this collection, *The Truth About Otis Battersby* and *Mission Budapest* were published in 2022 and 2023 and are available in both print and eBook formats. Born in New York, she has lived in Miami and London, and now resides in Tampa with husband John, and the furry, endearing Duffy.